THE ROOKERY

A Penny Green Mystery Book 2

EMILY ORGAN

THE ROOKERY

Emily Organ

Books in the Penny Green Series:
Limelight
The Rookery
The Maid's Secret
The Inventor
Curse of the Poppy
The Bermondsey Poisoner

ALSO BY EMILY ORGAN

Penny Green Series:
Limelight
The Rookery
The Maid's Secret
The Inventor
Curse of the Poppy
The Bermondsey Poisoner

Runaway Girl Series:
Runaway Girl
Forgotten Child
Sins of the Father

CHAPTER 1

My dearest Penny,

I feel certain that you would adore Bogota. The cool, rarefied air here is a welcome respite from the oppressive heat of the lowlands. The city sits on a plateau that is eight thousand feet above the level of the sea and I arrived here after a four-day mule ride from the port of Honda on the River Magdalena.

The many pretty villas here would delight you, draped as they are in bougainvillea, jasmine and ipomoea of startling blue. The parks are a joy to explore with their palm trees, fountains and statues, and there is an impressive cathedral in La Plaza de Bolivar, a museum and an observatory close by. The library contains fifty thousand volumes—

"This is the most recent map we have of Colombia, Miss Green," whispered the reading room clerk.

I folded away my father's letter as the clerk grinned and unrolled the map across my desk. He was a sandy-haired man with spectacles. New to his job, he appeared eager to please.

1

"I do apologise," he continued. "There's not enough room on these desks to view all of it."

"Thank you. I can see the River Magdalena now." I traced its winding route from the Caribbean Sea down to the eastern branch of the Andes with my finger. "And here's Honda. I can see now how my father would have made the journey to Bogota. Thank you, Mr Edwards."

The electric lights flickered.

"Oh dear," said Mr Edwards, glancing around. "I hope they remain lit. They went out last week and we had to ask everyone to leave as it was too dingy to work."

I looked up at the great dome above our heads. The pallid daylight filtering through the arched windows wouldn't provide enough light to read by.

"How are you finding the book?" He was referring to *An Historical, Geographical and Topographical Description of the United States of Colombia*, which lay somewhere beneath the map.

"It's rather detailed, but it will be useful when I find the relevant information in it."

"Of course. Your father's letters must contain some fascinating accounts."

"They do, as do his diaries. This is the first time I've collected everything together. My mother and sister have given me what they had, and the British Museum's natural history department also has some papers of his. I'm going to put everything he wrote together in a book."

"What an excellent idea, Miss Green. Your father is no longer alive?" His brow furrowed, as though he felt uncomfortable asking the question.

"We don't think so. He went missing almost nine years ago in Amazonia, which is an extensive area, as you can imagine. I've learnt that his final travels were in Colombia, on the edge of the Amazon jungle. I read through many of his papers shortly after he died, but I remember so little from them. Perhaps it was because I was still mourning." I felt my throat tighten. "But now I am ready to read everything through again, and I should like to remember him by putting it all into the book."

"It's a sad story, but what a marvellous way to keep the memory of your father alive. What was his name?"

"Frederick Brinsley Green."

"I shall look forward to reading your book about him." He grinned again and I grew concerned that he might expect the book to be something of a masterpiece.

"It will take me rather a long time to write, so I'm afraid you may need to wait a few years yet. And it will only be of interest to someone who wishes to read about plant hunting in South America."

"That might appeal to more people than you realise, Miss Green! I'm always keen to learn about new topics."

"I shall keep you informed of my progress."

"Please do."

I glanced at the reading room clock. "Goodness, look at the time. I'm going to miss my deadline." I jumped up out of my seat. "Thank you for your help, Mr Edwards."

"It's my pleasure. Let me help you pack your papers away. It can't be at all easy with one arm in a sling. How did you injure yourself?"

"I fell off an excitable pony in Hyde Park."

It was the same lie I had told everyone who was unaware of my involvement in the Lizzie Dixie case the previous autumn.

"Oh dear. I do hope you make a quick recovery, Miss Green. I have never got on well with ponies myself." He gathered up my father's diaries and letters into a neat pile.

"Me neither!" I opened my carpet bag and clumsily shovelled the diaries and papers inside it. "I should never have got on one in the first place! That'll teach me."

The bright flowers, scented shrubs and splashing fountains of Bogota continued to fill my mind as I stepped over the filthy ice heaps on Museum Street. The light was leaving the January sky for the day and I had heard that more snow was on its way. People bustled past me with their heads bent low and their collars turned up. A boy in a thin jacket was busy sweeping a crossing at the top of Drury Lane as a nearby clock chimed four.

I stopped to tighten my bonnet underneath my chin, holding my bag in my weaker hand as I did so. A cold wind brought flakes of ice with it, and I looked forward to warming myself in my lodgings that evening with a bowl of pea soup.

A boy knocked into me without warning. The forceful shove left me crumpled on the cold pavement with the breath knocked from me and my spectacles lying a short distance away. A lady in a fur-trimmed coat picked them up.

"Madam! Are you all right?"

I got to my feet and looked around for my carpet bag.

It was gone.

A broad young man in a shabby overcoat patted me on the shoulder. "I'll get 'im," he said, before chasing off after the boy.

I put my spectacles on and watched the man break into a run. Ahead of him, a lean youth ran across the road, dodging the horses and carriages as he went. In his hand was my bag.

My shabby carpet bag with all my father's precious letters and diaries in it.

CHAPTER 2

"Someone stop him!" I cried.

The young boy and the man turned into a narrow street by the Combe & Co cooperage and disappeared from my view.

"The nice gentleman chasing him will see to it," said the lady in the fur-trimmed coat. "They move fast those gutter-snipes, don't they? I like to think this street is safe, but I don't suppose it is being so close to St Giles' Rookery."

I knew that we were standing near to one of London's most notorious slums, but I had walked this way so often that I was accustomed to giving it little thought. The Rookery's residents were often out in Drury Lane trying to sell withered pieces of fruit and vegetables, or offering to carry bags in return for coins. I had never had reason to think that they would do me any harm.

"I need my bag. It has all my father's letters and diaries in it!"

"Let's find a copper," said the lady, patting my arm in a patronising manner, which irritated me. "The coppers will have that ruffian arrested."

"But I need my bag now!"

"Well, hopefully the nice gentleman who chased after the boy will get it for you. Now, somewhere around here there must be a bobby."

As the lady looked around her, I thanked her for her help and slipped away.

"What about the police?" she called after me as I ran off down the pavement and crossed the road between an omnibus and a cart. A driver cursed at me, but I concentrated on reaching the narrow street next to the cooperage.

What could the boy possibly want with my father's papers?

I hoped he would abandon my bag once he had taken my purse. My boots slipped on the patches of ice and my woollen dress and petticoats felt too heavy to run easily, but I managed as well as I could, stumbling along the dingy street. I could hear hammers in the cooperage, and up ahead of me loomed the walls of St Giles' workhouse. Shadowy figures lingered in doorways and I felt many pairs of eyes on me as I ran.

I was soon lost in the labyrinthian streets. An acrid malt smell from the brewery mingled with the stench of sewage and the air had a dirty grey hue. I reached a crossroads, where a couple stood arguing outside a noisy gin shop. Dirt-streaked children clung on to the woman's colourless dress and a young girl held a mewling baby. Not wishing to linger, I continued on ahead. Paint had splintered off the doorways, and the windows were patched with pieces of timber and rags. Someone had lined up old shoes for sale along a wall and a scrawny dog was chewing at something in the gutter.

Staircases leading to basements and cellar lights in the pavement hinted at the subterranean world into which the boy might have escaped. I didn't feel brave enough to venture down into those places and inquire as to whether anyone had seen him. I had heard about the cut-throats who dwelt there.

A dark gap opened up where a street had once stood. Scaffolding had been erected in order to construct new buildings, but I couldn't see any workmen nearby.

I grew breathless. My corset was too tight to allow me to run any further, so I slowed to walking pace. I passed a number of rowdy pubs and tumbledown lodging houses advertising beds for fourpence a night. An old man with a handcart passed me and a sallow-cheeked girl tried to sell me a hare skin. I politely declined and asked her whether she had seen a boy running past with a carpet bag. She shook her head in reply and a heaviness began to descend upon me. The boy could have hidden himself anywhere in this gloomy warren, and I realised I had little hope of finding him.

My fingers and toes were numb with cold by the time I reached Seven Dials: a place where seven streets converged, as the name suggests. I felt sure that one of the streets would lead me to The Strand, but I couldn't think which. The gas lamps had been lit and a man was leaning against one of them, drunkenly singing 'Molly Malone'. A twittering sound came from a shop selling caged birds, and rags and old furniture were piled up for sale outside it. A young woman stepped out from one of the pubs and approached me.

"What's a lady such as yerself doin' down 'ere alone?" She wore a man's jacket over a long, muddy skirt. Her eyes were sunken and shot with red.

"I'm trying to find my way to The Strand. A boy took my bag and I followed him here, but now I have no hope of finding him."

"It ain't safe fer a lady like yerself on yer own. Yer need to get yerself outta here. Follow tha' road." She pointed towards the narrowest one, which was signposted Little White Lion Street. "Keep goin' tha' way and yer'll get ter Covent Garden. Go careful now."

I thanked her and moved away as a man strode over to us.

I assumed he knew the young woman, but then he called out to me, "I can't find 'im! I done me best."

It was the man who had chased after the boy. From what I could see of him in the gas light, he had a handsome face with a broad forehead and square jaw. I guessed he was about twenty-five.

"Thank you for chasing after him," I said. "I appreciate your help."

A horrible cold sensation settled in the pit of my stomach. *All my father's letters and diaries were gone.*

"You shouldn't 'ave come 'ere, it ain't safe. And you're already 'urt. What's 'appened to yer arm?" asked the man.

"Just a fall from a pony; nothing serious. There's something very important to me in that bag. It's not valuable and means nothing to anyone else – just some papers belonging to my father – but if you do find the bag, you'll let me know, won't you?"

"Course I will. Reuben O'Donoghue's me name. I'll keep a look out fer it."

He grinned and I smiled in return.

"Thank you, Mr O'Donoghue. I'm Miss Green. Penny Green. I'll go and find a police constable and report the theft. Bow Street station is probably the nearest, isn't it? Not that the police will be able to do very much about it."

"Let me show yer the right way."

"There's no need, thank you. A lady just told me which way I should go."

I looked around for the young woman, but she had moved on.

"You'll need someone with yer, it's almost dark—"

I was about to reply when a scream pierced the air. My eyes met Reuben's and a chill gripped me.

"Jesus, Mary and Joseph! What's that noise?" His eyes grew wide.

Another scream rang out from a street behind him.

"Murder!" someone cried out. "Murder! Murder!"

CHAPTER 3

The call rallied everyone around us. Figures emerged from dark corners and the pubs emptied out into the street.

"Murder!"

"Where?"

"Who's bin murdered?"

Reuben ran in the direction from which the commotion was coming and I followed closely behind him. Soon we were part of a great throng of people in a narrow street. Some held lanterns, which illuminated a clamour of people around the entrance to a courtyard. Reuben pushed his way to the front of the crowd. His height allowed him to peer over their heads and see what was happening.

"It's one o' Keller's lads."

"'E 'ad it comin'."

I saw Reuben turn and look around, as if he were trying to find me. I pushed through the crowd to reach him.

"Mr O'Donoghue?"

"There you are, Miss Green! It's the boy. The boy what took your bag. It's 'im what's bin murdered!"

"It can't be him! We only saw him a few moments ago."

I was sure that Reuben must be mistaken. The boy who had snatched my bag had been running away only minutes earlier.

"Are you sure it's him?" I pressed.

"Yeah, I know the lad. Jack Burton. Boots, they called 'im. A street-arab."

I strained to hear what he was saying as the noisy crowd jostled against me.

"I kept callin' out to 'im to stop, but he kep' on runnin'. If only 'e'd stopped and then this wouldn't of 'appened to 'im." Reuben wiped the back of his hand across his eyes. "I done me best."

"You shouldn't blame yourself, Mr O'Donoghue. It seems someone wanted to punish him for his actions. He may have stolen my bag, but he didn't deserve this."

"He didn't. Ain't no one does."

I still felt sure that Reuben was mistaken.

It had to be a different boy.

I began to edge my way closer to the courtyard.

"It'll upset yer seein' 'im, Miss Green!" Reuben warned.

Nevertheless, I wanted to see for myself whether it was the same boy who had taken my bag.

"Please let me past!" I called out.

Someone shoved me with an elbow and I stumbled forward into the courtyard, where a number of lanterns sat clustered around a bundle on the ground. I saw the boy's feet first. One foot was still booted, while the other wore only a tattered sock, the mislaid boot lying close by on the cobbles. The boy was sprawled on his back, one arm resting on his chest. His face was white and the dark gash across his throat made me recoil.

"He's so young!" I cried out. "Can we cover him with something?"

"I'll use my overcoat," said a man standing close by.

"I've closed 'is eyes," said a short woman in a headscarf. "They was wide and starin'. I couldn't look at 'em no more."

The coat was placed over the boy's body, and it was then that I noticed a dark bundle lying next to his body.

My carpet bag.

"He didn't need to steal from me," I muttered. "He could have asked me for money and I would've given him some. This didn't need to happen. He didn't need to be murdered."

I stepped forward and picked up my bag. A dark puddle of blood had spread out around the boy's head and shoulders, and I felt certain that it must have reached my bag, although I couldn't see any blood on it. My father's papers and diaries were inside, as was my purse with the coins still in it.

"Why would someone do this?" I said to the woman in the headscarf. "They didn't even steal anything. My purse is still in my bag with the money in it! Did they kill him as some form of punishment?"

The lady looked up at me. In the lantern light, I could see that she was about fifty, with a sagging, lined face and sharp, twinkling eyes. Her ragged headscarf was tightly knotted under her chin.

"One o' the gangs might of done it."

"Does this sort of thing happen a lot here?"

"More than it should. I don't understand who'd 'ave done this ter Boots. 'E were usually a good lad. Nicked yer bag, did he?"

I nodded.

"He must've been 'ungry. Either that or the Earl told 'im to do it."

"The Earl?"

"Edward Keller, 'im of the Seven Dials Gang. Calls 'imself the Earl o' York. Boots was in 'is gang."

"What about the boy's mother? Has she been told?"

"Boots was a horphan."

I looked again at the body under the coat and struggled to comprehend that the same boy lying there had taken my bag and run away from me only half an hour previously. I shivered from my head to my toes, unsure whether it was due to the cold or the shock.

We were startled by a loud whistle.

"Move on! Hook it!"

The whistle was blown again.

"Back to yer 'omes!"

"I don't 'ave one," grumbled someone close by.

Three constables pushed their way into the courtyard. Two had truncheons in their hands to disperse the crowd, and the third shone his bullseye lantern over the boy's body. I winced as the dark puddle seeping out beneath the overcoat turned red in the lamplight.

"Inspector's on 'is way!" shouted one of the constables. "Who saw what 'appened?"

"He took my bag," I said.

"Who murdered 'im?"

"I don't know."

"You didn't see what 'appened?"

"No. He took my bag and ran off with it."

"Who saw what 'appened?" the constable shouted out across the courtyard.

"I found 'im," said the lady in the headscarf.

"Did you see what 'appened?"

"No, I jus' found 'im lyin' there in the corner. That's when I've went about shoutin' there's bin a murder."

The constable marched off, presumably in search of more informative witnesses.

"Why was he called Boots? Was he a bootblack?" I asked the lady in the headscarf.

"Sometimes 'e were, other times 'e were thievin'. There y'are, Mr 'Awkins! 'Ave you seen what they done ter Boots?"

A man with grey whiskers joined the woman. He wore a smart, dark suit but no overcoat, and I wondered whether he was the man who had laid his coat over the poor boy's body.

"A very sad day indeed, Mrs Nicholls."

Mrs Nicholls introduced me to Mr Hugo Hawkins and informed me that he was a missionary.

"I'm Penny Green," I said. "A news reporter."

"A lady news reporter?" quibbled Mrs Nicholls. "I ain't never seen one o' them afore."

"There aren't many of us."

"Are yer goin' ter be puttin' this murder in the newspapers?"

"Yes, I'll write something about it, but I'll wait to see what the police have to say first."

"It's a terrible business," said Mr Hawkins, shaking his head. "We should pray for him."

Mrs Nicholls and I bowed our heads as he said a short prayer. As we finished praying, a stocky man with a black bag bustled into the courtyard. He stooped over Jack's body, placed his bag down on the ground and removed the coat. I looked away, not wishing to see Jack's young face again.

"Looks like the police surgeon's here," said Mr Hawkins.

Another man in an ulster overcoat and top hat strode into the courtyard and began shouting. I guessed he was the inspector.

"Search the streets! Find the culprit! Expect him to be armed with a knife!"

"Who'd of done this?" asked Reuben O'Donoghue, who now stood by my side. "Why'd anyone wanna kill a boy?"

A number of lanterns were flashing around the yard by this point, the noise and mayhem of the crowd replaced by the busy yet focused activities of the police.

"I thought Boots 'ad bettered 'imself of late," said Mrs Nicholls.

"We managed to keep him coming to chapel for a while," said another missionary who had joined Mr Hawkins, "but his visits lapsed. Once these boys are in a gang with their friends, they find it impossible to leave. In fact, they often become too scared to leave."

I heard a horse and carriage making its way up the street, presumably to take Jack's body to the mortuary. The police surgeon stood to his feet and called over to the inspector.

"He passed away within the past hour, which puts the time of death at after a quarter to four."

"It was after four o'clock," I called out, but no one seemed to hear me.

"Thank you, Dr Anderson," replied the inspector. "Any sign yet of the murder weapon?" he shouted out to the constables scouring the yard with their lanterns.

They replied that there wasn't as the inspector strode over to us. In the dim light, I could see that he had dark, mutton-chop whiskers.

"Good evening, ladies and gentlemen. I'm Chief Inspector Fenton of Holborn Division. I understand you saw what happened to the boy?"

Mrs Nicholls, Reuben and I explained what had occurred earlier that evening. He wrote down the details in a notebook.

"And I know all of you here apart from you, ma'am." His eyes were on me. "Name?"

"Miss Penelope Green."

He wrote this down.

"And who's that at the back there?" he asked, looking over our heads. I turned to see a shadowy figure behind us and a curl of tobacco smoke rising up in the lamplight.

"Earl of York," came the gruff reply.

"Good evening, Mr Keller. Not seen you around for a while."

"Been busy, ain't I?"

"Any idea what happened to the boy?"

"Got 'is throat slit. Dunno who dunnit."

"I reckon yer got a fair idea," said Mrs Nicholls angrily.

"Never laid a finger on 'im. He were one of me best."

"And a lot o' good you did 'im!"

"That's enough," said Inspector Fenton.

Two constables wrapped a blanket around Jack's body and carried it out of the courtyard and into the carriage. I averted my eyes from the pool of blood.

"Mr O'Donoghue, you're required to report to Bow Street station at nine o'clock tomorrow morning."

"You'd better not go arrestin' me again," said Reuben. "I chased the boy, but I never killed 'im."

I was surprised to hear that Reuben had been arrested before and wondered what he might have done wrong.

"Miss Green and Mrs Nicholls, you are also requested to attend Bow Street station at your earliest convenience tomorrow morning. We'll need to take witness statements from you. Keller, I want to see you tomorrow too. Mr Hawkins and Mr Meares, did you see anything that might be useful in this investigation?"

"We arrived here shortly after hearing Mrs Nicholls shout that there'd been a murder."

"Perhaps you could also come along tomorrow, on the off-chance you saw anything suspicious."

The inspector put his notebook away and went to speak to the constables searching the courtyard.

As a news reporter, I should have been taking notes and asking questions, but I couldn't bring myself to do it at that moment. I felt too involved in the tragedy to be able to report on it. Instead, I hugged my bag in the cold, dark courtyard and wondered how a young boy could be so suddenly and violently murdered.

"Poor lad," said Mrs Nicholls, sadly.

"I suppose there is nothing more we can do now, other than report to the police station tomorrow morning," I said. "I'll go and write up the story for the paper. I wish you well, Mrs Nicholls."

"Call me Martha."

"I wish you well, Martha, and I hope that the person who did this to poor Jack will be caught very soon."

"He ain't the first," she replied.

"This has happened before?"

I felt astonished not to have heard about it.

"Yeah," said Martha. "Jack ain't the first what's 'ad 'is throat cut round 'ere."

"Regrettably, there have been two others," added Mr Hawkins.

"Folks think it's the 'usband what done Mrs O'Brien in," said Reuben.

"I don't think it's 'im," said Martha. "He ain't been seen for months. I don't reckon 'e come back and slit Ellen's throat and then run off again."

"Everyone says it's 'im," said Reuben.

"Course they does, 'cause they don't know who else to say done it."

"And there's Roger Yeomans," said Reuben.

"'E's another one what got 'is throat cut," said Martha.

"So *two* other people living in this area have had their throats cut?" I asked. "Did this happen recently?"

"Yeah, recent. Were Mrs O'Brien afore or after Christmas?"

"Boxing Day," replied Reuben.

"And then we've 'ad Mr Yeomans just recent."

"And what have the police done about these crimes?"

Martha shrugged. "Well, you've seen 'em. They come scurryin' in makin' a lotta fuss and pretendin' they's got it all under control. They picks up the body and leaves us to clean up afterwards. Nothin' else 'appens after that."

"They must do something."

"Maybe they does. But I ain't never known 'em ter do much."

CHAPTER 4

I reached the *Morning Express* offices on Fleet Street at half after five o'clock. A boy stood under the gas lamp outside our building, brazenly selling copies of *The Holborn Gazette*. I glared at him and prepared myself for the explanation I would have to give my editor for missing the deadline.

The printing presses were roaring in the basement as I climbed the narrow wooden stairs to the newsroom. Before I even pushed open the door I could hear laughter from my colleague, Edgar Fish. His laugh could be irritating, but on this occasion I hoped it would lift my gloomy mood.

The newsroom was a cluttered place with piles of paper on every surface and a grimy window looking out onto Fleet Street. A fire flickered in the small, black-tiled fireplace. Edgar had his feet on his desk and a notebook in his hand. A curly-haired and corpulent Frederick Potter sat at his desk nearby.

"Miss Green!" said Edgar. He was a young man with heavy features and small glinting eyes. "Where've you been? You've missed your deadline and Sherman's got a rod in pickle for you. What's the matter? You look bereft."

"I have a good deal to tell you," I replied, removing my gloves and coat. "Am I missing something amusing? I heard you laughing before I walked in."

"Yes!" said Edgar. "We've been working on anagrams of our names. You may call me A Fresh Dig if you like. Or perhaps Figs Heard if you prefer. And sitting over there is Prettier Frocked!"

Edgar roared with laughter, while Frederick scowled.

I took off my bonnet and long, fair waves of hair fell out of their pins. "What can you do with my name?" I asked as I tried to re-pin my hair into a respectable style.

Edgar pushed his tongue between his lips and scribbled on his notepad. "Not a great deal," he replied. "Genre Penny?"

"Not much of an anagram, is it?" I sat down at my desk with little idea as to whether my hair looked decent or not.

"I'll keep working on it."

"And why is there a boy selling *The Holborn Gazette* outside our door?"

I pulled my papers out of my bag and placed them on my desk.

"It's all Edgar's fault," said Frederick. "It seems the *Gazette* has a vendetta."

"I thought Edgar and Tom Clifford were good friends?"

"They were," said Frederick, "until Edgar stole Tom's story."

"I didn't steal it!" said Edgar, removing his feet from the desk and slamming down his notepad. "I've already explained that Tom told me about it indiscreetly."

"About what?"

"It's the most ridiculous story," said Frederick.

"It's not," said Edgar. "It's of great interest to our readers.

Tom and I were in Ye Olde Cheshire Cheese and he told me about a man who sold his fat wife's corpse to a physician."

"Why would he do that?"

"She was in a freak show; she was a giantess. But then she died and a physician wanted to procure her body because of her unusually large size. I didn't realise it was Tom's story, so I arranged an interview with the husband before he did."

"Why would you want to report on a story such as that?"

"Readers love stories like that!"

"Are you sure?"

"Of course! Once they've read about what's happening in Parliament and the situation in the Sudan, they like to read about men selling the corpses of their fat wives. We need more stories like that, don't you think, Potter?"

"I think there are other publications which are better suited to stories of this type," Frederick replied.

"You're meant to be on my side, Prettier Frocked."

Edgar tossed a screwed-up ball of paper at him as the newsroom door was flung open. The editor, William Sherman, strode in and the door slammed behind him.

"Watch out. Here's Sawmill Hire Man," said Edgar.

"What are you talking about, Fish?" barked Mr Sherman through his thick black moustache. He wore a blue waistcoat and his shirt sleeves were rolled up. His hair was oiled and parted to one side.

"It's an anagram of your name, sir."

"Have you done anything useful today?" Mr Sherman frowned and his bushy eyebrows met above his nose.

Edgar looked like a scolded schoolboy. "Yes, I wrote about Mr Barnum's white elephant travelling en route from Siam to Malta."

"Well done. Anyone seen Purves, our parliamentary reporter?"

We shook our heads and the editor spun round and glared at me.

"Miss Green! I was expecting your article on the sudden death of Eduard Lasker."

"Yes sir, it's here." I showed him the piece of paper I had painstakingly typewritten with my left hand.

"Well it's no good *here*, is it? The compositors needed it downstairs an hour ago. It's too late. I've had to fill in with an article about the illness of Sir Arthur Sullivan. This isn't good enough, Miss Green."

"If you could please let me explain, Mr Sherman. I was waylaid in St Giles' Rookery on my way here."

I told the editor about the boy who had taken my bag, and how he had been found murdered. Everyone listened in silence, and by the time I had finished Mr Sherman was leaning against the wall with a sombre expression on his face.

"Well, Miss Green, I don't often say this, but you appear to have a suitable excuse for missing your deadline. And after such an ordeal, I think a glass of sherry is in order. It isn't your favourite East India sherry, I'm afraid."

"Any sherry will do well, thank you sir."

Mr Sherman withdrew to his office and returned with four glasses and the bottle. "I suppose the men will be wanting some too, not that they've done anything of great use today."

He poured out our drinks. "Now, we need a story on this poor boy's murder for tomorrow's second edition. Can you work on that as quickly as possible, Miss Green?" He looked doubtfully at my right arm in its sling. "On second thoughts, I don't suppose you can write particularly quickly, can you?"

"I've been managing to typewrite with my left hand, but it's rather slow going. Might I dictate the story to your secretary, Miss Welton? Do you think she would mind?"

"That's not a bad idea, and in fact she could typewrite it.

Her fingers move rather swiftly on that machine now. Go and sit with Miss Welton and we'll get the story written up on the double."

I sipped my sherry and enjoyed the feeling of warmth in my chest. "The people I spoke to in St Giles today told me that this is the third murder in recent weeks."

"Well there's a lot of murder in the slums, Miss Green."

"But all three victims had their throats cut."

"The gangs are vicious in those parts."

"I don't know whether the gangs are involved. A man and a woman were both murdered recently. Did we report on those stories?"

"Mrs Ellen O'Brien," Edgar chipped in. "I wrote about that one. The husband is suspected and they're still looking for him."

"But the people I spoke to thought it unlikely that the husband had done it. What about the man who was murdered? Did you write about him?"

Edgar shook his head. "What was his name?"

"Yeomans, I think they said."

"Never heard of him."

"Forget about this for now, Miss Green, and just write your story about the boy," said Mr Sherman. "I want to be the first paper to get this news out tomorrow. We need to better *The Holborn Gazette* whenever and wherever possible."

CHAPTER 5

I arrived back at my lodgings shortly after nine o'clock that evening.

"It's not safe for a lady to be out on her own at this hour," said my landlady, Mrs Garnett, who was dusting the hallway table. She had a habit of lingering in the hallway whenever I was late home. "You should be accompanied."

"I travelled by cab."

"You should still be accompanied."

"Accompanied by whom?"

"A husband." She spoke as if acquiring a husband were as simple as buying one from the local market.

"A husband wouldn't like me doing this sort of work."

"He certainly wouldn't. He'd have you enjoying more lady-like pursuits."

Mrs Garnett frowned at me, but I could see an affectionate glint in her brown eyes. She enjoyed scolding me, probably because she didn't have anyone else to scold. A childless widow of about sixty, she had come to London from British West Africa as a child.

"Don't make the mistake of thinking you're too old, Miss

Green. You may be getting older, but you look younger than your years." She scrutinised my features.

"Thank you, Mrs Garnett."

"It's the nose," she said. "The nose is what spoils a lady's features as she gets older because it never stops growing. Fortunately for you, your nose is still dainty."

"There's hope for me yet, then. Is that what you mean?"

"You're fortunate you don't have your sister's nose."

"That's not fair on Eliza, Mrs Garnett."

"She has the same brow as you. From the eyes up you look similar. But her nose has lost its shape."

"But she does have a husband."

"That's true, and she should count her blessings. You need a husband too, Miss Green. What happened to that detective who used to call round for you?"

"Inspector James Blakely, you mean? Our discussions were only ever of a professional nature, Mrs Garnett. He's currently helping with a case in Manchester at present."

I hadn't seen James for many weeks, but I thought about him often.

"He's still all the way up there?"

"Yes... never mind. I must go and have something to eat."

"Yes, you must." She flicked her feather duster at me. "I've lit your stove for you."

After a hot bowl of soup with bread and butter, I began to feel warm for the first time that day.

I loosened my stays, unpinned my hair and took a seat at my writing desk with the edition of the *Morning Express* from Thursday 27th December 1883 laid out before me. I looked for the article Edgar had written about Mrs O'Brien's death and found that it comprised only a few lines at the bottom of a column on the seventh page.

As I began to read, Tiger jumped onto my desk and sat on the newspaper. "You always manage to sit on the column I'm reading, don't you?"

She purred and I gave her a stroke, before scrunching a piece of blotting paper into a ball and throwing it across the floor for her. She chased it and then patted it under my bed.

Police are requesting information regarding the whereabouts of the husband of Mrs Ellen O'Brien, a charwoman who was horrifically murdered a few yards from the front door of her home at 36 Nottingham Court yesterday.

Chief Inspector Fenton reported that the unfortunate woman's throat had been cut with a knife, and that the murder weapon has not yet been found.

Neighbours in Nottingham Court spoke of a disturbance between one o'clock and half past one in the morning. Mr Ayres, a fish porter, happened across the dreadful scene as he left for work at half past four.

Anyone with information on Mr O'Brien's whereabouts is requested to attend Bow Street police station as a matter of urgency.

The police clearly considered Mrs O'Brien's husband to be the culprit, and Martha Nicholls had said that he had been missing for some time. To compound the lack of progress on the case, the murder had occurred on Boxing Day, when many people would have been distracted by the Christmas celebrations.

Would the police ever consider that Mrs O'Brien might have been murdered by someone other than her husband?

I wondered what sort of woman she had been.

Had she been a mother? How were her loved ones faring after such an awful event?

I closed my eyes and winced as I pictured Jack Burton on the ground of the filthy courtyard. St Giles was a busy place, and the murderer would have had only a matter of minutes to commit his act. I shuddered. It was brazen and barbaric, and I couldn't understand the mind of someone who would do something like that.

And what of Mr Yeomans? I had yet to find out anything more about him and his death. The police would be asking me questions the following morning, but I also had some questions for them.

Were they going to carry out a proper investigation into Jack's death, or would it be forgotten as the others seemingly had been?

I climbed into bed that night with some of Father's letters to read before I went to sleep. I had underestimated how precious his papers were to me, and I realised that it wouldn't do to be carrying them around in my carpet bag any longer. If I hadn't managed to retrieve my bag, they would have been lost to me forever.

I unfolded the last letter he had sent me, the one I had been reading earlier in the British Library reading room, and continued where I had left off.

The people I encountered in Bogota range from the Indians of the rural areas to the sophisticated men and women of Spanish descent. I have also met with many wealthy Colombian merchants, as well as Germans, French, Dutch, and of course the English. The variety of people is impressive when you consider what a great undertaking it is to travel to this remote city in the Andes.

In the market, apples, potatoes, strawberries, mangoes, figs, cabbages, yams, bananas and of course the staple food, cassava root, are to be found. I also discovered packages of Morton's Ham and tins of Peek Freans biscuits. To think they have made the journey to Bogota all the way from Bermondsey!

Like my father, I felt astonished that an everyday item such as Peek Freans biscuits could be found so far away in the tropics. I was sure that he must have felt a bout of homesickness when he saw them at the market in Bogota. I often wondered how much he had missed his home and family while he was travelling.

Had he counted down the days until he would see us again?

Sadly, this letter in my hands was the last communication I had received from him. His last known destination was a distant waterfall, and no one could be certain whether he had ever reached it.

Tomorrow I plan to ride twenty miles south-west of Bogota to the falls of Tequendama. I have heard much of the orchids and tropical birds there, and am looking forward to the spectacle of the River Funza plunging from a height of five hundred feet. It must be a sight to behold!

I felt that putting his words together in a book might help me understand what had happened to him. I couldn't believe that he was still alive, for I felt sure he would have found a way to return to his wife and daughters had he been. But I hoped that if I could recreate his travels on paper I might find a clue to his final resting place.

And by writing for the *Morning Express*, I could hopefully tell London what was happening in the miserable slum in which I had found myself that day. If the public discovered that three people had been murdered in St Giles' Rookery in recent weeks, the police would have to do something about it.

CHAPTER 6

Snow fell during the night, and by the following morning the carriage wheels were churning laboriously through ice and mud. The omnibus eventually reached The Strand, and from there I trudged through the snow up to Bow Street. I had dressed myself in three pairs of stockings and a second woollen dress to provide another layer over my petticoats. Newspaper boys called out the news of Jack's murder, and it seemed to me that each of them bore an alarming resemblance to him.

Bow Street police station was an imposing building, clad in stone and adjacent to the new magistrates' court. Opposite stood the impressive, columned facade of the Royal Opera House, where a constable was trying to rouse a man from sleep in one of its doorways.

Once inside, I reported to the officer behind the desk and settled on a wooden bench to wait. The smell of tar soap hung in the air as a woman scrubbed at the floorboards.

Reuben O'Donoghue walked in with snow on his boots a few moments later. Once he had given the desk officer his name, he gave me a wide grin and sat down next to me, rubbing his hands together for warmth. He was clean-shaven and wore a neatly knotted blue neckerchief.

"You recovered yet, Miss Green?"

"I don't think I have. I slept badly."

"Don't suppose you're used to seein' someone what's been murdered, are you? We got your bag back, though."

"I can't stop thinking about the boy. He shouldn't have lost his life."

"It were proberly nothing to do with 'im thievin' yer bag. It were proberly someone who was after 'im anyways. One o' them gangs."

"What about the other two murders?"

"Mrs O'Brien? And someone else... Yeomans I fink 'is name was."

"Yes. What do you know about them?"

"O'Brien were found in the street early one morning, round Christmas time. Some poor fella on his way ter work found 'er and they's been looking for Mr O'Brien ever since as everyone's sayin' he done it."

"Do you know anything about Mr Yeomans?"

"Only that he were found out the back o' The Three Feathers. They says it were a robbery."

"Who says that?"

"The police."

"Do you think the same person could have murdered Mrs O'Brien and Mr Yeomans?"

"Like I said, one were done by O'Brien and Yeomans were a robbery. You think O'Brien robbed Yeomans?"

"I don't think so, because Martha told me Mr O'Brien hasn't been seen for a long time. Someone else could have killed Mrs O'Brien and the same person may have killed Mr Yeomans. They both had their throats cut, didn't they? And so did Jack."

"The same person mighta done all three?" Reuben's eyebrows knotted together.

"They could have done."

"You'd 'ave to 'ave a kink in the brain to do that kinda thing."

"Well, yes, you would."

"I don't think the same person's bin cuttin' people's throats. There's no reason ter. They's three different people and I think as Jack's bin murdered by a gang. Proberly the Daly Boys. Keller's 'ad a carry-on with them for ages."

A door to the left of the desk swung open and Chief Inspector Fenton strode out with a bundle of papers in one hand. His mutton-chop whiskers were tinged with grey and he had dark, narrow eyes.

"Miss Green? Mr O'Donoghue?" He pointed at us accusingly. "You shouldn't be sitting together like this. It gives you an opportunity to collude."

"Collude?" I asked. "About what?"

"To fabricate a story."

"There's no need to fabricate anything, I've come here this morning to tell you what happened. I'm making a witness statement."

The inspector scowled. "I don't like witnesses, suspects or anyone else finding opportunities to confer."

"I didn't realise we weren't allowed to speak, Inspector Fenton. Perhaps your colleague could have warned us."

I glanced at the officer behind the desk, who was attempting to shrink from view.

The inspector consulted the papers in his hand and stroked his whiskers. "Miss Green, can you come with me, please?"

Having originally considered my visit to be little more than a formality, the inspector's confrontational manner made me feel concerned that I had done something wrong. I gave Reuben a parting smile and followed Inspector Fenton. We passed through the door and along a whitewashed corridor, in which a smell of latrines mingled with soap.

We reached a small room with a table at the centre and a clock on the wall showed that it was ten minutes after nine. The room was lit by a gas lamp and a narrow window. Sitting at the table was a police officer with a large grey moustache and a crooked nose, which looked as though it had been broken once or twice. He stood up as we entered the room.

"This is Inspector Pilkington, and allow me to introduce myself to you again, Miss Green, as Chief Inspector Fenton, head of CID in Holborn E Division." He paused, as if allowing time for the noble title to sink in, before gesturing me to sit on the chair opposite them.

Once we were all seated, Inspector Fenton leafed through the papers in front of him, took a pen from his inside jacket pocket and dipped it into a pot of ink on the table.

"Miss Green, can you please tell me your full name?"

"Miss Penelope Jane Green."

He wrote this down.

"Age?"

"Thirty-four."

"Thirty-four and unmarried?"

"Yes."

"No husband? Never married?"

"No."

"Address?"

"Five Milton Street, Cripplegate."

"And have you an occupation?"

"I'm a news reporter."

"A news reporter, eh?" Inspector Fenton sat back in his chair and regarded me with renewed interest. "Which paper?"

"The *Morning Express*."

He wrote this down with an impressed nod of his head. "So now you find yourself in a story of your own?"

"I suppose I do. Rather reluctantly, I must add."

"Yes, it's rather a sorry state of affairs."

"Are you any closer to finding out who did it?"

"Not yet, Miss Green. We have many people to speak to, and I'm certain that the conversation we're about to have will assist us immensely."

"I don't think it will, Inspector. I didn't really see anything. I can't see how I can be of much help."

"Everyone says that," he replied. "Let's get on with it, shall we?"

He pushed his piece of paper towards Inspector Pilkington, indicating that he should continue with the writing.

I told the two detectives what I could remember from the time I had left the reading room to the moment when Jack Burton had been found dead. Inspector Pilkington wrote everything down while Inspector Fenton asked the questions. A map was produced so that I could attempt to show them the route I had taken through St Giles. I admitted that much of it was guesswork, but they were patient with me and by the end of our conversation they had as thorough an account as I could possibly give.

"Do you have any suspicions yourself, Miss Green, about who might have committed the crime?"

"None at all. I'm not familiar with the area or the people who live there. I can recall a lone gentleman, who I assumed was a gang member, standing with us in the courtyard. I could make a wild guess that perhaps the murder was the result of a gang feud."

"But that is only a wild guess, as you say. You have no evidence with which to corroborate this view?"

"None."

"I would like to discuss again when you first saw Mr

O'Donoghue. That would have been shortly after four o'clock?"

"Yes. I heard the clocks chime four and then my bag was taken by Jack Burton. Moments later, Mr O'Donoghue informed me that he would run after the boy."

"So you saw Mr O'Donoghue pursue the boy across Drury Lane and into a street, which you have identified on the map as Short's Gardens?"

"Yes."

Inspector Fenton took the pages of notes back from Inspector Pilkington before continuing.

"And we have ascertained that the time of death for the deceased was between a quarter past and twenty minutes past four o'clock. Did you see Mr O'Donoghue between the time of your bag being taken and the boy being found murdered?"

"No."

"Do you know where he was?"

"He was following the boy."

"Where exactly?"

"Somewhere in St Giles."

"But you don't know exactly where?"

"No." I shifted uncomfortably as I realised what Inspector Fenton was implying.

"And you next saw Mr O'Donoghue where?"

"At Seven Dials."

"At approximately what time?"

"I can't be certain, but I know now that it was after Jack was killed, so I suppose it must have been about half past four."

"You suppose? You do not carry a watch?"

I shook my head.

"And you didn't happen to see a clock?"

"No."

"Very well. And from which direction did Mr O'Donoghue approach you?"

"I couldn't say. I had got myself quite lost by that stage."

"You mentioned that a young lady pointed you in the direction of Little White Lion Street?"

I nodded.

"Did Mr O'Donoghue appear from that direction?"

"No."

"He came from the opposite direction?"

"Yes, I think so."

Inspector Fenton unfolded the map again and pointed at Seven Dials.

"The street opposite Little White Lion Street is Great White Lion Street. Do you think he might have come from there?"

I stared at the area of the map where his large finger was pressed.

"No. I think it more likely that he approached me from Great St Andrew Street or Queen Street."

"Which?"

"I can't be certain which."

"Very well." I looked again at the map, aware that the courtyard where Jack had been found was just off Queen Street.

"Inspector Fenton, if you think that Mr O'Donoghue had anything to do with Jack's death, I will say now that he could not have done it. He wouldn't have done it. He helped me."

"He helped you because a street urchin pinched your bag."

"Yes, but he wouldn't have harmed him."

"How else would he have retrieved your bag?"

"I'm sure he would have simply asked the boy for it."

The inspector snorted as if he perceived my comment to be naive.

"If he'd killed Jack, he would have returned to me with my bag," I continued. "He wouldn't have left it lying by Jack's side."

"How do you know that he was returning to you? He may have been walking away from the scene of his crime with every intention of escaping the area when he unexpectedly came across you. Presumably he was expecting you to have remained on Drury Lane. However, he wasn't walking in the direction of Drury Lane, was he?"

"I suppose he was still looking for Jack."

"But you merely suppose that, Miss Green? You cannot know it for sure."

"I don't know Mr O'Donoghue well, but I can tell that he wouldn't have done such a thing to Jack. Besides, he had no blood on his clothes."

"Can you be certain? It was almost dark when you saw him the second time."

"I would have noticed. And he would have been bothered or flustered, or out of breath in some way. I know he didn't do it, Inspector!"

CHAPTER 7

Inspector Fenton regarded me with his narrow eyes. "I can understand your defence of Mr O'Donoghue," he said. "After all, he is a charming man who appeared to help you in your hour of need. However, Mr O'Donoghue is no stranger to the officers here at Bow Street station."

"Perhaps not, but has he ever murdered anyone?"

"Not to our knowledge, Miss Green, but there is always a first time."

"A criminal is not necessarily a murderer."

"Not always, no."

"Inspector Fenton, have you ever considered that the same person could have committed all three murders?"

"*Three* murders?" He raised an eyebrow.

"Two other people have been murdered in St Giles recently. Mrs O'Brien and Mr Yeomans. Have you found the people responsible for their deaths?"

"Mrs O'Brien was killed by her husband, who is currently missing."

"But perhaps he didn't do it."

"There is no evidence pointing to anyone else. And as for

Mr Yeomans, he was murdered after an argument at The Three Feathers public house. No suspect has been arrested, but we suspect that it was a fellow drunkard. The regular customers of The Three Feathers are rather uncooperative, so it has been difficult to flush the suspect out. In these communities, you find that people often protect each other."

"Mr O'Donoghue told me that the motive for Mr Yeomans' murder was robbery."

"If Mr O'Donoghue has more information about the murder of Mr Yeomans, I shall be extremely interested to hear it."

"I hear that Mrs O'Brien and Mr Yeomans both had their throats cut in the same manner as Jack Burton."

"It is a common method of killing."

"But do you not think it something of a coincidence?"

"There is no similarity between the three victims, Miss Green. Now that concludes our interview." He glanced at the clock, which indicated that it was ten o'clock. "We must get down to the business of speaking to Mr O'Donoghue." Inspector Fenton got up from his chair.

"Did they know each other?"

"Who?"

"The three people who were murdered. Perhaps they all knew each other and their murderer?"

"Miss Green, it seems to me that you are clutching at straws in an attempt to create an entertaining tale for your readers. We are not in the business of entertaining here. We are in the business of solving crimes."

"Do you not even wish to consider the possibility? If three people have been murdered by the same person, there is a case for involving Scotland Yard."

Inspector Fenton's face reddened. "Are you trying to tell me how to do my job, Miss Green? There is no need for the

Yard to be involved. We are quite capable of managing our own affairs."

"Perhaps I might ask Inspector Blakely what he makes of it." I said this, despite the fact that I had no idea how to contact James in Manchester.

"Blakely? What does he have to do with this? Just a moment." He pointed a thick finger at me. "Are you the lady reporter who was embroiled with Blakely in the Lizzie Dixie case? Now I understand why you have your arm in a sling. I should have realised. You're a good friend of the Yard, aren't you?"

"Not particularly. There are plenty of detectives there who have never warmed to me."

"Hardly a surprise, I suppose, Miss Green. You are, after all, an ink slinger, and those of your profession have a reputation for meddling, spreading false rumours and generally hindering the business of the police."

"Perhaps the less reputable members of my profession would do such a thing, but I would not, Inspector Fenton."

He leant forward across the table, so that he could look down at me. "Why would you choose a profession such as this, Miss Green? It is hardly a suitable calling for the fairer sex."

I had noticed a hard look in his eye ever since I had first mentioned Scotland Yard.

"I think women are *perfect* for news reporting," said Inspector Pilkington snidely. "Naturally nosy." He tapped the side of his crooked nose and laughed.

I ignored the comment.

"I like to inform people and uncover the truth, Inspector Fenton. Too often, the truth is kept hidden."

"And it's kept hidden for a good reason."

"However uncomfortable it may make you, people have a right to know."

"Do they? Has it ever occurred to you, Miss Green, that if we tell the public everything that happens in our investigations they would be swarming all over London like a plague of locusts trying to solve crimes? Everyone from Mrs Grundy to 'Arry and his gal 'Arriet."

"I don't expect to report on all the details of a crime, Inspector. I merely think that people—"

"That's enough now, Miss Green. We need to speak to your friend, Mr O'Donoghue."

Inspector Fenton turned away from me, so I bit my tongue, picked up my gloves and bag, and left the room. The two inspectors walked behind me into the waiting area, where Reuben O'Donoghue was still sitting on the bench.

Reuben doffed his hat when he saw me.

"Thank you again for your help yesterday, Mr O'Donoghue."

"I didn't do much."

"But you certainly tried."

"I done me best, I s'pose. God rest 'is soul, poor boy."

"Are Mrs Nicholls and the missionaries not yet arrived?" I asked.

"Ain't seen 'em."

"Good day to you, Miss Green," said Inspector Fenton, impatient for me to leave.

I bid him farewell and pushed open the door. More snow had settled on the steps and pavement outside.

"Now then, Mr O'Donoghue. Consider yourself in custody," came Fenton's voice from behind me.

I let the door slam closed again and turned around. "You're arresting him?"

"I said *good day to you, Miss Green.*"

The inspector had a deep scowl on his face and maintained a firm hold on Reuben's arm. Reuben's face was pale.

"But he didn't do it, Inspector! I told you that!"

"The judge and the jury shall decide upon his fate, not you, Miss Green. It would be best for you to leave now before you find yourself in danger of impeding a police investigation."

Reuben watched me, his eyes wide and his forehead creased.

How different he looked now from the man who had chased after Jack in an attempt to retrieve my bag.

I wanted to stay and help him, but I knew I would likely find myself in trouble if I tried to do anything more. I turned and left the police station, resolving to do whatever I could to make sure the real killer was caught.

CHAPTER 8

There was no further snow the following day, but that which had already fallen sat in dirty frozen mounds swept up from doorways, paths and roads. After a morning at work in the reading room, I walked down Museum Street and Drury Lane, then turned into Short's Gardens, the road Reuben had chased Jack Burton along two days previously.

The inquest into Jack's death had taken place that morning at St Giles' Coroner's Court and returned a verdict of wilful murder by a person or persons unknown. As yet, there was no further evidence that Reuben O'Donoghue had killed the boy, and the coroner had urged the police to solve the case as quickly as possible.

The maze of grimy streets and passageways soon enveloped me. I clutched my carpet bag to my chest as I passed a cluster of children dressed in ragged clothes and throwing snowballs. In the street beyond the workhouse, a man with a withered hand played an accordion while a monkey in a makeshift dress skipped about on the cobbles. The monkey performer had drawn quite a crowd. Women chattered, babies cried and men leant up against doorways with their hands in their pockets, some of them swaying with drink. An old man with an eyepatch had cleared the snow and ice from one side of the lane to lay out numerous little glass bottles for sale at twopence each.

I came across two missionaries speaking to a woman in a doorway. One held a collection of pamphlets, while the other carried a pile of blankets. I asked the three of them where I could find Martha Nicholls, and fortunately the woman knew her. Following her directions, I eventually found the dismal courtyard where Jack had lost his life. I couldn't help glancing at the spot where he was found, which was covered with a blanket of smooth white snow. It was the only part of the courtyard that hadn't been swept. I felt a lump rise into my throat.

Shirts, petticoats and aprons hung stiffly from ropes that had been strung up between the buildings, and a stout woman in a headscarf was bent over a washtub. Another woman was sorting furs into piles as three children played by the privies. Her face was gaunt and she paused to produce a loud, rattling cough. I approached the laundry woman, who was scrubbing furiously at a washboard.

"Mrs Nicholls?" I said gently.

She stopped her work and looked up.

"The news reporter!"

Her face opened out into a toothless smile and she dried her hands on her apron. "Miss Green, ain't it? Yer s'posed to call me Martha."

Her nose and cheeks were red with cold, and she wore several old coats and scarves. I looked up at the broken and glassless windows in the building behind her.

"Is this where you live? Do you have a fire to keep you warm?"

"Yeah, and I got coal. I'm one o' the lucky ones. Winston

gives me it. Susan over there's 'aving to burn 'er table." Martha gestured towards the sunken-cheeked woman. "She won't take me coal."

"Who's Winston?"

She grinned proudly. "Me son. 'E's done well for 'imself. Got out of 'ere and works as a clerk in Guilford Street. 'E lives in Red Lion Square. Always got ink on 'is fingers."

"As have I." I laughed.

"You must be clever like 'im, then. It ain't no thanks to me that 'e's got to where 'e is. 'E went to Barnardo's down in Stepney. I couldn't afford ter keep 'im. 'E got 'is schoolin' there, and now 'e's cleverer than what his father ever were. Anyways, what can I do fer yer?"

"I hope you don't mind me visiting you. It's about Jack's murder. Have you heard that Reuben O'Donoghue has been arrested as a suspect?"

"Yeah, but I don't think he done it. I can't see 'im as bein' the murderin' type."

"That's what I think. The police need to be looking for someone else, don't they? Have you heard anything more about who else might have done it?"

"Ain't no one knows for sure. Some of 'em's sayin' it's the Daly Boys. That's a gang."

"Reuben mentioned them to me. But I've been thinking more about Mrs O'Brien and Mr Yeomans, and I'm wondering if you could tell me where their bodies were found. I'd like to see for myself what similarities there may be between their murders and the murder of Jack Burton."

"I ain't gonna tell yer."

"You won't?" I felt my heart sink.

"Nah! I'll take yer there meself!" Martha cackled at her joke and jabbed me with her elbow. "C'mon. Neither of 'em's far from 'ere. I'll take yer to where they found Roger first."

I walked with Martha through a maze of alleyways, past tumbledown shops, pubs and gin houses. We passed people trying to sell anything they could get their hands on, from shoelaces, matches, cress and song bills to sorry-looking apples and pears. Martha greeted many of them along the way.

"I hope I'm not keeping you from your work," I said.

"Think nothin' of it, none of it's dryin' any'ow. Mr Larcombe won't get 'is shirts back today. They're all 'angin' frozen on the line." Martha laughed. "I'm 'oping as the pump won't get frozen this winter. Trick is to wrap rags round it. I done that last year and it never froze once. I've wrapped on extra this week. What's 'appened to yer arm?"

"I fell off a pony."

"You got a pony? Where d'yer keep it?"

"Not my own pony; it was one from the riding stables in Hyde Park. Tell me about Jack. Did you know him well?"

"Not too well. 'E often 'ad a smile on 'is face, and when 'e were goin' straight he were shinin' boots on Shaftesbury Havenue."

"How old was he?"

"Proberly fourteen."

"And you think he was an orphan?"

"Yeah, I fink so. 'E lived wiv the Earl o' York and some lads down King's 'Ead Yard."

"And when he wasn't going straight, he was thieving?"

"Yeah, just nickin' silk 'ankerchiefs, snuff boxes, shirt pins. The usual. The Earl tells the lads to go out and not come back till they got money or summink they can sell."

"It doesn't sound as though Jack was malicious. He simply took my bag because of his difficult circumstances."

"Same as a lotta the lads. They don't wanna be nickin' stuff, does they? They does it 'cause they thinks they got no choice."

"I wonder if he knew his killer."

Martha shrugged her shoulders. "There's no way o' knowin', is there? Look, there's some toffs what 'ave come lookin' round."

Gathered by a pawnbroker's shop was a small group of people wearing common clothes, but they appeared clean and well-fed. They were listening intently to a woman wearing a brown velvet coat and a colourful feathered hat.

"The toffs pays money ter come lookin' round places like this," said Martha. "These lot'll 'ave just been in the pop-shop. Next they'll 'ave a look in a few 'ouses to see 'ow many people 'ave ter live in each one, and they'll go in the pub too. Them togs ain't what they normally wears. They reckons they looks like us!"

She cackled.

"That woman there's Mrs Baxter. She charges 'em a fine price ter look round and tells 'em she's gonna share the money out among us. Can't say I've seen any of it meself. She takes the ladies down the work'ouse so's they can get them-selves a slavey while they're down 'ere."

We neared the group and could hear Mrs Baxter talking. She stood in front of the greasy, latticed window of the pawn-broker's shop, in which jewellery, ornaments and keepsakes were stacked high.

"But when her father found out about the love affair, she threw herself off that roof there!" she said, pointing upwards.

Her words were met with startled gasps.

"And her ghost has walked this lane every night since!"

Martha chuckled. "They believes ev'ry word of it."

Mrs Baxter turned to look at us. She was a wide-faced woman with a heavy jaw and copper-coloured eyes.

"Martha Nicholls!" she said as we approached the group.

"Mornin', Mrs Baxter. Sad news about Boots, ain't it?"

Mrs Baxter's face became solemn. "Terribly sad."

She turned back to her tour group. "You may have heard that one of the boys here was tragically murdered two days ago. He had his throat cut."

Her voice became choked and there was a murmur of condolence in reply.

"I'll take you to the place where he was found murdered at the end of our tour. Meanwhile, Martha here was once followed by Polly Maguire's ghost the whole night!"

"You poor woman," said a well-spoken lady in a shabby tweed coat with missing buttons. She held out some coins to Martha, who refused them.

"I ain't in need o' charity, thank you, ma'am."

We walked on. "Were you really followed by Polly Maguire's ghost?" I asked.

"It were summink. I dunno if it were 'er or not. Anyways, come on. Mrs Baxter likes tellin' tales, and it's what people wants to 'ear, ain't it?"

We crossed Endell Street and entered a narrow alleyway between the wash houses and the workhouse. I could hear children playing beyond the workhouse's high wall. A dishevelled man and his dog sat at the base of the wall next to a dirty snow heap.

"Round 'ere," said Martha, leading me down a left turn. "This 'ere's the back o' the pub where Roger went drinkin'. The Three Feathers. See it?"

We stood in a fetid yard looking at a ramshackle, timbered pub slumped against the buildings either side of it.

"The men comes out the back 'ere when they needs ter do their business. People think that's what Roger were doin' when he were killed." She made a cutting gesture across her throat. "The landlord's found 'im the next mornin' lyin' in 'is blood. I think he were over there." She pointed at an icy puddle by a broken handcart.

"And no one knows who killed him?"

"Ev'ryone's thinkin' it were someone what was in the pub with 'im. 'E weren't an 'appy drunk; 'e were one what got into rows 'n' that. He weren't popular. 'E'd worked down the docks till 'e lost 'is leg."

"He was missing a leg?"

"'E 'ad a peg. Walked around all askew on 'is peg leg."

"So he would have struggled to defend himself."

"'E 'ad a punch on 'im. 'E were a boxer once. But wiv 'is peg 'e 'ad no balance."

I pictured Roger Yeomans staggering drunkenly about on his peg leg. It was quite possible that he hadn't been very like-able, but he sounded as though he had been a vulnerable man all the same. He had likely been an easy target for a cowardly killer.

"And when was he found?"

"We'nsd'y third o' Jan'ry"

"The third? Just six days ago?"

"Yeah, it'd be about that."

"Do you think the landlord would mind if we asked him a little more about Roger?"

"No! Don't yer be goin' in there!"

"Why not?"

"Yer wouldn't last long, honestly yer wouldn't. The place is full o' thieves 'n' whores and the landlord ain't someone yer wanna go talkin' to." Martha leant in closer and whispered. "Word is, 'e ate a man's kidneys."

"How?" I asked in disbelief.

Martha shrugged. "I'm only sayin' what I 'eard."

"Perhaps you can show me where Mrs O'Brien was found."

"Course. Follow me, deary."

"They's knockin' 'ouses down," said Martha as we passed a

street of half-demolished buildings. "Soon they'll 'ave knocked everythin' down and don't ask me where we're s'posed ter live after that. They won't want us in them fancy new ones! Mebbe I'll 'ave died afore that day arrives." She cackled again. "This 'ere's Nottin'am Court."

It was a narrow, dingy street lined with houses that had seen better days.

"'Ello, Martha!" called out a young boy as he ran past us.

A little girl sat in a doorway with a kitten in her arms, her dress was thin and a tattered shawl covered her shoulders. She looked up at us with large, wary eyes.

"Mornin' Hettie," said Martha. Nearby two young boys fought over some marbles. The older one shoved the other one backwards and he fell, hitting his head on the cobbles.

"Careful now!" shouted Martha, righting the startled child. "Yer almost knocked Will's brains out John! Where's yer ma got to?"

John looked about five years old and he pointed sullenly at a doorway. The shouts of an arguing couple could be heard from within.

"That's Molly in there," said Martha, with a disapproving tone to her voice. "Be'ave yerselves, boys, till yer ma comes out."

I looked again at Hettie and worried about her with only a thin dress to wear in the cold. She wasn't the first child I'd seen dressed in such a way and I knew, with a heavy heart, that she wouldn't be the last. I wished there was something I could do about it.

We walked on.

"Mrs O'Brien lived just along 'ere," said Martha. "Y'know the toffs what we saw just now? Well, some on 'em used ter come lookin' round Mrs O'Brien's 'ouse ter see what poor folk lives like. She 'ranged it wiv Mrs Baxter and got tuppence each time. Quite a lotta folks want the toffs ter come lookin' round 'cause they gets money outta it. The man in the mask's bin seen along 'ere 'n' all."

"Who's the man in the mask? Another ghost?"

"Nah, he's real enough. A few folks 'ave said as what they've seen 'im."

"Have you seen him?"

"Nah."

"And he wears a mask, you say? What sort of mask?"

"Like one what they wears in the theatre, or so I've 'eard."

"And he's been seen on this street?"

"Yeah, but only night-times."

"What about the night Mrs O'Brien was murdered?"

"Dunno."

We reached a door with planks of wood nailed across it.

"'Ere," said Martha. "Mrs O'Brien was found by 'er front door 'ere." She poked at the cobbles with her patched-up boot. "Irish she was. 'Usband's Irish 'n' all."

"And this was just after Christmas?"

"Yeah. Twenny-seventh, and they reckons she were murdered on the twenny-sixth. Mr Ayres found 'er about four in the mornin'. Still recoverin' from the shock of it, 'e is. 'E's 'ad problems with 'is nerves ever since."

"And her throat was cut?"

"Yeah. Hev'ryone says it's 'im what done it."

"The husband? Mr O'Brien?"

"Yeah, he ain't been seen for the best part of a year. They reckons 'e ran outta money and come back, and then 'e's cut 'is wife's throat and gone off with the money what she 'ad."

"Did anyone see him?"

"Nah, no one seen 'im."

"So he might not have come back?"

"Might not've. No one saw no one else round 'ere, but it's as good a hexplanation as we got."

I looked up the street with the leaden sky over the dark

buildings and the scantily clad children playing among the mounds of dirty snow. I felt a heavy, despondent sensation in my chest.

"Even if Reuben O'Donoghue did kill Jack," I ventured, "he wouldn't have killed Mrs O'Brien and Mr Yeomans as well, would he?"

"'Ard to imagine it. I don't think he woulda done. Trouble is, the bobbies knows 'im 'n' 'e's been harrested afore now, so it's easier for 'em when they got someone they know."

"What's he been arrested for?"

"Fightin'. The bobbies remembers about the fights 'e's got into and they remembers a face, don't they?"

We walked back up Nottingham Court.

"Did Jack, Mrs O'Brien and Mr Yeomans know each other?"

"Yeah. Mr Yeomans were married to Mrs O'Brien's sister, though they 'ad a fallin' out, and Mr Yeomans used ter pay Jack to run errands for 'im."

"What sort of errands?"

"Just gettin' stuff for 'im; whatever 'e needed. And Mr Yeomans were friendly with the Earl o' York."

"Is that so?"

I recalled the shady leader of the Seven Dials Gang loitering in the courtyard the night that Jack was murdered.

If the victims had all known each other, had they also known their assailant?

We reached the pawnbroker's shop and I tried to thank Martha Nicholls for her time by offering her a shilling, but she wouldn't take it.

"Yer needs to meet our Winston," she said.

"Your son?"

"Yeah. 'E thinks there's summink amiss 'n' all. Yer've both got clever minds, I can tell. Yer needs ter speak to 'im."

CHAPTER 9

The lights flickered off in the reading room and the silence was broken by a chorus of groans and curses.

"Not again!" a red-whiskered man seated opposite me called out.

"The wonders of electricity," said my neighbour, a pale man with dark, beady eyes. "Bring back the gas lamps, I say. At least they were reliable."

I returned to my notes, which were difficult to read in the increasing gloom. It was only mid-afternoon, but heavy snow clouds were pushing the light out of the day.

"Good afternoon, Miss Green," whispered a voice in my ear. "How is your work on the book progressing?"

I turned to see a set of olive green eyes staring at me through a pair of spectacle lenses.

"You startled me, Mr Edwards!"

"Oh, did I?" He took a step back. "I do apologise. I'm terribly sorry. I shouldn't have disturbed you."

"Please don't worry. The book will take me a while yet as I have to work on something more urgent for now."

"You're managing to write well with your left hand." He glanced down at my notes.

"Not really. It's a struggle to read what I've written if I'm honest."

"I suppose the moral of the story is not to get on an excitable pony!"

"Exactly that. Is there some trouble with the lights again?"

"Sadly, yes." He tutted. "We have someone looking at the electricity at this very moment, so hopefully full light will be restored shortly. Let me know if you would like me to fetch the map of Colombia again, Miss Green."

I thanked him and he moved on.

"Very attentive that clerk, isn't he?" whispered the red-whiskered man to the pale man next to me. "If one is a lady, that is."

"You can't blame the fellow," replied my neighbour. "Having a few ladies around the place rather brightens it up, doesn't it?"

"Indeed, gentlemen," I replied. "My sole reason for working here is to brighten up your surroundings."

The red-whiskered man rolled his eyes.

I looked back at the notes I had made since my walk with Martha. I had written down everything I could remember and had also drawn some crude maps, marking the location of each victim with a cross. I had made a note of the dates and approximate times of their murders and then written down their connections with each other. I read and reread my words, feeling increasingly certain that the three murders had been carried out by the same person.

The Head Librarian announced from the upper gallery that work was being done to restore the electricity, but, should it fail, the reading room would be closed due to poor light.

"Darn it!" called out the red-whiskered man. "How on earth is one supposed to finish one's thesis?"

Jack Burton, Ellen O'Brien and Roger Yeomans.

I turned the names over in my mind.

Was anyone in the Holborn police division interested in finding out what had happened to them, or were they simply content to arrest Reuben O'Donoghue and place the blame on him? Did Inspector Fenton know something I didn't, or was he just being lackadaisical?

I found a clean sheet of paper and began to write out the reasons why I thought the murders were linked and why they should be considered as part of a single investigation. My plan was to take the paper into Bow Street police station the following day and give it to Inspector Fenton. I wanted to write that I thought the case was a matter for Scotland Yard, but I knew that would anger him.

The lights flickered back on.

"Hurrah!" shouted the red-whiskered man.

"Miss Green," whispered a familiar voice. I looked up to find Edgar Fish standing next to me in his dark grey frock coat and top hat. "What are you working on?" He stared closely at my notes. "Did Sherman ask you to do that?"

"No, it's just something I'm looking into."

"The murder in St Giles?"

"Yes. I think the wrong man has been arrested."

"Oh dear." Edgar shook his head. "The last time you got involved in something like this, you lost your job."

"But I was reinstated because I was, in fact, correct."

Edgar sighed. "Why not do what I do? Simply work on the stories Sherman tells you to. You always insist on giving yourself additional work to do."

"I was there," I whispered to Edgar. "I saw the boy. He had my bag. Someone killed him after he ran off with *my bag*. Two other people have also been killed."

"I know: Mrs O'Brien and a drunkard. Look, I think

you're creating a tempest in a teacup here. It's not worth your time. You'll antagonise people and generally make things rather ticklish for yourself. *Again*."

"Have you visited St Giles recently?"

"No, and I can't say that I plan to."

"It's a thoroughly miserable place. There are children in rags running around barefoot in the snow, and I met a lady who was having to burn her own table for firewood."

Edgar chuckled.

"Why is that amusing?" I hissed.

"It's not amusing, but you are, Miss Green. You seem to think that by showing an interest in these murders you are somehow helping the people who live there."

"It's not quite like that."

"There's nothing you can do about their situation, Miss Green, other than thank God himself that you're not living there. The slums have been there for hundreds of years; the people who live there now are the children, grandchildren and great grandchildren of slum-dwellers. They are trapped in poverty. It's a terribly sad fact, and yet we must accept it. The slums will continue to be there long after you and I have had our day."

"But does it not seem unfair to you?"

"Of course it's unfair. And we must be grateful we are not the ones who have been dealt the bad hand. The churches and chapels can help the poor. I believe the slums are inundated with missions these days. And the police are there to solve the crimes. There is little else for you to do, unless of course you wish to become a philanthropist?"

"I certainly would if I had the money."

"Fish!" came a harsh whisper from behind us. We turned to see Tom Clifford from *The Holborn Gazette*. His pork pie hat was pushed back on his head and his slack jaw chewed persistently on a piece of tobacco.

"I don't often see you in the library, Tom," whispered Edgar.

"Don't often come 'ere, that's why." He continued to chew and stare at Edgar.

"Can I help you, Clifford?" asked Fish.

I thought it odd to see the two of them confront each other in this manner, as they had once been good friends.

"I think you should talk outside," I whispered. "The people around us are trying to work."

"*Trying* being the operative word," said the red-whiskered man.

"Nothing much to talk about," said Tom. "Just exchanging pleasantries. Thieved any more stories recently, Fish?"

"I don't steal stories."

"No? Then how comes you stole mine?"

"It wasn't much of a story, though, was it?" I said.

"Keep out of it, woman!" Tom jabbed a tobacco-stained finger in my direction.

"Don't you dare speak to a lady in that manner!" said Edgar in a raised voice, which made everyone around us look up and stare.

"I can talk to her however I like!" retorted Tom. "She works for the *Morning Express*, don't she? She's as worthless as you are!"

"How dare you!"

Edgar gave Tom a shove on the shoulder. Tom responded by pushing both of Edgar's shoulders, and Edgar fell back against my chair.

"Oi!" shouted the red-whiskered man, rising to his feet.

Edgar raised his fist and lunged at Tom, who ducked out of the way with a laugh.

"Stop that this instant!" Mr Edwards ran over and stood between them, his sandy hair flopping over his spectacles. "There is to be no fighting in the reading room!"

He pushed his hair out of his eyes and gave me a glance that suggested he was disappointed to see me consorting with such men. The Head Librarian, a plump, round-faced man, marched over from his desk into the centre of the room.

Edgar and Tom straightened their jackets and glared at each other.

The Head Librarian held out his hand. "Reading tickets, please."

"You're expelling us?" said Edgar in dismay. "But we're journalists!"

"You could be the Prince Consort for all I care. Reading tickets, please!"

Edgar and Tom rummaged about in their pockets before handing him their cards.

"Thank you. You are no longer permitted to visit the reading room. You too, madam."

The Head Librarian turned to me and I stared back, open-mouthed.

"Are you not with these two gentlemen?" he said. "Your reading ticket, please."

"No, not Miss Green. She had nothing to do with it," said Edgar. "She was busy working and I interrupted her and then *he* interrupted me. Miss Green is blameless."

The Head Librarian stared at me, his eyes blue and slightly bulging. "Blameless? Really? Most fights usually take place over some woman or other."

"The lady is blameless," added my pale neighbour. "I witnessed the entire encounter."

"Thank you, sir. Miss Green you have a reprieve. Out you go, gentlemen!" He pointed at the door.

"Thank you," I said to the pale man, relieved that I hadn't lost my reading ticket. I looked up at Mr Edwards, but he simply shook his head and walked away.

CHAPTER 10

I t was early evening by the time I returned to Bow Street police station. Polished carriages stopped on the opposite side of the street, depositing men in top hats and women in evening gowns at the Royal Opera House. Ahead of me, two constables wrestled a red-faced man in through the door of the station. I followed them and asked at the desk for Inspector Fenton.

The red-faced man loudly protested his innocence and tried to struggle free from the constables, receiving three truncheon blows for his trouble.

"Chief Inspector Fenton ain't 'ere, madam," said the desk officer.

"How about Inspector Pilkington?"

I wanted to hand my papers directly to Fenton, but I supposed that Pilkington would have to do. The bobby nodded and I took a seat on the bench. The red-faced man was bustled through the door beside the desk and Inspector Pilkington appeared soon afterwards. He wore his overcoat, as if he were about to leave after a day's work.

"Miss Green, what can I do for you?"

He glanced over at the door as though he would rather be on his way home than talking to me. I got to my feet.

"Thank you for agreeing to see me, Inspector Pilkington." I opened my carpet bag and pulled out the pages of notes I had written in the reading room. "I have been back to St Giles and spoken with a resident there who told me more about the murders of Mrs O'Brien and Mr Yeomans. I have discovered they knew one another and that Mr Yeomans also knew Jack Burton."

Inspector Pilkington gazed down his crooked nose at me. "Is that all, Miss Green?"

I gritted my teeth and continued. "Inspector, my suggestion is that a single perpetrator murdered these three victims. The manner of death is the same, and each was murdered when it was dark."

"There's a lot of darkness at this time of year, Miss Green."

"I realise that, but do you not see the similarities? I find it difficult to believe that three separate people have decided to cut someone's throat within the same area in the past fortnight. Do you not think it a coincidence?"

"I can't deny that it appears to be a coincidence, Miss Green, but stranger things have happened. Especially in St Giles' Rookery."

"I've written everything down. Look, I even drew some maps. Can you see how small the area within which the murders were committed is?"

"Yes, I see. And we have maps here at the station, too." A faint smile lifted one corner of his mouth.

"I can't help but think you're not taking me seriously, Inspector."

"Miss Green you're a news reporter, not a detective. I have no doubt that you would make a good detective. Your notes are certainly very thorough. But may I suggest that you concentrate on your profession and allow me to concentrate on mine?"

"Do you not think it unlikely that Mr O'Donoghue could have committed all three murders?"

"We have further questions to put to Mr O'Donoghue, Miss Green."

"You're going to question him about Mrs O'Brien and Mr Yeomans?"

"It would not be proper to impart any further information about our investigations, especially not to a news reporter, Miss Green. Now, if you will excuse me, I'm finished for the day."

He turned to walk towards the door and I felt a rising sense of frustration.

"You need to keep looking for the murderer, Inspector! Mr O'Donoghue is innocent, and while you're concentrating your efforts on him, the man who has committed these three murders is still roaming the streets! Does it not occur to you that he might strike again, Inspector?"

"That would be most unexpected." He paused by the door and I hoped that he was considering my words.

"Are you not at least prepared to entertain the idea? Here, take my notes and please show them to Chief Inspector Fenton."

His lip raised in a sneer, but he took the pieces of paper from my hand.

"Perhaps I am wrong," I continued, "but surely every possibility should be considered? It would be rather careless detective work, otherwise."

His eyes narrowed. "Thank you, and that really is all now, Miss Green. The hour is late and you should be making your way home. The streets around here are no place for a lady wandering about on her own."

CHAPTER 11

The mercury continued to drop and small icicles hung inside the window of my lodgings. The water pump in Mrs Garnett's yard had frozen and I had to visit the baths in Ironmonger Row before starting my work for the day. Once again, I wore three pairs of stockings and the extra woollen dress to keep me warm.

As I walked to the reading room, I couldn't help thinking about Martha and the residents of St Giles, and how they were managing in this cold with no proper doors and windows, and with little fuel to burn. I made a short detour to buy some tea and hot buttered toast from a stall by the brewery on Castle Street.

Despite the cold, Martha was in her yard scrubbing at her washing tub when I arrived.

"Your pump hasn't frozen?"

"Nah, and it ain't gonna freeze neither. Got the rags wrapped round it, ain't I?"

She was wearing more coats than the last time I had seen her and had three headscarves knotted under her chin. When

I gave her the tea and toast she laughed, sending a large cloud of breath into the freezing air.

"Yer don't need ter be bringin' me breakfast."

"But it's extremely cold."

"I seen more winters than just about any of 'em livin' round 'ere. I ain't been carried off by the consumption yet. I'll give this ter Susan. She needs it more than what I does."

Martha took the tea and toast to the sunken-cheeked woman who was once again in the yard sorting furs. I sadly watched her divide the toast among her children before suffering another coughing fit.

"Does she need to see a doctor?" I asked Martha quietly.

"Proberly. I've told 'er she needs to go over the work'ouse. They got doctors there, see. But she won't 'ave it; she's too proud for the work'ouse. She'll be all right. The missionaries'll check on 'er, and they'll 'ave some soup on the go today. Lemme show yer."

The mission was on Neal Street, in a red-brick building which looked to have once been a warehouse. It had been turned into a makeshift chapel, with a wooden cross nailed up on the door and a painted sign which read: 'The Mission of Faith, Hope and Charity. Everyone welcome.'

About two dozen men, women and children were queuing up alongside a row of trestle tables. They cradled tin bowls in their hands. Steam rose up from the large soup kettles as the missionaries dipped their ladles into them.

"Told yer," said Martha. "Already got the soup goin' on this mis'rable cold mornin'. They looks after us. They tells us we should believe in Jesus, and we all pretends we does so we gets our soup!"

She cackled and looked over at the small crowd around us. "Seems like just about hev'ryone's 'ere this mornin'. There's the Earl o' York."

In the daylight, I could see that he was a short, lean man

with a keen, shrew-like face and a thin moustache. A clay pipe was clasped between his lips, and he wore a top hat and a dark blue, velvet overcoat, which was several sizes too large for him. A gold watch chain hung across his cream, brocaded waistcoat.

"He looks rather well-dressed to be a gang leader," I muttered.

"'E fancies 'imself as a swell. Them togs'll be from the rag shops down Lumber Court. Wiv a bitta work you can get 'em all cleaned up nice."

A cold wind whipped down the street, carrying with it stinging flakes of ice.

"Are you going to have some soup?" I asked Martha.

"I'll let some o' the others 'ave a go first. They needs it more than an old woman like me. The urchins needs it the most."

"Mrs Nicholls!" one of the missionaries called out, waving.

We walked over to him as he continued to serve out the soup.

"This is Mr 'Ugo 'Awkins," said Martha. "Remember 'im?"

"I think so," I replied. "You were in the yard on the night that Jack died, weren't you, Mr Hawkins?"

He nodded solemnly. "I was indeed. Miss Green, isn't it? Nice to see you in the light of day."

He stood slightly shorter than me and was about forty-five, with close-set blue eyes. Large ears protruded from beneath his felt hat and he had thick grey side-whiskers.

"It's a pleasure to see you again, Mr Hawkins," I said. "How good of you to be serving soup on a cold day such as this."

"It's the Christian way, and the very least we can do for the people who are in need of food. If you have any spare coins, Miss Green, the mission is always in need of donations."

He gestured towards a plate that had some coins on it and then he filled a bowl held out by a thin girl with matted hair.

"An extra spoonful for you, child," he said, before turning back to face us. "It was a sad day yesterday, wasn't it, Mrs Nicholls?"

I placed a sixpence on the plate.

"Yeah, we 'ad young Jack's funeral."

"It was his funeral yesterday?" I realised I should have asked when it was. "I should have liked to come."

"Yer busy," said Martha. "Yer one o' them women what's got a proper profession. I'd 'ave liked a proper profession if I'd 'ad any brains between me ears. Well, look who it is!"

She watched as a young, broad-shouldered man with fair whiskers approached us.

"Winston!"

Her son wore a grey tweed overcoat and a bowler hat. Martha walked over and gave him a warm embrace.

"'Ere's me Winston!" she said proudly, pulling him over by the arm to meet me.

She introduced us and told Winston what I did for a living.

"A news reporter, Miss Green? How interesting. A *lady* news reporter?"

"There aren't many of us."

"Next to none, I should imagine."

Winston struggled to look me in the eye and I noticed that his whiskers had been cultivated to compensate for a receding chin.

"'Ow comes yer not workin'?" Martha asked her son.

"Everything's frozen up, Ma; even the ink in the inkwells. They told us we can have the day off."

"A day off! That's nice, ain't it?"

"It would be if they were paying us for it."

Another gust of icy wind made Winston clasp his hat tightly.

"This weather would freeze the tail off a brass monkey. Have you had some soup, Ma?"

"Not yet, but I will. Look, 'ere's Mr Meares," said Martha as another missionary joined us. "Mr Meares was there that night with Mr 'Awkins. You remembers 'im, don't yer, Miss Green?"

"Yes, of course." My memories of him were of little more than a shadowy figure in the yard. I could now see that he was a tall, freckle-faced young man with grey eyes and a dimpled chin. He had a straw-coloured moustache and a smiling, cheerful demeanour.

"Miss Green! I remember. The poor boy took your bag, didn't he?"

"Yes."

"And I see that you have had it returned to you."

I looked down at the carpet bag in my hand. "Yes, although I don't suppose it matters when you consider that a young boy lost his life in the process."

"St Giles is a dangerous place," said David Meares. "At least you remained safe during the incident, Miss Green. We've become rather used to it, I'm afraid. We worked in the slums in Salford for a few years, didn't we Hugo?"

The older man nodded in reply and gave his protégé a smile.

"At least Reuben O'Donoghue's been arrested for the murder," said Winston.

"I'm still not sure why," I said. "He was trying to help me. He chased after Jack when the poor boy took my bag."

"And then cut his throat when he caught up with him!" said Winston.

"No, he couldn't have done it."

"Who else did it, then?" Winston's voice had an unpleasant nasal whine to it.

"I don't know, but Mr O'Donoghue was simply being helpful."

Winston laughed. "I'm not sure about that! Have you told her, Ma?"

"Told 'er what?"

"About Reuben O'Donoghue. That ne'er-do-well."

"'E's 'ad 'is moments."

"*He's had his moments,*" repeated Winston. "That's 'Ma speak' for, 'He's a murderer.' Miss Green, did you know that Mr O'Donoghue once punched a man so hard he broke his jaw?"

This time, he fixed his pale eyes on me, as if he hoped I would show some sign of revulsion. I struggled to believe that he was talking about the same man I had met.

"Sadly, there are many in St Giles who have troubled lives," said David. "They remind me of myself, as I was in a similar situation until I met Hugo. I'm indebted to him for showing me the right path. That's why the mission is here, in fact. If we can help these people live in the Christian way, St Giles' Rookery will be changed forever."

"It'll take more than that," scoffed Winston.

"I hope to visit Mr O'Donoghue while he's in custody," continued David, ignoring Winston's comment. "A time of prayer will give the man some solace. He has given the mission some generous donations in the past, and we have tried our best to help him mend his ways."

"No chance of that." Winston laughed. "He's too busy fighting with his fists and knives in The King's Head."

"Really?" I thought of Reuben's smile and struggled to imagine such a violent side to his character.

"Yeah, so it's no surprise it's come to this. Murder was the next rung on the ladder for him," said Winston.

"Very sad," added David.

There was a pause in the conversation, during which I found myself sombrely staring at the cobbles beneath my feet. I thought of the notes I had given to Inspector Pilkington about the murders and how I had insisted that Reuben O'Donoghue was innocent of Jack's murder.

Had I been mistaken?

CHAPTER 12

"Penelope, you're late," said my sister Eliza as a waiter showed me to her table.

She rose from her seat and we embraced.

"I'm sorry, Ellie, I'm rather busy with my work at present."

We sat down and I removed my gloves.

"You're trying to do too much again, no doubt. I don't know how you're going to find enough time to write the book about Father."

We had agreed to meet for lunch in the Fitzroy Dining Rooms; a smart restaurant with gleaming white tablecloths and an elaborately corniced ceiling. Voices hummed around us, cutlery chinked and the smell of roasted meat made my stomach grumble.

Like me, Eliza was blonde-haired and brown-eyed. She was three years my junior and married to a lawyer, George Billington-Grieg. Her energies were devoted to the West London Women's Society, which boasted a membership of more than seventy women and was forging strong links with the National Society for Women's Suffrage.

"Did you ride here on your bicycle?" I asked.

"Of course. The Maître d'Hôtel kindly found space for it by the kitchens. Did I tell you someone tried to steal it a few weeks ago? I'd left it by the stationers on Queen's Road while I made the briefest of shopping visits, and I stepped out onto the street to find some fellow trying to ride off on it! He didn't succeed, of course. He hadn't a clue what to do with the pedals. I hurled the paperweight I had just purchased at him and it hit his back! Then off he scarpered. Fortunately, the paperweight survived unscathed."

"And your bicycle was also unscathed?"

"It was."

Eliza called over to the waiter. "Could you take our order, please?"

She turned back to face me and lowered her voice. "Much as I adore this restaurant, it wouldn't do to be sitting here all afternoon."

"You're wearing a new jacket, Ellie. It suits you very well."

"Thank you! It's double-worsted, which is much needed in this weather."

Her jacket was red and she wore it over a loose divided skirt in a matching shade. Her clothing allowed her to ride her bicycle without suffering the indecency of her skirts riding up.

"The cuffs on your jacket look a little frayed," said Eliza.

I examined the green velvet sleeves on the jacket that had become a firm favourite of mine. Unfortunately, Eliza's observation was accurate.

"Have you bought any new clothes recently?" she probed.

"Not recently."

"I know you're busy, Penelope, but you need to take a little more care over your appearance. I know many married women who have allowed their standards to slip a little over the years, but when you're looking for a husband it's important to—"

Thankfully we were interrupted by the waiter arriving to take our order.

"How's the arm?" asked Eliza once the waiter had left.

"I hope to stop wearing the sling in a week or two."

"It must be a terrible inconvenience."

"It is rather, and I think it singled me out as a target for a young bag pincher. With my arm in a sling, he must have seen that I would be unable to put up much of a fight."

"He took your bag?" Eliza's eyes widened.

"Yes, but fortunately I got it back. It had Father's letters and diaries in it."

"Oh, Penelope, that's terrible. You could have lost everything!"

"I shall be more careful with his papers from now on. But that's not the worst of it."

I told Eliza about Jack's murder and the other murders I had heard about in St Giles. She listened intently as we dined on mock turtle soup.

"Well I never! I read all about the boy's murder and didn't have an inkling that you had been involved!" She mopped up the last of her soup with a wedge of bread. "You take a lot of risks in your line of work."

"I wasn't working when my bag was taken, Ellie. I was simply walking down the street."

She gave me a doubtful look. "I worry about you. Look at you sitting there with your arm in a sling from all that terrible business last year and now, before your arm's even healed, you're embroiled in something new! I can't help but think that if you had someone looking after you—"

"Not *this* conversation again." I sighed.

"Yes. And of course you know all this, I've told you

enough times, but married women don't find themselves in the scrapes you do, Penelope."

"Are you suggesting that's a good or a bad thing?"

Eliza rubbed her temples. "I don't suppose it's either really. But you know what I mean, don't you? A husband would... I'm not sure how to put this without causing offence." She took a sip of wine. "A husband would ensure that you looked after yourself."

"A husband would prohibit me from working. Just as George does with you."

My sister flinched as though this remark had wounded her. "Not necessarily. A husband mightn't stop you at all. As for George, that's just how he is. He's proud and he doesn't want anybody entertaining the idea that he doesn't earn enough to support his family. It's the way he was brought up by his father. I have very little time for my father-in-law, as you well know."

"But you should like to have a profession, shouldn't you?"

"Yes, and I've made some amends with my voluntary work. Besides, we aren't talking about me, Penelope. We're talking about you."

"I'm happy as I am, Ellie."

"Are you sure? I worry about you almost as much as I worry about my own children. I suppose that... well, I just wish that you were settled."

Eliza rested her hand on mine.

"I *am* settled, and I have Tiger," I replied. "This is what I always wanted to do. You remember me wanting to be a writer even as a child, don't you?"

"I do indeed. You used to make us read all your stories!"

"And you remember how much Father encouraged me?"

"He was extremely encouraging, although I don't think he expected you to take off to London. I think he anticipated you remaining in Derbyshire and becoming a writer there."

"I wanted to come to London. I like an adventure, just as he did."

"But you shouldn't be putting your life at risk as he did."

"This is what I have always wanted to do. And I enjoy my work. Most of the time, at least."

"What do you mean by *most of the time?*"

"This week has been rather difficult, and I'm concerned that I may have made a mistake." I dabbed at a splash of soup on my chin with my serviette.

"Oh dear. What sort of mistake?"

"I told you just now that the police have arrested Reuben O'Donoghue, the man who chased after Jack. I couldn't believe that he would kill a boy so brutally in that manner. He just doesn't seem the sort to do it. On two occasions now I've appealed to the detectives at Bow Street station to let poor Reuben go free."

"So that is your mistake?" she asked.

"Well, there have been three murders in St Giles in recent weeks."

"That's dreadful!"

"And I think they've been committed by the same person. For a while I couldn't possibly imagine that Reuben might have murdered three people. I spent some time visiting the scenes of the murders. I wrote down my thoughts and drew some simple maps."

"Maps?" Eliza raised an eyebrow.

"Yes, just so that I could understand what had happened and when. And then I gave my notes to one of the detectives, asking him to consider the possibility that the murders had all been carried out by one person, and that this person could not possibly have been Reuben O'Donoghue."

"Do you have any evidence to support this theory?"

"Not especially."

"So this is something you've put together on a whim? A hunch that perhaps this man is not the guilty party?"

"I realise now that this is what I've done. It didn't seem that way while I was working on it. At the time I was certain, absolutely certain, that the three victims had been murdered by the same person and that Reuben was completely innocent of any involvement in their deaths. But having spoken to a few people, it seems Reuben may not be as charming as he first seemed."

"Isn't that always the case?"

"Yes, it is. I should have known better, shouldn't I?"

"You always have been rather impulsive, Penelope. It wouldn't do you any harm to give matters a little more thought before you decide to act."

"I'm worried that I've made myself appear rather foolish."

"If you've been undertaking your own investigations and given written reports and maps to the police, then I would say that you probably have been rather foolish. Can you still say with any certainty that this Reuben fellow is innocent?"

"I don't know. Having been convinced that he was, I've heard certain things said about him which suggest he is a rather violent man."

"So now you regret trying to demonstrate that Reuben is innocent as he may be guilty after all?"

"Yes. I'm worried that I may have been rather rash."

"It sounds as though you have been. I would leave the investigating to the police from now on."

"But they don't understand what has been happening in St Giles!"

"And you do?"

"I like to think that I do," I said after a pause. "But perhaps I am also mistaken about that."

CHAPTER 13

"**A**h, Miss Green. My favourite lady news reporter," said Edgar when I arrived in the newsroom.

"Perhaps the *only* lady news reporter you know of?"

"No, I know dozens of them and you're my absolute favourite."

"You're an abominable liar, Edgar. What do you want?"

I took my papers out of my bag and sat down at my desk.

"With all this General Gordon business going on, Sherman's asked me to write an article about the Sudan."

"That should present you with an enjoyable challenge."

"It requires rather a lot of research."

"You don't know anything about the Sudan?"

"I know a moderate amount. But a few historical and geographical books would certainly enlighten me."

"Such as those found in the British Library's reading room?"

Edgar cleared his throat. "Which is a pity, because I am no longer allowed inside the reading room."

Frederick Potter paused from his work and looked up. "Why are you not allowed in there?" he asked.

"Edgar's had his reading ticket taken away from him," I said.

"Why?"

"For fighting with Tom Clifford," I explained.

"You had a fight with Tom Clifford in the reading room of the British Library?" Frederick slapped his desk and threw his head back in laughter.

"I fail to see why it's so amusing," said Edgar.

"It could only happen to you, couldn't it?" said Frederick, wiping tears of mirth from his eyes. "That's the funniest thing I've heard this year!"

"It's only the fourteenth of January. So far, competition for the year's funniest event is rather scarce."

"Did Tom Clifford also have his reading ticket taken away?"

Edgar nodded and Frederick laughed again.

"His editor, Cropper, is going to be hopping mad. What did Sherman say? He can't have been happy."

Edgar said nothing.

"*You haven't told him?*" said Frederick. "Even funnier!"

"Hilarious," said Edgar.

"You have to tell Mr Sherman," I said. "Access to the reading room is essential for your work."

"I am absolutely *not* telling Sherman that I've had my reading ticket confiscated. I will find a way to appeal. Perhaps my father will write a favourable letter to the Head Librarian."

"Is it a lifetime confiscation?" I asked.

"How should I know? He didn't show any sign of returning it soon, did he? Miss Green, when you are next in the reading room – which I'm hoping you will be within the next day or two – would you mind taking down some notes about the Sudan for me?"

"How am I supposed to find the time, Edgar?"

"You manage to find time to do other things, such as wandering around St Giles trying to solve murder cases."

"I've been working on the story of Jack Burton's murder."

"You've been doing more than that, though, haven't you? I saw your notes. You're trying to do the police's work for them."

"I am *not*."

I took offence at the suggestion, even though I knew there was an element of truth to it.

"Anyhow, my reporting on the matter will be limited to Mr O'Donoghue's trial from now on."

"Is that so? Miss Green, don't forget that I defended you when the Head Librarian also threatened to take away your reading ticket."

"That's correct, you did. Thank you, Edgar."

"See what a gentleman I am?" said Edgar to Frederick. "I made sure that Miss Green would not be expelled from the reading room."

"Extremely honourable of you, Fish."

"You'd think she would happily repay me in some manner, wouldn't you?"

I sighed. "What is your deadline for the Sudan article?"

"Thursday. Are you going to do the research for me?"

"If you're not going to tell Sherman about the ban, I suppose I have very little choice, don't I? I can't be doing your research for you indefinitely, though. You will have to decide whether to tell Mr Sherman what happened or find a way to get your reading ticket back."

"I'll get it back, Miss Green, don't you worry. My father will pull some strings for me, as he usually does."

Mr Sherman entered the newsroom with a slam of the door.

"Morning," he grunted.

"It's Mr Small Aim Whiner," said Edgar removing his pencil from behind his ear as though he were about to do some work.

"Is that another of your anagrams, Fish? If only you devoted as much brain time to something useful. In fact, you should be in the reading room. Your article on the Sudan will require a good deal of research."

"Yes, of course," said Edgar, giving me an uneasy glance.

I noticed Frederick stifling a snigger.

"Miss Green, there is news on the Jack Burton case," said Mr Sherman. "E Division has announced this morning that their suspect, Mr O'Donoghue, has been released."

"Released?" I said with surprise.

"That's what you wanted, isn't it?" said Edgar.

"I'm not sure any more."

"It is of no importance what Miss Green or any other of us think about that news. The police are the ones armed with the facts and they have made the decision to release him, which means, of course, that the suspect is still at large."

I felt a horrible, heavy feeling in my chest, worried that my notes about Reuben O'Donoghue's innocence had influenced the decision to release him.

Surely they hadn't paid too much attention to anything I had written?

"Have they released him because they've found another suspect?" I asked.

"They haven't said," replied Mr Sherman. "It's your job to find out, so I suggest you have a conversation with Inspector Fenton and find out which direction they are taking the Jack Burton investigation in now."

"I will."

"So what are you waiting for? Fish, off to the reading room with you. Miss Green, you need to get out there and uncover what's going on."

I gathered up my papers and put them back in my bag. I couldn't face the detectives at Bow Street station again. I had already pestered them with my misinformation and now I had to decide whether I could, in good conscience, stand by it.

Had I been right or had I encouraged them to release a triple murderer?

CHAPTER 14

I walked from Fleet Street to Drury Lane with my bonnet pulled down firmly over my ears. Lampposts and signs were spectral in the heavy fog, and the ice underfoot showed no sign of melting. The fresh air and flowery scents of the Andes came to mind and I empathised with my father's yearning for exotic destinations. He had told me that the best months for travel in South America were between October and July, which enabled him to avoid many harsh winters back home.

I hadn't decided what I was to say to Inspector Fenton and Inspector Pilkington, so I walked past the turning to Bow Street, drank a coffee at a street stall, and then continued on towards the British Museum. The reading room was usually a welcome retreat, but as I got closer I was reminded of the embarrassing fracas between Edgar and Tom Clifford, along with Mr Edwards' look of disapproval. He had been helpful with my South American research, but I was concerned that I had disappointed him. Perhaps he would no longer help me with the map of Colombia should I need to see it again.

I could just about discern the railings of the museum in the fog up ahead. As I prepared to cross the street, I caught sight of a familiar figure up ahead.

I dashed across the road and saw that the familiar-looking man had turned in through the gate of the museum. He was little more than a silhouette in a bowler hat and overcoat in the fog, but his comportment was unmistakable. I ran to catch up with him and almost slipped on the ice as I hurtled through the gate.

The man was walking steadily towards the grand columns of the museum entrance.

"James!" I called out.

I suddenly hoped that I hadn't been mistaken.

Was it really James?

The man turned to face me.

"Penny?"

We strode towards each other and I felt an enormous grin spread across my face.

"James! What are you doing here? I thought you were in Manchester!"

"I was." He returned my grin. "I was. Goodness, it's lovely to see you again."

We held each other's gaze and I felt a strong urge to embrace him as I would a long-lost friend.

"I was coming to see if you were in the reading room," he said.

"You were looking for me?"

"Yes."

His eyes were the same bright, twinkling blue I remembered and his cheeks were flushed slightly with the cold. He had grown dark whiskers across each jaw, which gave him the appearance of a more mature gentleman. I felt a flutter of joy in my chest.

"Your sling." I looked down at his arm. "You don't have to wear it any longer?"

"No, everything is just about healed. You're still encumbered, I see."

"Yes. It's good to see you again, James."

"And you too, Penny. Do you have time to pay a visit to our old haunt over the road?"

He nodded in the direction of the Museum Tavern.

"Of course. I'd love to."

It was a little before noon and the Museum Tavern was quieter than usual.

"I suppose it's rather early for a sherry?" said James.

"Perhaps so, but I think your return from Manchester is sufficient cause for celebration."

We sat with our drinks at a partitioned table by one of the etched-glass windows. Mirrors reflected the flickering gaslight and pipe smoke hung in the air.

"How are you?" I asked.

"I'm well, thank you, Penny. The case in Manchester was resolved satisfactorily."

"And the future Mrs Blakely must be pleased to have you returned. How is she?"

He seemed surprised by the personal nature of my question.

"She is very well, thank you. Very well indeed."

He took off his overcoat and hung it on the partition behind him. He wore a smart grey jacket and waistcoat, and as he sat down I noticed that the gold pin in his dark green tie was in the shape of a horseshoe. I realised that I was once again wearing my green jacket with the frayed velvet cuffs. I wished I had heeded Eliza's advice and bought myself something new to wear.

"Do you have a date yet for your rearranged wedding?" I asked.

"Yes, yes. It was supposed to take place at the end of this month, but Manchester rather altered our plans, so the future Mrs Blakely and her mother have settled on September."

"A lovely time of year to be married."

"Isn't it? Yes." James took a sip of stout and pursed his lips together.

"I don't think you have ever told me her name," I ventured. For some reason, I wanted to build up a clearer idea of James' fiancée in my mind.

"Who?"

"Your wife-to-be?"

"Oh, of course. Charlotte."

"Charlotte Blakely sounds rather lovely."

"Does it? Well, I suppose it does, yes." The thought leapt into my mind that Penny Blakely sounded even better, but I pushed the idea away, feeling my cheeks begin to redden at the notion that I had even considered it.

"So you've had an interesting few days?" asked James.

"Yes, you could describe it as such."

"I hear that you paid a visit to CID in E Division. Chief Inspector Fenton?"

"Oh dear, has the word spread? I have spoken to Fenton and Pilkington, and I can't say that I care a great deal for either inspector."

James laughed. "You've been trying to swim against the stream again."

"I don't think I managed the situation very well. It was a terrible shock to see the boy murdered in that way. I don't mean *see*, as such. I didn't actually see it happen, thank goodness. But one moment he was running off with my bag and the next moment he was found with his throat cut. And there he was laid out on the ground. Dead."

I stared at the wood grain of the table as the unwanted image flooded into my mind once again.

"I can't stop thinking about him. I don't bear him any ill-will at all, even though he took my bag from me. He only did it because he was so desperate. And then I was convinced that Reuben O'Donoghue had only been helping me and couldn't have had anything to do with it. He seemed such a nice man... He was friendly and handsome."

"Handsome men cannot be murderers, eh?" James smiled.

"Oh, well, I realise now that they could be! I had no idea he'd been in so much trouble in the past. It was only when I spoke to some of the people living in St Giles that I realised what a violent man he was. So now I feel rather ashamed that I tried to convince Fenton and Pilkington that he was innocent. I've made rather a mess of things and would be quite happy now to have nothing further to do with it, except that my editor, Mr Sherman, wants me to continue covering the story, so now I must return to Bow Street and ask Fenton for further information relating to the investigation."

I drained my sherry.

"I must learn to think before I act," I continued. "My sister keeps reminding me to do so."

"Perhaps. But this is what I like about you, Penny. You care."

"About what?"

"About people and fairness. You're a determined person and perhaps that means you irritate the authorities, but the authorities need someone irritating them, don't they? If no one's challenging them, there's a risk that they won't do their work properly. I suppose that has become the role of the news reporter now. In the past, you would simply have written about events as they happened, but these days news reporting has become a more persistent quest for truth and justice."

"Yes, I think it has. Thank you, James. You're already making me feel a little better about it."

"So continue making a nuisance of yourself, I say."

"But perhaps only when I can be sure of my convictions. I thought Reuben O'Donoghue was innocent, but now I'm worried that he is, in fact, guilty. And now he has likely been released because I was so insistent that he hadn't committed the crime. And what evidence did I have? Nothing other than a hunch."

"Probably quite a good hunch, I'd say."

"Why?"

"I don't think Reuben O'Donoghue is the culprit. He may have got himself into a number of sticky situations in the past, but I don't think he murdered Jack Burton."

"Have you looked at the case?"

James nodded. "Witnesses have confirmed that Mr O'Donoghue was not at the scene of the murder. He was close by, as you know, but not in the courtyard. The police have released him on that basis."

"Not because I asked them to?"

"No, Penny. They consider you to be nothing more than an interfering news reporter. However, they read your notes and I have put them into the case file at the Yard."

"You read my notes?" I felt my face grow hot again.

"Yes. You've done some useful work, and your friend at the Yard, Chief Inspector Cullen—"

"He's *not* my friend!"

"I know, I was using sarcasm. Cullen, your friend at the Yard, has asked me to consider the possibility that the three recent murders in St Giles might have been committed by the same person."

I exhaled with great relief. "That's what I've been waiting to hear. James, I'm so pleased! I thought I'd made a considerable mistake. And to think that you'll be working on the case!"

I resisted another urge to embrace him.

"It's certainly an interesting one. And I'm looking forward to hearing all about the people you've spoken to so far in St Giles. The clues must be in there somewhere. There's one thing which worries me, though."

I didn't like the solemn look on his face. "What's that?"

"If we're looking for someone who has killed three people within three weeks, then the chances that he's about to strike again are extremely high."

CHAPTER 15

Two days later I joined the throng of reporters hurrying from Fleet Street to St Giles. The fog had lifted, but the morning had dawned cold and grey.

"Who is it? Do we know who it is yet?"

"A man. A shopkeeper."

"I heard he was a publican."

"It's up at the pop-shop."

I tried not to pay much attention to the rumours floating around me; the facts would be known once we arrived there. I followed the crowd down Long Acre, up Endell Street and left into Castle Street. The crowd became a crush as we turned into Nottingham Court and passed the place where Mrs O'Brien had been murdered.

People were fighting with their elbows and umbrellas to get through the throng, while residents hung out of their windows to watch the spectacle. There were shouts and cries, and several constables tried to discourage us from walking any further.

"Six apples for sixpence!" shouted an enterprising costermonger with a basket of pitiful-looking fruit. "A dozen for tenpence! Did yer 'ear me, sir? A dozen for tenpence! Gimme a shillin' and I'll give yer fifteen of 'em!"

"Let me through! Press!" I called.

My colleagues echoed my cries.

"I got a good view o' the murder from me window," said a woman with a baby strapped to her back. "Yer can look out me window for two shillings! Who wants to look out me window for two shillings?"

We pushed our way to the top of the street, where the pawnbroker's shop stood, and I thought I caught a glimpse of Tom Clifford's pork-pie hat in amongst the crowd.

"Move away!" shouted the police officers. "Move back! Make some space!"

I could see Chief Inspector Fenton in the doorway of the pawnbroker's shop with two constables at his side, and I wondered whether James had arrived there yet.

"Move away!"

The people in front of me were shoved backwards and someone trod on my toes. I began to feel panicked. There were too many people there for such a small space.

"All the gentlemen from the press over here!" came a shout.

I followed the voice to where Fenton stood.

"Not you, sir. You're not press, are you? Press only!"

I felt encouraged that Fenton was making time for the news reporters. He knew that he would make life easier for himself by giving us what we wanted now, or so I conjectured.

I jostled with my colleagues to get closer to Fenton, and felt an elbow dig into my side as Tom Clifford pushed past.

"Steady, gentlemen, steady," said Fenton. "We don't want any more murders here today."

"What's happened?" called out a reporter.

"All in good time," said Fenton. "Can everyone hear me? Splendid."

He straightened his tie and retrieved a notebook from his pocket. He cleared his throat and glanced around at the crowd, as though he were enjoying this moment of undivided attention.

I held my notebook and pencil ready, and Inspector Fenton peered at his notes before reading them out to us.

"At approximately twenty past eight this morning, Constable Burns was walking his usual route along Queen Street when a concerned gentleman approached him to say that the pawnbroker's shop had not yet opened for the day. The gentleman in question was keen to pawn a spectacles case and had failed to rouse the occupant of the shop, a Mr Ernest Larcombe.

"The gentleman informed Constable Burns that it was most unusual for Mr Larcombe's shop to be closed at such an hour, as the pawnbroker was in the habit of opening at half after seven o'clock each morning. Constable Burns then took it upon himself to rouse Mr Larcombe by knocking on the door and windows with some vehemence. He, too, was unsuccessful in rousing him.

"It was then deemed necessary to gain entrance to the shop to establish the welfare of the occupant. This was undertaken by accessing a window at the rear of the property, which had been left open. Once inside the shop, Constable Burns discovered the occupant, Mr Ernest Larcombe, lying behind the counter on the floor of his establishment. The pawnbroker's throat had been cut in a manner which was incompatible with life.

"It was Constable Burns' immediate supposition that the pawnbroker had been murdered the previous evening and had lain undiscovered throughout the night."

"What time was he murdered?"

"The investigation has only just begun and, at the present time, the last sighting of Mr Larcombe alive was yesterday evening at seven o'clock."

"Where's his wife?"

"We're trying to establish her whereabouts. The residents of St Giles can rest assured that a number of auxiliary police constables have been brought into the area and that there is no need for panic. Thank you, gentlemen, that is all for now. We must carry on with our investigation."

"Did the wife do it?"

Inspector Fenton ignored the question and began to move away as the reporters scribbled in their notebooks. I pushed past them to get closer to the inspector.

"Inspector Fenton, do you think this could be the work of the same person who killed Jack Burton?"

"Good morning, Miss Green." He fixed me with his narrow eyes. "It's too early to say, I'm afraid. At the moment, we're trying to find witnesses and locate the murder weapon. Perhaps your friend Inspector Blakely will consider your question in greater detail when he arrives."

"He's not my friend, he's a colleague. You must be pleased that the Yard is now helping you?"

"The Yard would be more helpful if its detectives arrived promptly."

The inspector checked his watch just before he was accosted by a reporter from the *News of the World*.

I peered through the grimy, latticed casement of the pawnbroker's shop, but I couldn't see past the clutter piled up in the windows. A china shepherdess stood next to a tarnished silver cup, while an emerald brooch lay among a number of pocket watches and a pair of bent spectacles rested atop a pile of silk handkerchiefs.

"It's Miss Green, isn't it?" said a nasal voice.

I turned to see Winston Nicholls standing beside me.

"Not another one," he added, wiping the window glass with his sleeve and trying to ascertain what was happening inside. "I've a good mind to move Ma to my house. It's not safe here any more. Do they know who did it? A swindled customer, perhaps?"

"They don't know yet."

"I don't suppose it's an enormous coincidence that this happened after Reuben O'Donoghue was released. Where's the man now? I doubt he's at his own shop in Lumber Court."

"He has a shop?"

"Yes, he's in the rag trade."

"Did Reuben know Mr Larcombe?"

"Everyone knows Mr Larcombe." He gave me a brief glance with his pale eyes before looking away again.

"What was he like?"

"A swindler and a drunkard. Just about everything you see in that window is stolen; most of it by the Seven Dials Gang. The police should have done something about Larcombe years ago."

"Penny, how are you?"

I turned away from the window and was relieved to see James standing nearby. He regarded me with solemn blue eyes which almost matched the colour of his tie.

"Rather saddened," I said. "Your prediction came true."

"I don't suppose it was a difficult prediction to make." He glanced at Winston as if wondering who he was.

"This is Winston Nicholls," I said. "His mother is Martha, whom I've visited a few times now. She told me about the other murders in St Giles."

"She sounds like a useful person to be speaking to. Hello, Mr Nicholls. I'm Detective Inspector Blakely from Scotland Yard."

"The Yard!"

It was the first time I had seen Winston smile.

"A proper detective from the Yard!" He continued. "What do you think so far? Four people with their throats cut in three weeks. A man with a grievance? An act of revenge? Or someone with an appalling thirst for gore?"

James frowned but remained polite. "I've only just joined the investigation, so there is much to do, as you can imagine, Mr Nicholls."

"If you need any help, Inspector, I'm happy to oblige."

"Do you live here?"

"No, but Ma does. I live in Red Lion Square in Holborn."

"And you have an occupation?"

"Clerk."

"If I do need to speak to you about anything, Mr Nicholls, be reassured that I shall come and find you."

"I've a lot of ideas about the murders, you see."

"Is that so?"

"All committed in the hours of darkness and the same manner of death each time. Audacious attacks wouldn't you say, Inspector? Do you think it was a mistake to release Reuben O'Donoghue? He's a troublemaker if ever there was one."

"E Division have their reasons for releasing him, Mr Nicholls."

"That may be so, but what does the Yard say? I urge you to reconsider O'Donoghue as a suspect, Inspector Blakely. I think it'd be of great service if you were able to establish where that man is at this present time, and what he's doing. Washing the blood from his clothing, perhaps?"

"We will leave no stone unturned, Mr Nicholls."

James took his notebook from his pocket and leafed through its pages.

"Because the murderer will have a lot of blood on him,

won't he, Inspector? You can't cut a man's throat without making a great deal of mess."

"Thank you for your opinion, Mr Nicholls, but I must examine the scene of the crime and see what clues, if any, the perpetrator has left behind."

I expected Mr Nicholls to take this as his cue to leave, but still he persisted. "You'd be looking for a young man with some strength in him, I suspect. He'd be strong enough to overpower his victims because I should think they'd all have put up a fierce struggle. And who wouldn't? A man's desire to stay alive is extremely strong, wouldn't you say, Inspector?"

The door of the pawnbroker's shop opened and Inspector Fenton pushed his head out. "So you're finally here then, eh Blakely? You took your time."

"Meet me at the Tavern at six o'clock if you can," James said to me quietly, before stepping past the two constables guarding the shop door.

"Goodbye, Mr Nicholls. Please send my best wishes to your mother," I said. "I hope she is not too upset by this latest murder."

"Oh, she will be. There was a time when this place was safe. Many people will now be too frightened to leave their homes."

I saw Tom Clifford swaggering over to us out of the corner of my eye.

"The Scotland Yard detective's here now, eh?" he said, spitting a globule of chewing tobacco onto the icy ground.

"You shouldn't spit in front of a lady," said Winston.

"Lady? This is Miss Green we're talking about."

Tom gave me an unpleasant leer.

"You're the Yard's favourite, aren't you, Miss Green? There's little chance of any other newspaper getting time with Blakely now. Doesn't really seem fair, does it, sir? Sorry, I don't know your name."

I introduced the two men. Winston immediately began to talk about the murders and Tom listened intently.

I realised this was the perfect opportunity to depart and headed off to find some other local people to interview.

CHAPTER 16

All the tables were taken at The Museum Tavern that evening, so James and I found a place to stand by the staircase at the back of the pub. The air was filled with tobacco smoke, chatter and laughter. James hung his overcoat and jacket on a coat stand and stood with his shirt sleeves rolled up and a pewter tankard in one hand. I noticed that today his tie pin was topped with a small gold star.

"I'll be interested to read your news article when it's published in the morning," he said. "Did you find anyone with useful information in St Giles today?"

"Some of Larcombe's customers and a neighbour. They all described him in a similar manner: rather short-tempered, friendly when he'd had a drink and often cantankerous. He had lived in St Giles for about fifteen years, and prior to that had been living in Clerkenwell, close to the King's Cross end, where he'd also run a pawnbroker's shop. He was married, but his wife was often away. Some think she was staying with a daughter who in poor health, but someone else suggested it was a maiden aunt. Either way, it seems she was helping to look after a family member of some description."

"Or perhaps someone she chose the company of over him," suggested James. "I've taken statements from eight people today and their views of Mr Larcombe largely match the description you've been given. The inquest will be held within the next day or so, and we'll hear more from the witnesses then. CID in E Division are trying to find his wife. I'm struggling to understand why the pawnbroker was attacked. If it had been an isolated incident, I'd be tempted to speculate that it could have been a falling out with a customer or a burglary gone wrong. But because of the other murders in the area recently, I feel certain that the attacker is the same man."

"Perhaps it's a different killer this time and he's simply copying the other murders?"

"We can't rule that out. I suppose there could be more than one murderer. But to have two people in the locality who could kill so brutally would be unusual, I think. Tell me who you've spoken to in St Giles so far."

I held James' tankard of porter while he fetched his notebook from his overcoat pocket. "Are you all right holding my drink with your injured hand?"

"It's my arm which is injured."

"Yes, but even so. Doing anything much with your hand will put strain on your arm. How long until the sling can come off?"

"Another two weeks, my doctor tells me. Have you heard about the man in the mask?"

"Yes, now that sounds rather queer. Several witnesses have mentioned him to me." He flicked through the pages of his notebook. "There are some pertinent sightings of him, in fact. On the night that Roger Yeomans died, a man wearing a mask was seen over on Broad Street at half past eleven. He was seen again at half past three in the morning on Betterton Street. There is also a sighting of him on the seventh of January, the day that Jack Burton was murdered. A man wearing a mask was seen shortly after sundown on Tower Street."

"About the time Jack was murdered?"

"Yes."

"And what sort of mask was it?"

"Apparently, the sort of mask an actor would wear on the stage. It's dark in colour and covers the eyes and nose. A Pulcinella-style mask, if you like. Perhaps it's an actor from Drury Lane having a bit of fun."

"Let's hope so. Otherwise, he sounds rather sinister."

"He could be. The mask would be the perfect thing for concealing someone's identity. E Division are making enquiries about further sightings and are asking the theatres if any of their actors are walking about St Giles in costume. Now, tell me who you spoke to today."

By the time I had finished giving James the particulars of the people I had interviewed, a table had become available and we sat down. James bought us another drink and consulted his notebook again.

As he bent his head over his notes, his brow furrowed in thought, he absent-mindedly tapped the end of his pencil on the table. I watched him closely and pictured him standing at the altar with Charlotte. She would wear a beautiful dress, perhaps similar to my sister's, which had been made of white satin trimmed with lace and orange blossom. I imagined the happy couple illuminated by beams of sunlight from a colourful stained-glass window.

"Which church are you getting married in?" I asked.

"What?" He looked up at me with a puzzled expression. "Oh. St John the Baptist in Croydon. Why do you ask?"

"I don't think I've asked you before."

"The future Mrs Blakely and her parents live in Croydon."
He returned to his notebook. "So, in summary, we have Ellen
O'Brien found close to her home in Nottingham Court on
the twenty-seventh of December. Then we have Roger
Yeomans on the second of January, Jack Burton on the
seventh and Ernest Larcombe the pawnbroker on the
fifteenth. All of them have had their throats cut. Judging by
the examinations of the E Division police surgeon, it seems
the incisions have been made from left to right while the
victim was lying on the ground. By ensuring that the victims
are on the ground, the murderer is taking care not to get too
much blood on his clothing, although there must surely still
be a fair amount."

"He must have some considerable strength to get his
victims onto the ground before he uses his knife," I said.

"It's interesting you should say that, because something
peculiar was found in Mr Larcombe's mouth."

"Really?"

"A rag which had been soaked in chloroform. I imagine
the attacker would have held the rag over the pawnbroker's
nose and mouth to render him unconscious before adminis-
tering the fatal wound."

"That must have taken some doing in itself."

"Yes, Mr Larcombe must have put up a struggle. It would
have taken him two or three minutes to succumb."

"So the murderer was carrying a bottle of chloroform
with him?"

"It would seem so. I suspect he hid himself somewhere in
the shop and waited for the pawnbroker to lock up for the
day. The police surgeon estimates that the time of death was
between seven and eight o'clock yesterday evening. Mr
Larcombe was last seen by a customer who visited his shop
shortly before Mr Larcombe closed up at seven. The
customer didn't see anyone else inside, which suggests our

man was perhaps hiding somewhere. It's full of curios that place. Very easy to hide away."

"Mr Nicholls intimated that many of the items at the pawnbroker's shop were stolen."

"They might have been. There's a great deal of criminality in the area. So once Mr Larcombe had closed his shop, the killer poured some chloroform onto a rag, emerged from his hiding place and caught the pawnbroker unawares. He approached him from behind, perhaps, and got the rag over his face before his victim could react. By all accounts, Mr Larcombe was a fit man in his forties, so he should have been able to defend himself well in a fair fight."

"So there would have been a struggle in the shop for a short while and then the pawnbroker would have collapsed to the floor? And after that, the attacker used his knife on him?"

"Yes, I think so, and the fact that the rag was pushed into his mouth suggests it was used to restrict his airway as well. It was a brutal attack, during which the murderer did all he could to ensure that the pawnbroker was certainly dead. Photographs are going to be taken of the pawnbroker's eyes in the hope that they hold the image of the murderer."

"Could that really happen?"

"I don't know. It's a new idea that the eyes retain the last image beheld before death. It's called optography."

"And does it work?"

"A scientist in Germany claims to have found that it works in rabbits. But it's a new idea, as I say."

"I've not heard of it before. If it works, solving the murder should be easy! I can't imagine it being so straightforward, however. How do you think the killer got out of the shop unseen?"

"A window was left open in the pawnbroker's accommodation at the back. He probably escaped that way, because the shop door remained locked. It seems his wife was not in the property at the time, as you said. E Division are still trying to find her."

"Do you think the killer could have colluded with his wife?"

"It is a line of enquiry that we may consider. But I think it's rather likely that this is the same man who cut the throats of the previous three victims. The question we need to answer is, why did he do it?"

"But chloroform wasn't used in the other murders."

"Sadly, because it probably wasn't needed. Mr Yeomans was drunk and only had one leg. Mrs O'Brien and Jack Burton were both of a smaller build. It is likely that our killer found it quite easy to overpower them."

As with the other murders, I couldn't understand the motive. "So this despicable man went to the pawnbroker's shop armed with chloroform and a knife, and laid in wait for his moment to attack. Then it was not a chance killing; he deliberately targeted the man. But why?"

"Once we understand that, we will be closer to discovering the killer's identity, but for the time being we must continue with our investigations. We know the motive could not have been robbery, because the day's takings were left alone in the shop along with a whole range of valuables. Perhaps our man helped himself to something, but there is no way of telling. This is a similar case to Jack's murder, when the killer could have taken your bag with him and helped himself to the money in your purse. Instead, he just left it there, didn't he?"

"Jack's murder was so swift. He was attacked and killed within a matter of minutes, and yet the murderer took more time with Mr Larcombe. I suppose that's because he knew he might have been discovered at any moment in that courtyard, while in the pawnbroker's shop he was hidden from view. Where might he have obtained the chloroform?"

"It's found in many household apothecary kits, although the rag found in Mr Larcombe's mouth had been soaked in quite some significant amount. The kits usually contain small bottles, so we need to remain on the lookout for someone buying large quantities from an apothecary. There is no doubt that he may try to use this method again."

"On whom? And when?" I shivered. "I can't bear the thought of anyone else suffering in this way. Surely he's done enough?"

"I would like to think so, but this man is clearly a degenerate. There's no telling what he's capable of."

CHAPTER 17

"Understanding how the victims knew each other has to give us a clue to the murderer, doesn't it?" I said. "I've discovered that Jack ran errands for Mr Larcombe as well as for Mr Yeomans. Jack was a member of the Seven Dials Gang. It's led by Edward Keller, who calls himself the Earl of York."

"I've been finding out about them. One of the gang's activities is to run messages for people. They also move around money and stolen property. I don't know enough about Ernest Larcombe's character yet, but it is not unheard of for pawnbrokers to collude with gangs and thieves in criminal activity, pawning stolen watches and jewellery, for example. However, I don't think that's why he was killed. I think it must be something less obvious than his criminal activities, just as it was with Jack."

"Might he have fallen out with Keller?"

"It's a possibility, and the other victims may also have done so. I certainly need to interview Keller and find out whether he can enlighten me any further. I've yet to find a connection between three of the victims and Mrs O'Brien."

"Mr Yeomans was once married to her sister."

"Ah, was he indeed?" James wrote this down.

"I'm not sure why that should mean that the two of them had to be murdered, but it's a connection that Mrs Nicholls told me about."

"And the rather queer man we met earlier is her son?"

"Yes."

"I can't say that I took to him. He said a number of strange things. I suppose these murders are rather shocking, and they obviously affect people in many different ways. He must be worried about his mother living so close to these crime scenes."

"I suppose you hadn't anticipated a case as challenging as this on your return to London."

"No, and I could have done with something a little more straightforward." James sat back in his seat and glanced over at a man sitting beside the bar, who was refilling his pipe. "It's almost enough to persuade me to smoke tobacco again."

"What's stopping you?"

"The future Mrs Blakely abhors the smell of pipe smoke."

"But she isn't here."

"True," he smiled. "The odour lingers though, doesn't it?" He took a sip of stout. "Tell me what else you've been working on recently, Penny. I need to stop thinking about the murders for a moment."

"Well, until this unfortunate business with Jack Burton occurred I had just begun writing a book."

"A book?" His face brightened. "That's impressive news indeed! What about?"

"It's on the subject of my father's plant-hunting travels. I've wanted to collect together all his letters and diaries and publish them in one volume for a number of years now, and that is what I've started doing. My mother and sister have given me all the papers they had and I have a fair few myself."

"And your father's papers were in your bag when Jack took it, isn't that right?"

"Yes, so it was an enormous relief not to have lost them permanently."

"You had a close shave. To think that Frederick Barnsley Green's papers were almost lost for good!"

"I keep them all safe in my room now to avoid that ever happening again. You're welcome to come and visit me if you would like to see them."

"I'd like to."

He smiled again and I felt my cheeks grow hot. I knew it was inappropriate to invite James to my room, but I couldn't help suggesting it. Besides, I knew that he would be interested in seeing my father's papers.

"I think it's an admirable task, Penny. You have a lot of patience."

"Having a little more time to do it would be preferable. I have so enjoyed rereading his letters and diaries. There are many details I had forgotten. In his last letter to me, he mentioned seeing tins of Peek Freans biscuits in the market in Bogota. Isn't that astonishing? After reading that, I bought myself a tin of the same biscuits. Whenever I look at the tin I think of my father, and it helps me feel closer to him." I paused to quickly dab at my eyes with my handkerchief. "It's quite ridiculous, when you think about it, that I need to look at a tin of biscuits to create an association with my own father!"

"Why do you need to feel close to him?"

"I miss him." I heard my voice waver. "He was away a lot on his travels, but when he was home I could see how very like him I was. And although he didn't want me to move to London initially, I felt as though he understood my need to journey off on my own and pursue a profession which would take me into all manner of risky places and situations."

James looked at my arm in its sling. "I'm not certain he would have approved of some of the danger involved."

"Perhaps not."

"He would no doubt be proud of you for having kept such a calm head during the incident. Some people would have run screaming from the room."

"From what I've read of my father, he also seemed to remain calm in the face of adversity. He found himself in a whole range of sticky situations. He was almost shipwrecked in the Atlantic on one occasion and survived a bite from a venomous snake another time."

"It sounds as though it will be a fascinating book." James finished off his stout. "Is your father the only person who truly understood you, do you think?"

"Perhaps he is. My mother and sister are less inclined to understand my profession, they seem determined to see me settled with a husband instead."

"Sensible advice."

"I consider it rather dull advice."

"You don't harbour any wish to be married and settled?"

"No. And I'm not entirely happy to be in London at this present time, either. With the harsh winter and these terrible killings, I think I would much rather be travelling on a steamboat up the River Magdalena watching brightly coloured kingfishers dive into the water, while the alligators lay basking on the sandbanks."

James laughed. "Somehow, Penny, I feel sure that one day you'll be doing just that."

We exchanged a long smile. Then he suddenly appeared startled and checked his pocket watch.

"Goodness, it's late and I must help you find a hansom cab. Before we leave, I need to tell you that I think that the St Giles murderer has been practising."

"Practising ways to murder people?"

"I've heard talk of a few seemingly random attacks. Having spoken to people in St Giles today, I have gleaned that these attacks were similar in nature. They were carried out at night and nothing was stolen from any of the victims."

"Might these victims be able to give us a description of the man?"

"I should hope so."

"Why didn't the police do anything about these attacks?"

"Few of them were reported as the assailant chose his victims carefully. Many of them are prostitutes, drunks or criminals, who would rather have as little to do with the police as possible. The man is clearly familiar with the people who live and work in St Giles, and he must know the layout of the streets very well to escape as quickly as he does."

"Have you managed to speak to any of the victims?"

"Not yet, but I plan to visit a lady tomorrow who claims that she was attacked by a mystery assailant one evening. Would you like to accompany me? She'll probably be wary of speaking to a detective, but I think your presence might encourage her to speak more freely in my company. You mustn't identify her in your newspaper, though."

"Can I mention that the killer may have attacked other people before embarking on this murdering spree?"

"Yes, please do. I think it would be useful to print that, as it may encourage more people who have encountered or witnessed this man to come forward. Please choose your words carefully, however, as we need to minimise panic."

"I will, although I think some newspapers will particularly enjoy printing such lurid stories."

"I'm sure they will. I'm learning that the press can be both a help and a hindrance, in equal measure."

CHAPTER 18

"Read all about the St Giles murders!" shouted a paper boy. "Four of 'em's 'ad their throats slit!" He made a cutting gesture across his neck as I walked past him. "'Eard abaht the murders, lady?" he called.

'Another St Giles Horror', 'Murder in St Giles', 'Another Shocking Murder', screamed the newspaper headlines. *The Illustrated Londoner* carried a large drawing of a miserly-faced Mr Larcombe with thinning hair, a dark moustache and a long, pointed chin. Smaller pictures around him depicted the scene of the crime, the discovery of the murder, the conveyance of the body to the mortuary and a map of St Giles. There were even illustrations of the detectives working on the case, which included a poor, yet amusing, likeness of James.

The killer had been branded 'the St Giles Monster' by many, and some newspapers had commissioned artists to draw what they thought he might look like, with a black hat and cloak, and a sinister black mask. Some even speculated that 'Spring-heeled Jack' had returned to wreak fresh terror on the streets of London. There were sightings of suspicious-looking figures and even ghosts in many areas of the capital, and some claimed to have been terrified by a man with glowing eyes and claws.

In the absence of evidence to the contrary, it was difficult to argue with the hysteria. People were understandably frightened. Each day I awoke feeling nervous that there would be news of another murder.

Mr Larcombe's inquest was held at St Giles' Coroner's Court and hordes of people filled the narrow street outside the red-brick building. Once again, the verdict was recorded as wilful murder at the hands of a person or persons unknown.

More snow had fallen during the week, and when I met James at Seven Dials late in the afternoon on the Friday, a pall of grimy frozen fog hung over the city. My nose was so cold that I felt sure it had turned an unbecoming shade of red. I wore a new skirt and fitted jacket, both of blue wool with a black velvet trim. A row of two dozen black glass buttons fastened my jacket and although I felt happy to be wearing a new outfit, it didn't keep me as warm as I would have liked.

Unusually for James, he was a few minutes late arriving.

"I'm sorry. I received an unexpected visit from my grandmother."

"Is she all right?"

"She is, but my grandfather isn't. He's very unwell."

"I'm sorry to hear it. He's the grandfather you help with the gardening?"

"Yes. Fortunately, there's nothing to do in his garden now as we've just dug up the last of the leeks." He rubbed his gloved hands together for warmth. "You look very smart today, Penny."

"Thank you." I smiled.

"Still wishing you were on a steamboat on the River Magdalena?"

"I'd like either to be on the steamboat or watching the beans dry on a sun-drenched coffee plantation."

"Ah, that does sound pleasant. I expect the coffee has a superior taste in Colombia."

"Yes, apparently the quality of the beans deteriorates during the crossing of the Atlantic."

"That's a pity. The only solution is to travel there yourself and drink it at source, then."

"I'm afraid it is."

"Shall we go there next week?"

We both laughed and James nodded in the direction in which we were about to walk.

"The woman we need to speak to is often found at the lodging houses on Mercer Street. I thought that if we met close to sundown we might find her in that area looking for a bed for the night."

We walked along Mercer Street, passing a noisy pub. Many of the people milling around us had Irish accents and a couple of mean-eyed men carried thick sticks of wood with rounded clubs at the ends.

"I see they're armed with their shillelaghs," said James. "I'm not sure whether they're doing so in response to the recent murders, or whether it's a usual habit for them."

"How have the past few days been?"

James sighed. "The Yard has received so many reports of the man in the mask now that I have to question whether they can all be genuine. There have also been reports of a group of men loitering suspiciously outside the pawnbroker's several hours before Mr Larcombe was murdered, and varying descriptions of a man seen running away from the shop at nine o'clock in the evening.

"Some witnesses say he had brown whiskers and others

say he had a thick orange moustache. A customer of Mr Larcombe's says he saw a man hiding behind some shelving in the pawnbroker's shop a week before Mr Larcombe was murdered. There's so much to follow up on that we barely have enough men to do the work. Thankfully, Chief Inspector Cullen is doing more work on the case, which is especially important now that the Home Secretary is asking for regular reports on progress."

"And I suppose the difficulty is in deciding which witnesses have seen something helpful and which are fabricating tales."

"Yes, the skill lies in determining between what's relevant and what's hogwash."

We stopped halfway along a row of shabby buildings. "Let's try here," said James.

A dirty yellow blind in the window was inscribed with: 'Dorney's Good Lodgings. Single Bed. 4d.'

We walked up the steps and James inquired as to whether Sarah Fisher was inside. A woman with a hacking cough told us to go next door to the lodging house called Parker's.

A short, thick-set man at the door of Parker's eyed us suspiciously as we approached.

"Are you the schools' inspector?" he asked James.

"No, I'm Detective Inspector Blakely and I'm investigating the St Giles murders."

A flash of interest flickered across the man's face. "Is that so?"

"I'd like to speak to Sarah Fisher. Is she here?"

"What, you think she done the murders?" The man cackled.

"I have heard that she was attacked a few weeks ago and I'm wondering if the perpetrator was the same man who has been carrying out these terrible killings."

The man nodded. "You'll find 'er somewhere round 'ere,

but just speak to 'er and no one else. I don't want yer wanderin' round harrestin' people for what they may or may not've done. You'll be keepin' me customers away. Police hofficers ain't good fer business."

"I won't be marching anyone down to the station, Mr Parker, you have my word."

"Well, 'ave a look around then." He made a wide gesture with his chubby arm. "The men's rooms is hon the first floor and the ladies hon the second. If she hain't there, 'ave a look in the kitchen."

We thanked Mr Parker and made our way up a flight of wooden stairs with a number of steps missing.

"I'll check the men's rooms," said James, "and you look on the ladies' floor. I'll meet you in the hallway downstairs."

I continued up the greasy staircase, my boots clomping noisily on the flimsy timber. I could hear the scuttle of rats ahead of me as I rounded the stairs and found myself in a grim, dingy corridor. Leading off from it were several doorways, which opened out into rooms filled with small, timber-framed truckle beds lying side by side. Some had torn and discoloured bedding on them, while others were bare wood. The windows were covered with rags, and I guessed that these rooms would be packed full of people once night fell.

For now, there were only a few women and girls in the rooms, including an old lady who was fast asleep, snoring loudly. There was a strong odour of unwashed bodies.

I asked if anyone knew where Sarah Fisher was, and those who acknowledged me shook their heads in reply. I stepped over broken floorboards and peered in at each doorway, aware that I was being regarded with great suspicion.

"Don't tell me yer one o' them missionaries," said a thin woman who was trying to comfort a crying baby. "Always on at us abaht goin' ter chapel."

"I'm not a missionary. I'm looking for Sarah Fisher."

"Ain't seen 'er."

I couldn't decide whether she was telling the truth or simply didn't want to help me.

Eventually, I made my way down to the hallway, my mood darkened by the sight of the miserable rooms I had already looked around.

James was waiting for me.

"No sign of her? I suggest we try the kitchen," he said.

"Must we? I would sooner leave."

The kitchen was in the basement and the sound of drunken singing drifted up the rickety staircase. Most of the occupants sat around a long table and a large coke fire burnt fiercely in the fireplace. The low ceiling was blackened with soot and the walls were patchy with damp.

A filthy-looking man lounged in a chair in the corner chewing on a fish, and in another corner a couple sat locked in an embrace. I felt aware that my face might easily display sadness and disgust, so I wore a faint smile and tried to present myself as unthreateningly as possible.

A few people turned to look at us as we entered the stifling room, while others continued to sing or argue.

"This isn't the sort of song a lady should hear," commented James.

"They're all words I've heard before," I replied.

James cleared his throat. "May I have a moment of your attention, please, ladies and gentlemen?"

"It's a copper!" shouted out a man with a yellow, wizened face.

He pulled off his wooden leg and brandished it. I noticed another man quickly shovelling something into his pockets.

"I ain't done nuffink," said an old lady, who took a swig from a tin cup. "Don't come nowhere near me, 'cause I ain't done nuffink. I'm as pure as the driven snow."

The man eating the fish howled with laughter.

"I'm Inspector James Blakely and no one is in trouble. I'm in need of your assistance."

"What? Ain't you come for Whelk-'Ead?" asked the old lady.

"Who's Whelk-Head?" asked James.

"'Im!" A gnarled finger was pointed at the man eating the fish. "Hev'ryone always comes for Whelk-'Ead!"

"I have no need to speak to Mr Whelk-Head unless he knows the whereabouts of Sarah Fisher," said James.

"She's 'ere."

The one-legged man pointed his wooden prosthetic in the direction of a dark-skinned woman sitting on a bench by the fire. She got to her feet and stared at us warily. She wore a woollen skirt of faded blue and a red shawl over a jacket which had been clumsily patched and repaired. She looked to be no older than seventeen.

"Hello, Miss Fisher. Is miss correct, or should I say missus?" asked James.

"Miss."

"Please don't worry, you're not in trouble. I need to ask you some questions. Is there somewhere more private where we can talk? My friend here, Penny Green, will accompany us."

"Private?" cackled the old lady. "Round 'ere?"

"Try the yard," said Mr Whelk-Head.

"Thank you," said James. "Do you mind if we talk in the yard, Miss Fisher?"

She shrugged and the three of us moved outside.

It was a relief to be outside again, even though the air was far from clean and fresh in the yard by the privies.

"I didn't see who it was," said Sarah when James asked her about the attack.

"Which street were you on?"

"Clark's Buildings."

Her voice was quiet and she fidgeted nervously with the fringing of her shawl. Her features were dimly lit by the light from the kitchen and our breath hung frozen in the air.

"What time of day was it?"

"Evenin'."

"It was dark?"

"Yeah."

"You've already told me you think it occurred during the first week of December. Where were you headed?"

"Can't remember. I needed money."

"Did you see the man before he attacked you?"

"No."

"And what did he do exactly?"

"'E put a rag over me nose and mouth. It 'ad an 'orrible smell."

"And as you didn't see him before he did this, I'm assuming that he was behind you?"

"Yeah."

"The man crept up behind you while you were walking?"

"Yeah."

"And what did you do when he put the rag over your nose and mouth?"

"I tried to push 'im off. And I screamed as best I could."

"And what was his response?"

"He pulled me onto me back."

"He pulled you backwards so that you fell onto the ground?"

"Yeah."

"And did you do anything as this happened?"

"Yeah, I fought 'im. I dug me nails into 'is 'ands, and I kicked wiv me legs, and I cried out. It 'urt what 'e were doin' and that rag smelt somethin' rotten."

"Could you see his face?"

"Nah."

"Could you see if he was wearing a particular type of hat?"

"He 'ad an 'at on. Dunno what sort."

"Did he have whiskers?"

"Yeah, I fink so."

"Did he speak at all? Or make any noise?"

"Nah."

"And how did you get away?"

"Someone came alongside o' me. I was kickin' me boots on the ground and they made a noise. An' I cried out some, and someone 'eard it."

"So your attacker was disturbed?"

"Yeah, 'e let go and run off."

"And do you know in which direction?"

"Down the 'Igh Street."

"Did you see anything more of what he looked like as he was running away?"

"Black coat. Nuffink else."

"How long was his coat, would you say?"

"Long."

"Did you see the colour of his trousers?"

"Nah."

"And what of his stature? Would you describe him as a tall man? Short man?"

"In between."

"Large? Thin?"

"Just normal."

"And strong?"

"Yeah, 'e were strong a'right. But a coward 'cause he done a runner soon as someone else come along."

"And who was that other person? Did you speak to him or her?"

"Yeah, it were a man what 'elped me up and asked if I was a'right."

"Did the man tell you his name?"

"Nah."

"And what did you say to the man?"

"Just told 'im I was a'right and then 'e walked off one way and I walked the other."

"Would you recognise him if you saw him again?"

"Dunno. It were dark. 'E were an Irishman."

"And where did you go after the attack?"

Sarah shrugged. "I felt a bit faint 'cause o' the smell on the rag. But I 'ad to get some money, didn't I?"

I guessed that there was only one way a woman in her position could acquire money on the streets at night.

"Were you injured?" I asked.

"Nah, not much."

"And do you feel recovered from the attack now, Miss Fisher, or does it still worry you?"

"I'm more scared now. 'Specially wiv all them murders 'appenin'."

"Do you make sure you're safely indoors when night falls?"

"I try ter. It ain't always easy."

I wished there was something I could do to help keep this young woman off the streets.

"This is where you usually stay, is it?" I gestured toward the lodging house where the sound of drunken singing was drifting up from the basement again. I had struggled to walk around the place for ten minutes and couldn't imagine how awful it would be if I had to rely on it for shelter.

"When I can pay fer a bed."

"And what happens when you can't?"

"There's doorways, under bridges and carts. That sorta thing."

"Miss Fisher, what do you suppose your attacker was attempting to do to you?" asked James.

"Murder, for some reason. Dunno why."

"And he would have persisted, you think, if the Irishman had not come to your aid?"

"Proberly, yeah. I could've been dead. I 'ad a lucky escape."

"You did, Miss Fisher. Indeed, you did."

After James had bid her goodnight, I slipped a shilling into her hand.

CHAPTER 19

We left Mercer Street and turned into Long Acre. It was dark, but the night was brightened by pools of gaslight reflected in the snow. There were only a few people about; most had likely been driven indoors by the cold.

"A rag placed over her mouth which smelt bad. It sounds suspiciously like the attacker tried to subdue her with chloroform," James said.

"It has to be the same man who killed Mr Larcombe, doesn't it?"

"There's quite a similarity. She really did have a lucky escape, as she says. If that Irishman hadn't turned up, she would have been overpowered by the chloroform and the attacker would have surely cut her throat."

I felt nauseous. "What sort of man does something like that to a defenceless girl like Sarah?"

"She needs to stay off the streets at night."

"But I think that people should be able to walk about at night without someone trying to murder them. What she needs is somewhere safe to stay and a life which doesn't force her onto the streets. There are lots of people like Sarah here. They're easy prey for this monstrous man." My jaw clenched with anger.

"It's a shame she didn't see much of her attacker, as we could do with a decent description of him. I'll ask E Division to carry out enquiries in and around Clark's Buildings and see if they can find anyone who saw or heard anything on the night that Sarah was attacked. It would be even better if they could find the Irishman who helped Sarah, as he may be able to give us a more detailed description of the attacker." James glanced around us. "It looks like the fog has lifted a little. Let me find a cab to take you home."

"There's no need. I'll get on the underground railway at Charing Cross."

"I don't like the thought of you travelling home alone in the dark with this monster about. You've just heard what he did to Sarah Fisher."

"It's not late, and the killer seems set on terrorising only the residents of St Giles. I'll feel much safer once we've left this area."

"Quick, in here!"

James grabbed my arm and pulled me into a doorway.

"What?"

"Shush! I think someone might be following us."

We were hiding in the doorway of a grocer's shop in deep shadow as the nearest gas lamp was several yards away.

"Who?" I whispered.

My heart began to thud. James was so close by that I could smell his cologne and hear his gentle breathing.

"I don't know yet."

He peered out of the doorway and looked back up the street in the direction from which we had just walked.

"I think he's stopped in a doorway too," he whispered. "I can't see him now."

"When did you catch sight of him?"

"I thought someone was following us after we left the lodging house, and I looked back and saw a figure behind us once we had walked a short stretch."

"Is it the man in the mask?"

"It's difficult to see at the moment."

"The murderer?"

I felt an unpleasant tingling sensation at the back of my neck.

"Don't worry, Penny. When you're working on a well-known case, all manner of queer folk will take an interest in what you're doing. I'm sure the chap means no harm. Let's walk on and see what happens. Take my arm if it helps you feel safer."

I did as he suggested and we walked on down Long Acre.

"There's a shortcut through this way," said James, suddenly leading me down a dark, covered walkway. "This lane zig-zags somewhat, but it will bring us out on Garrick Street."

"I can barely see a thing!"

We walked briskly, our feet slipping in the snow. Ahead of us I saw the warm glow of a pub.

"The Lamb and Flag," said James. "We must have a drink in there one evening. It's said to be one of Charles Dickens' favourite pubs, although many other public houses make the same claim."

He looked over his shoulder.

"Is he there?" I asked.

"I'm not sure."

We reached Garrick Street and continued to walk as quickly as we could. The snow had made my green woollen skirt damp and heavy.

"If a hansom cab appears now, may I suggest that we hail it, Penny? You need to get home safely."

I didn't like the worried tone in James' voice.

"The man's still following us, isn't he?"

"There's someone behind us still. I don't know whether it's the same man or not."

"What do you think he'll do if we stop and wait for him?"

"I'm not sure. Shall we try it? I have my revolver with me in case of any trouble."

We stopped at the top of Bedford Street and turned just in time to see the dark figure disappear into the shadows.

"He's following us all right, isn't he?" said James.

I gripped his arm tighter.

"Let's see what he does when we walk back towards him," I said.

"Are you sure?"

"What can he do? There are two of us and only one of him. And you have your revolver."

"I don't want to put you in danger, Penny. That's precisely the reason why I suggested that we find you a cab."

"I want to find out who he is! It may even be that good-for-nothing reporter from *The Holborn Gazette*, Tom Clifford."

"Very well, we shall go and see. But let's be careful."

We walked back up the street over our smudged footprints in the snow.

"He hasn't moved yet," whispered James.

We continued to retrace our steps, drawing nearer to the place where we had last seen him.

"He must be close to the Garrick Club," said James. "I wonder if he's a member!" he added with a quiet laugh.

Then I felt him jump. "Look! There he goes! We've flushed out the fox!"

The man sprinted out from the shadows a few doorways ahead of us, then ran across the street into a road on the opposite side.

"He's gone up Hart Street," said James. "Should we follow?"

"I'm not sure."

"Come on, let's see where he goes."

I let James take my hand as we ran across the road and up towards Hart Street. Ahead of us, the man was still running. He turned sharply to his left.

"There are a number of passageways here which lead up to Long Acre," said James. "He's probably heading back to St Giles. Let's leave him to it. We could be playing this game of cat and mouse all evening."

"But who is he?" I said.

I felt a shiver run down my spine.

"I don't know."

CHAPTER 20

"That machine makes an infernal racket, Miss Green."

I paused from my typewriting and stared at Edgar.

"It's not as loud as the printing presses."

"No, but they're in the basement. That contraption you're typewriting on is merely yards away from me. What's wrong with the inaudible pen and paper?"

"Have you looked at the notes I compiled for you on the Sudan yet?"

"Yes, and they look fairly comprehensive, thank you. There's a good deal there that I can use. But I need a little more on Khartoum."

Frederick snorted. "If I know Miss Green, she's probably spent most of the weekend in the reading room writing all that down for you. And with her left hand too! You're an ungrateful oaf."

"Well said, Frederick!" I added. "Has your father managed to pull any strings yet, Edgar?"

"He's working on it. Don't forget that it's your fault I had my reading ticket confiscated in the first place."

"It's *my fault* you came to blows with Tom Clifford?"

"I think so. I'm just trying to recall the sequence of events now."

"It takes two to fight."

The newsroom door slammed shut behind Mr Sherman as he strode in with a copy of *The Holborn Gazette* and flung it down next to the typewriter.

"Seen this morning's edition, Miss Green?"

"Not yet."

"Turn to page three."

I did as I was told and saw an article about Ernest Larcombe's murder. Halfway down the column was a headline in a small yet eye-catching font: 'Interview with the Pawnbroker's Wife'.

"You spent much of last week down in St Giles, didn't you? Why the deuce didn't you speak to Larcombe's wife?"

"I couldn't find her. Even the police couldn't find her on the morning after the murder. Inspector Fenton told us they were trying to establish her whereabouts."

"Tom Clifford clearly established her whereabouts. Why couldn't you manage to do so? Especially seeing as you're constantly on the arm of Inspector Blakely!"

"That's the problem," said Edgar.

"What is?" barked Mr Sherman.

"Miss Green being on the schoolboy inspector's arm. She was too distracted by him to find the wife for an interview."

"Is that right, Miss Green? Is Blakely too much of a distraction for you?"

"Not at all! On the contrary, we have spoken to a woman who we think was attacked by the killer. He was disturbed by an Irishman and fortunately she escaped from his clutches."

"That's capital. Are you working on that now?"

"Yes, sir."

"And we have a description of the attacker?"

"Not much of a description, sir."

"Because *The Holborn Gazette* has a description."

"Really? How?"

"Have a read for yourself. There." Mr Sherman jabbed his forefinger at the second column within the same story.

"An account from a witness by the name of Winston Nicholls," I said. "No, this is wrong. Winston Nicholls wasn't a witness. He's the son of a woman who lives in St Giles and is a rather peculiar man."

"It says that he witnessed a masked man leaving the pawnbroker's shop late on the evening of the murder."

"If he did, then he didn't mention it to me. I saw him the morning after the murder."

"Perhaps he mentioned it to the police."

"Maybe he did, but if so Inspector Blakely is not aware of it. I know that much."

"Perhaps Blakely needs to be speaking directly to E Division."

"As far as I'm aware, the two units speak regularly."

Mr Sherman sighed. "We could waste our time discussing the whys and wherefores this morning, Miss Green, but the fact of the matter is *The Holborn Gazette*'s coverage of Larcombe's murder trumps ours. Your work on this is in the suds. I don't expect to pick up a rival newspaper on a Monday morning to discover that its reporters are a step ahead of my own. The public out there is hungry for information and, with three columns of exclusive news, *The Gazette* is printing exactly they want to read! I even heard people talking about *The Gazette* in the Turkish baths yesterday evening."

"They may be printing what the people want to read, but I'm not sure that a great deal of it is accurate. Winston

Nicholls is not a witness. I don't know how he is claiming to have seen the murderer."

"Have we any evidence that *The Gazette* is reporting inaccurate news?"

"Only that Winston Nicholls is not a witness."

"You know that for sure?"

"I would need to check."

"You'd need to check. So that means you don't know for sure."

"I will check, Mr Sherman, and fully establish the facts."

"*The Holborn Gazette* purports to be reporting the facts."

"I believe their 'facts' have been somewhat embellished."

"Would you indeed?"

"Tom Clifford is not a man I consider to be careful in his reporting."

"Penny's right," said Edgar. "He's a deplorable fellow."

"He may be deplorable, but at the present time he is no doubt keeping his editor happy. Tell me more about this woman who was attacked. Can we say for sure that it was the St Giles murderer who assailed her?"

"There's a strong possibility. It seems the attacker attempted to sedate her with chloroform, the substance also used to overpower Mr Larcombe."

"Readers aren't interested in possibilities, Miss Green. They want to know that the same man attacked this poor woman and that she narrowly escaped death at his hands. They want to discover what he looked like and exactly what he did, so they can look out for him themselves. There are many concerned people out there who are desperate to know more, and it's our job to feed them what they want. That's what *The Gazette* is doing. Now, get your story written about the woman who was attacked and give me plenty of time to read it as it will no doubt require some alterations."

He glanced around the room, scowling. "No sign of

Purves yet? Send him to my office without delay when he arrives."

Mr Sherman left the room with another slam of the door.

"Tom Clifford lies!" I said to Edgar. "He makes his stories up, doesn't he? When I was in St Giles there was no sign of the pawnbroker's wife. For all we know, he's concocted the interview and no one will question him because he claims to have a piece of exclusive news. And Winston Nicholls is not even a witness!"

"So you have said a few times now."

I thumped my desk in anger. "I don't see how I'm supposed to outdo Tom Clifford unless I begin creating stories myself, and I refuse to do that. It's not how news reporting is supposed to be."

"You know what your problem is, Miss Green?"

"What?" I hissed.

"You take your job rather too seriously. Sometimes you're so determined to establish the exact truth that you miss out on interesting opportunities."

"What do you mean?"

"Gossip, rumour, that sort of thing. You don't really have an ear to the ground, do you? You're good at spending your time in learned places, such as the reading room, and you have highly accomplished writing skills, but I suppose the fact that you're a woman hinders you slightly when it comes to accessing the best sources of news."

"And where might they be found?"

"In the taverns."

"I suppose you mean Ye Olde Cheshire Cheese?"

"Yes. Frederick owes his living to it, as do I. Tom Clifford certainly does. How about we go there once we're finished here?"

"I've worked with you for seven years, Edgar, and you have

never once invited me to join you in Ye Olde Cheshire Cheese."

"There you go, you see. You're pleasantly surprised now, aren't you?"

CHAPTER 21

I sat with Edgar and Frederick at a table in one of the many quaint, wood panelled-rooms on offer in Ye Olde Cheshire Cheese.

"There's a wide choice on the menu, Miss Green," said Edgar. "You can choose between the chop or the steak."

"Sometimes you can get a sausage here," added Frederick, rubbing his large stomach.

"Occasionally sausage or eggs, but usually chop or steak. Have you got a light, Potter?"

The men lit their pipes as I sipped my sherry and glanced around the busy room, recognising some of the faces from Fleet Street. I saw one other woman there, who I was sure worked on one of the periodicals.

"There are quite a few reporters from the *News of the World* here," I said.

"There are always hordes here from the *News of the World*," said Edgar. "How they find the time to do their reporting and writing I'll never know."

"Perhaps they do most of it here."

"Highly likely."

We ordered our food from the waiter and Edgar had just opened his mouth to speak when he was interrupted by a roar of laughter behind us. We turned to see Tom Clifford and his colleagues chuckling at a neighbouring table and Edgar groaned.

"Is there a single place in this city you can go to without bumping into someone from *The Holborn Gazette?*"

"In their defence, this is the pub which everyone on Fleet Street comes to, so it's not much of a surprise, is it?" said Frederick.

"Perhaps we need to find a new pub," said Edgar.

"But isn't this the place where you can have your ear to the ground?" I asked.

"Anyway, forget about *The Gazette*," said Frederick. "Their circulation may be up, but it'll fall again. Just wait and see."

"Why should it fall?" I asked.

"Because it's a tawdry newspaper. It doesn't have the pedigree of the *Morning Express*."

"That's what will carry us through? Our pedigree?"

"Of course. Other papers will come and go, but the *Express* will stay its course," Frederick replied.

"If only Sherman believed that," said Edgar. "He's got the needle about our circulation, and don't forget that he has the proprietor, Mr Conway, breathing down his neck. No wonder he's getting into a stew about Tom Clifford's reporting on the murders. London hasn't seen anything like this for years and people want to buy the newspapers each day so they can find out whether another poor fellow has been murdered or if the killer's been found.

"It's times like these that present us with our prime opportunity to procure more readers. A large number of the masses can read now, and we need them to buy our paper rather than any of the others. To do that, our reporting needs to be more entertaining. Look how popular the penny dreadfuls are! If you've ever read one, you'll know what utter tosh they contain. But tosh is what the masses want to read.

"The *Morning Express* may have pedigree. But if we don't cater for all those readers out there, and rely purely on the old guard, our circulation is certain to spiral downwards. You laughed at me concerning the story of the man selling his fat wife's corpse, but that's the direction in which we're heading. Tom Clifford has the right idea, much as I dislike to admit such a thing."

He glared in the direction of Tom and his colleagues.

"But don't you think he might be making his stories up?" I asked quietly.

"He is probably elaborating on the truth. And he has done so for quite some time now."

"Well, he won't get away with it for much longer," said Frederick. "We're merely seeing a temporary craze for sensationalist stories. The fad will pass and people will demand quality again."

"I wouldn't be so sure," I said, draining my sherry.

"I don't blame Sherman for losing his rag this morning," said Edgar. "Although I know you've been working hard, Miss Green, I also believe there's more you could be doing to grab the reader's attention. Think about how involved you are in all this. The boy who was murdered had stolen your bag! Why not write a piece about how you discovered him on the ground with his throat cut?"

"I didn't discover him; someone else did."

"But you saw him."

I nodded in reply.

"Then write about what you saw! What was it like to witness the corpse of a poor boy who had been savagely murdered just moments earlier?"

"It was awful." I felt tears prick the backs of my eyes. I didn't like to think about poor Jack and how he had suffered.

"I can't write about it. It doesn't seem respectful to write about him in that way. People should be allowed to remember him as he was."

"As a thief, you mean?" Edgar smirked. "It may not seem respectful to you, but it's what people want to read. Don't you see that?"

"How would you feel if the death of your son was described so publicly in a newspaper?"

"I'd be devastated if anything of the sort happened to my son. But you must detach yourself from such thoughts, Miss Green. The boy was neither my son nor yours. He was a thief, and he was also the victim of an exceptionally dangerous man who is still roaming the streets of St Giles! Now, don't tell me there's no story in that. You must commit it to paper and give it to Sherman. He would be extremely grateful for it."

Frederick placed another glass of sherry in my hand and I gratefully took a large sip.

Could I really write about the boy's death so graphically?

The more I considered it, the more convinced I became that I couldn't. Even though he had been a thief, Jack had undoubtedly been born with a good heart. A short lifetime in the slums had turned him into a criminal, and I believed that, following his tragic demise, he deserved to rest in peace.

"You are very quiet now, Miss Green. I apologise if my last words were rather strong."

"There was sense in them." I took another sip of my drink. "But I don't think I can do that sort of news reporting."

"Perhaps you would be better off reporting on the society dinners and balls?"

"Perhaps I would, but I cannot think of anything more tedious."

"It would be, but don't forget, Miss Green, that our job is to make the dullest of events seem interesting to our readers.

That's the skill of a journalist. You may not like Tom Clifford's method of exaggerating the truth, but perhaps you have been adding your own embellishments to your work without actually realising it. Every story requires embellishment to make it interesting, does it not?"

"Yes, Edgar, you're right. I suppose I'm doing that already without realising." I finished my drink and rested my shoulders against the back of the bench, feeling slightly carefree after two sherries. "We don't often find the opportunity for conversations like this, do we? When we're in the office we're so busy with our work and very often end up sparring over something."

I watched Edgar take off his jacket and roll up his shirt sleeves. We hadn't always worked well together and there was still a faintly venomous glint in Edgar's eye, but I felt that we could perhaps work more harmoniously from this time onwards.

"There's always a deadline hanging over our heads, and although we work together there's a sense of competition, isn't there?" he replied. "We all want to be the one who is patted on the back by Sherman. We all want to be given the important story. In fact, truth be told, I'm rather envious that you're reporting on the St Giles murders. I wouldn't mind having a go at that story myself."

"At the present time, I would say that you are welcome to it."

"You don't mean that, Miss Green."

"I'm not sure whether I'm really suited to some of this news reporting."

"Of course you are. You're responding to what I said a few moments ago, aren't you? That's why I apologised for my words being a little strong. You don't have to do what I say."

"But it's the right thing to do, isn't it? I need to forget

about any emotional attachment to the boy and write a lurid story about his death."

"I wouldn't go that far, Miss Green. Really, I wouldn't."

"Do you think it's because I'm a woman?"

"What do you mean?"

"Perhaps I'm more sensitive with regard to reporting on such events. Perhaps if I were a man I should find it easier."

"There's no doubt that you're sensitive, Miss Green, but I don't think you would find it any easier if you were a man."

"Look at the people standing around us," I said. "Most of them are men. Perhaps news reporting is better suited to the masculine population."

"What are you saying? This is the very opposite of what you usually stand for, Miss Green! I know I sometimes joke about female reporters and poor bad grammar, but I only speak in jest. I believe that you are just as well-suited to this job as any man I know, including myself."

"That's kind of you to say, Edgar."

"I'll be brutally honest with you." He leant forward and fixed me with his earnest gaze. "Do I think women make good news reporters? On the whole, I would say no. But you're a little different, Miss Green. You've worked on Fleet Street for ten years and you do your job extremely well. I have faith in you."

Our eyes locked and his cheeks reddened, so he busied himself with refilling his pipe.

"And I'm only saying this because I have drunk two tankards of beer.," he added. "You won't ever hear me say such a thing when we're in the newsroom. That wouldn't be right, would it? Well, look who it is! Your schoolboy inspector."

I turned to look over my shoulder and saw James weaving his way between the tables towards us wearing his bowler hat.

CHAPTER 22

"James! How did you find us here?"

I moved along the bench to make space for him to sit down with us.

"I'm a detective, remember?" He grinned and took off his hat. "Good evening, Mr Fish. Mr Potter."

"Jam Keys Label!" said Edgar.

"I beg your pardon?"

"It's just one of Edgar's infernal anagrams," I said. "He concocts them while I'm busy in the reading room doing his work for him. Why are you here? Please don't tell me there's been another murder."

I felt a sudden sinking sensation in my chest.

"No, just some intriguing correspondence."

He removed some folded pieces of paper from the inside pocket of his jacket while Frederick ordered more drinks from the waiter.

"Tell me what you think about these. You know Winston Nicholls, don't you?"

I groaned. "Yes, according to *The Holborn Gazette* he witnessed the murderer leaving the pawnbroker's shop."

"Did he? Well, it's the first I've heard of it. Perhaps Inspector Fenton is aware, although he hasn't said anything to that effect."

"Winston says the murderer wore a mask. I think it's more likely that he or Tom Clifford invented the story."

"I shall have to speak to him and find out more, especially in light of these letters he's sent us."

He passed me three pieces of parchment, handwritten in sloping blue ink.

"Tom Clifford is just over there." I pointed him out. "You can speak to him about Nicholls in a moment."

I read the first letter.

Dear Inspector Blakely

I have spent many hours studying the murder scenes in St Giles and I can tell you that the murderer is most certainly Mr O'Donoghue. He was arrested for the murder of Jack Burton, but later released. I saw him going into the pawnbroker's shop on the day of Mr Larcombe's murder. I thought nothing of it until I heard that Mr Larcombe had been murdered. Mr O'Donoghue is a violent man and he is responsible for the murders of Mrs O'Brien, Mr Yeomans, Master Burton and Mr Larcombe. You must arrest him at once.

Winston Nicholls

"How confusing," I said. "He told Tom Clifford that he saw the masked murderer leaving the pawnbroker's shop after Mr Larcombe's murder, yet in this letter he says that he saw

Reuben O'Donoghue going into the pawnbroker's shop, presumably before Mr Larcombe was murdered."

"I believe so."

"But in his interview in *The Holborn Gazette*, he didn't mention Reuben O'Donoghue at all. I don't understand him."

"It's as clear as mud, isn't it?" said James. "There are two more letters to read."

I perused the second letter.

It is a great shame that you do not employ me as a detective at Scotland Yard. I tell you now that I know who the murderer is, and what's more, I can lead you to him. I have seen the man with my own eyes and if you do not arrest him forthwith he surely will kill again.

The third read:

I am worried for the safety of my mother. She lives by the courtyard where Master Burton was murdered. If there are any more murders in St Giles, she will have to move as she is not safe. Why do you not arrest the man? His name is Reuben O'Donoghue. He was arrested once and then released. The police do not know what they are doing. I hope that you do.

"Most peculiar," I said, handing the letters back to James.

"Do you have any insight into Winston Nicholls' state of mind?"

"Sadly, I don't. I have had only two conversations with him, and on both occasions I found his manner to be rather odd. He seems unable to look anyone in the eye. His mother is a friendly, pleasant lady, however."

"Do we know for sure that he is a clerk, or is that only what he tells his mother? From what I've heard, he spends a good deal of his time hanging about in St Giles."

"I couldn't say for sure. I know very little about the man."

"I'll interview him properly and find out more, although I have to say I'm wary of doing so. I think he considers himself to be more of an expert on this investigation than any police officer, but we do occasionally encounter men such as him and we must entertain what they tell us, as we could miss a trick if we were to ignore them completely."

"Let's hope that he has something useful to tell you and it isn't a complete waste of your time."

"Have you encountered anyone in St Giles by the name of Adam?"

I considered this question while I thought about all the people I had met during my visits.

"No."

"Because I have another letter here from someone who calls himself Adam. It was sent to Bow Street station."

James unfolded the letter and handed it to me.

"Could this actually be another letter from Winston, although he calls himself Adam?" I asked.

"I don't think so. Look, the handwriting and paper are quite different."

"Goodness," I said, my hand beginning to tremble. "This man claims to be the murderer!"

You took your time to wake up. No one noticed me after the woman in Nottingham Court and the man in The Three Feathers. It was the boy what did it, and after the shopkeeper they're all running scared.

Adam D.V.

"*It was the boy what did it*. What does he mean by that?"

"I think he means that Jack's murder was what finally got the Yard involved."

"Well, he's not wrong about that. I still despair at the fact that E Division did so little about the deaths of Mrs O'Brien and Mr Yeomans. But do you think this letter is actually from the murderer?"

"Of course not!" interjected Edgar. "These people are all time-wasters. You can't take them seriously. You should have seen how many fishy letters the *Morning Express* received at the time of the Lizzie Dixie case last year."

"I remember," I said. "We were sent a lot of bewildering letters, many of which made little sense."

"It's not unusual for the Yard to receive letters about crimes," said James, "and there's no telling whether Adam has any connection to the murders. He doesn't give away any information here which isn't already public knowledge, so this letter could have come from anyone, I suppose. I was interested to find out whether you had come across someone by that name, but as you haven't I shall add it to the case file with Mr Nicholls' letters and wait to see whether we receive any more."

"Adam D.V. He tells you his first name but not his surname. What can the letters D and V stand for?"

"It doesn't matter," said Edgar. "He cannot be sane. Just ignore it."

"That's the challenge of detective work," said James, folding up the letters and putting them back in his pocket. "You have to determine which elements deserve your attention after discounting all the red herrings."

"I don't envy you," I said, finishing off my sherry. "I really don't."

James ordered a chop and Edgar ordered two bottles of wine, and we ate and drank together.

When we had finished eating, James went to speak to Tom Clifford for a while, and by the time he returned I realised that my head felt rather fuddled.

"So, what did Tom say?" I asked.

"Penny, your words are slurred. I think we need to get you home."

"Yes, that's probably a good idea," I replied.

I noticed Edgar smiling at me, and for some reason I began to giggle.

"She's three sheets to the wind!" laughed Frederick.

"So are you," said Edgar.

"What did Tom Clifford say?" I asked after I had recovered from my laughing fit.

"Penny you have just asked me that same question!" James laughed. "It's no use me telling you now, as you won't remember. I'll tell you when you're sober."

"Oh." I sank forward and rested my forehead on the tablecloth.

I heard Edgar and Frederick talking, but I didn't raise my head because it felt so comfortable where it was. I closed my eyes and decided that I could quite happily sleep there.

I felt a hand on my shoulder.

"Come on, Penny, I'll escort you home," said James.

"There's no need. Just carry on talking and I'll have a rest."

"Not here, you won't. Come on."

The icy air cleared my head slightly and James quickly found a cab. We both got in.

"There's no need for you to travel with me," I said. "I'll be fine now."

"No, I insist. It's late and I intend to ask the driver to take me to my house after dropping you safely at Milton Street."

I felt pleased to have James sitting beside me. I told myself it was the chill in the air that encouraged me to lean in a little closer to keep warm, so that our shoulders were touching slightly. He didn't object, nor did he edge away from me. The lights in the street were spinning slightly.

"Why are you helping me home? You don't need to help me home."

"I want to make sure you get back to your lodgings safely."

"But you don't have to. Why are you?"

"Because I want you to be safe."

"Why?"

"Because if I don't ensure that you return home safely, I shall be worried about you."

"You'd be worried about me? Why?"

"Penny, you sound like my little niece asking *why* all the time."

"Why?" I began giggling again.

"That's enough. Get some sleep! You almost fell asleep at the dinner table just now."

"I can't sleep, I'm not comfortable."

"Here, you can rest against my shoulder."

I happily leant up against James and closed my eyes. I could smell the wool of his coat mingling with his pleasant eau de cologne.

I thought again of James and the future Mrs Blakely standing together at the altar.

"You must be looking forward to being married," I said.

"It will certainly be a new chapter."

"It's a shame."

"Penny, don't."

I sat up. "Don't what? *It's a shame*. That's all I said."

His face was cloaked in shadow, but I could tell that he was looking out at the street ahead.

"Am I not allowed to say *it's a shame*?"

"I thought you wanted to sleep."

"You didn't answer my question."

"Penny, you're tipsy. We can't talk sensibly when you're tipsy."

"So you're not going to speak to me, then?"

"I didn't say that."

"It's a shame you're getting married. There, I said it. I said it sensibly, too."

I watched him as he turned to look at me.

"Oh, Penny, you're insufferable. Do you know that?"

We passed a gas lamp, and for a brief moment I saw his face. His eyes were open wide and fixed on mine.

I felt a strong instinct to kiss him and acted on it without further thought. My lips were against his only for a moment. His mouth was warm and the slight stubble on his chin rubbed against my face and sent a tingle down my spine.

He pulled away.

"Penny, it wouldn't be right."

The night air suddenly felt cold on my face again, and I quickly turned away.

"You're drunk and I'm engaged to be married," he added.

"I know. I'm sorry. I shouldn't have done that. Please forget that I did it. I'll ask the cab to stop and walk the rest of the way."

"I said I would accompany you home."

"I expect you wish you'd never offered to do so now."

"No, I don't."

James sighed and I pushed myself into the far side of the carriage and hugged my bag. My whole body felt tense with shame and regret. *What if James now thought of me as a woman with loose morals? Perhaps he thought me disgraceful for drinking too much sherry and requiring an escort home?* I silently urged the horse to walk faster and bring the calamitous journey to an end.

CHAPTER 23

"**A**re you feelin' a'right today, Miss Green? Yer lookin' peaky."

Martha was busy scrubbing a shirt collar on her washboard, the suds foaming up around her red knuckles.

"I'm fine, thank you. Just tired."

I didn't want to admit that I was suffering from the effects of the sherry the night before. My stomach kept turning, but the smell of the soap was refreshing.

The snow and ice had melted away and a smoky fog was curling itself around the rooftops. A small pot of flowers had been placed in the corner where Jack had been found and Susan was sharing the toast I had given her among her children by the privies. I wondered whether she would eat any of it herself and then my thoughts turned to Sarah Fisher. I wondered if she was managing to stay off the streets at night.

"Poor Mr Larcombe, God rest 'is soul," said Martha. "No one wants ter be out on the streets now 'less they can 'elp it. Problem is, people 'ave ter get out and get a bitta money, don't they? No one can stay indoors the 'ole time. It's worryin' me. Who knows but I could be next!"

"Of course you won't be, Martha."

"'Ow d'yer know that? I might be! The killer ain't choosy. He's done two men, a boy and a woman. There ain't no particular type what 'e's goin' for. It could be me as much as the next person."

"Why don't you go and stay with Winston?"

"Nah, I'm stayin' 'ere. I were born in St Giles, and that's where I stays. I ain't lettin' some murderer frighten me off. And there's a lotta people 'ere what can't get away. They're stuck 'ere, so I'm stayin' wiv 'em."

"Winston appears to have some theories about who the killer might be."

Martha laughed. "Oh, 'e would! 'E's got an opinion on hev'rythin'. 'E's been writin' letters about it all, and 'e were in the newspaper, weren't he? Weren't yours, were it?"

"It was *The Holborn Gazette*."

"That's the one. I always knew he were a clever 'un. Reckons 'e can solve it all afore the police can, he does. Proberly ain't too difficult. The coppers ain't doin' much, are they?"

"It's a difficult case for them, Martha, but Scotland Yard is involved now and I'm sure they'll soon catch the man."

Talk of the Yard brought James to mind. My toes curled as I thought about the journey we had shared in the cab. Hopefully, I would be able to avoid him until I felt fully recovered from the embarrassment. I cleared my throat and tried to occupy my thoughts with work.

"Martha, can you tell me where I might find Ed Keller?"

I wanted to obtain an interview which Mr Sherman would appreciate.

Martha stopped scrubbing and gave me a sharp look.

"The Earl o' York? Yer don't wanna be talkin' to 'im. 'E'd give you a punch on the nose by way of an 'ow-de-do."

"I need to interview him for the *Morning Express*."

"You won't get nothin' from 'im. And there's no tellin' what 'e'd do to a pretty young girl such as yerself."

I smiled at the vague compliment. "I'm not a girl, Martha. I'm almost thirty-five."

She stopped scrubbing again and looked me over. "Thir'y-five? Yer don't look a day over twenny-eight."

She resumed her scrubbing.

"That's very kind of you. Didn't you say he lived in King's Head Yard?"

"I don't remember sayin' that."

"You told me Jack lived there with Ed Keller and some of the other boys."

"Don't remember."

"Please, Martha, I'm certain you told me he lived in King's Head Yard. Is that far from here?"

She shook her head and glared at me. "Miss Green, yer don't give up, do yer?"

"I'm a news reporter."

She pointed a soapy finger at me and her jowls quivered with anger.

"Yer don't wanna be goin' nowhere near King's 'Ead Yard or the Earl o' York or none of them street-arabs! We don't want anuvver murder on our 'ands, do we?"

"You think they would murder me?"

"King's 'Ead Yard ain't no place for a lady!"

"I want to interview Ed Keller. Perhaps he might like to be interviewed."

"Nah, not 'im."

"I've spoken to some quite unpleasant people in my time, Martha."

"None as bad as 'im, I can tell yer."

"You'd be surprised at how many people like him enjoy speaking to the press. They seem pleased to have their say."

"Not 'im."

"But he does live in King's Head Yard?"

"I ain't sayin'."

"You've already confirmed it, Martha. Thank you. I'll find the place and I will be careful. I've done this sort of thing before."

I said goodbye and turned to leave.

"Wait!" she called out from behind me. "If yer gonna be brainless, then don't do it on yer own."

I turned to face her again. "Martha, I don't expect you to come with me."

"There's no chance o' that! You think I'm goin' anywhere near King's 'Ead Yard? Yer need a man wiv yer."

She dried her hands on her apron and I prepared myself to argue in the event that she suggested I take her son. Fortunately, she had someone else in mind.

"Let's ask one o' the missionaries."

"It's not a sensible idea, Miss Green. I would urge you to reconsider," said David Meares, his freckled face crumpled with concern.

"Yer won't change 'er mind, I've already tried me best," said Martha. "Yer've got ter go wiv 'er, else she's goin' by 'erself and that ain't safe."

The simple altar at the far end of the chapel was ablaze with candles. Martha and I stood by the doorway with Mr Meares and Mr Hawkins in the flickering gloom.

"I shall accompany you, Miss Green," said Hugo Hawkins, his close-set eyes sparkling in the candlelight. "Ed Keller and I usually see eye-to-eye."

"Not always," said David.

"I said *usually*. Sometimes he comes up here to pray with us."

"What do you want to speak to him about, Miss Green?" asked David.

"I'm interested to find out what such a prominent gang leader thinks about the murders. Perhaps he has something to do with them."

"That's a matter for the police."

"I realise that, but it would still be of interest to find out whether he knows anything. And I should like to ask him about Jack Burton. I still think about Jack a good deal."

"We all does," added Martha.

"Well, I can't guarantee that Keller will give you a warm welcome," said Hugo, "but we can try. Can you run fast in your skirts, Miss Green?"

"Not very fast."

"I didn't think so, but we will take care and God will watch over us. Please don't antagonise Keller with any tricky questions."

"I'll come too!" said David cheerfully.

"Really? I wouldn't wish to inconvenience you both. I know that you're busy."

"There's safety in numbers,"

"There yer go, Penny. Two strappin' men ter look after yer."

"Thank you. I'm very grateful to you all for your help."

"I must say that it's rather reckless of the editor of your newspaper to ask a young woman to venture into such a dangerous part of London," said Hugo.

"It wasn't his idea," I replied. "It was mine."

The two missionaries exchanged a glance and Martha sighed.

CHAPTER 24

"Did you know Mr Larcombe well?" I asked the missionaries as we walked towards King's Head Yard.

The fog was thickening and creeping down into the narrow streets, and it had a disorientating effect. I thought I was familiar with St Giles by now, but the weather had changed that. I felt grateful for the missionaries' company.

"We knew him, but not very well," replied David.

"He was once a good man," said Hugo, "but there was some trouble with the wife and it led him to drink."

"Had he not always been a drinker?"

"Well yes, but it made him drink more. He had deteriorated noticeably over the past year," David continued.

"But he still managed to look after his shop?" I asked.

"It seems so, although he wasn't averse to consorting with people of a dubious nature."

"Do you think he might have been murdered by a criminal associate?"

"It's possible. I wouldn't discount it," said Hugo.

"I'm quite convinced that a fellow criminal murdered him," said David. "He was a drunkard and had argued with many people. He may have owed money or someone may have owed him money. You know how it is with these people."

I was startled by the sound of raised voices close by and discerned the figures of two men in the fog ahead of us, one much taller than the other.

"She asked me for help!" said a well-spoken man's voice.

His companion began to reply but fell quiet as he noticed us approach.

As we drew closer, I saw that the taller man was Reuben O'Donoghue. The other man was about fifty years of age with an orangey-grey moustache and a top hat.

"Is everything all right, gentlemen?" asked Hugo.

"Of course, Mr Hawkins. Mr Meares. Miss Green." Reuben doffed his hat and gave me a smile.

"I've said all I need to," said the short man. "Good day, gentlemen. Madam."

He gave a slight bow and scurried away, leaving Reuben to shrug nonchalantly and saunter on past us.

"I wonder what was going on there," said David.

"Mr 'Awkins! Mr Meares!"

The limping figure of a woman loomed out of the fog ahead of us. There was no bonnet or hat on her head, but she wore many layers of grimy clothing and had a woollen shawl clasped around her shoulders.

"Can I trouble yer for a sixpence?"

She pushed her matted hair out of her sunken eyes and held out a dirty hand.

"I needs a bed fer tonight. I slept in a doorway in Broker's Alley last night and woke with wermin crawlin' all over me. And the cold... I've 'ad enough o' the cold. I was stayin' down Parker's, but the deppity says I'm trouble. 'E's kicked me out and me sister's kicked me out 'n' all. I ain't got no money fer a bed."

"Have we seen you at Chapel recently, Maggie?" asked Hugo.

She scratched the back of her neck. "Well, it ain't been easy recently. Most o' the times I bin tryin' ter find money to get a bed fer the night. But I promise I'll come ter chapel tomorrer. I'll be there tomorrer."

"Don't forget that we serve soup each day in the winter."

"Yeah, I'll come and get a soup tomorrer. That's what I'll do."

She tentatively held her hand out again.

"But I need a bed fer tonight, I won't be able ter stand that cold again. It'll be the death o' me."

There was a long pause before I opened my handbag, rummaged about for my purse and gave Maggie a shilling.

"Oh lor! Bless yer, ma'am. Bless yer." She curtsied.

"Please make sure you find somewhere safe to sleep tonight," I said, thinking of the attack on poor Sarah Fisher.

"I will! I will! Thank you. God bless yer."

Maggie limped away and the missionaries both turned to face me.

"You realise that she'll spend that coin on gin down at The Three Feathers?" said Hugo.

"She would be foolish to do that."

"These people *are* foolish!" said David. "That's why we don't allow them to become accustomed to money. She'll need more coins tomorrow and more the day after that."

"Your shilling could have done far more good in the hands of the mission," added Hugo. "With such a donation, we could provide food and prayer for these people and steer them away from the dangers of alcohol."

"She needed a bed for the night," I retorted. "No one

should be wandering the streets after dark with a killer on the loose. I gave her enough money for gin *and* a bed."

"We always encourage temperance," said Hugo.

"Probably a good idea," I said, mindful of the ill-effects of my indulgence the previous evening.

I took another shilling from my purse and gave it to Hugo Hawkins.

"Does that seem fair now?" I asked sharply.

"Thank you."

"Are we almost at King's Head Yard?"

"Almost," Hugo replied stiffly.

We turned into a foul-smelling walkway and emerged into a murky courtyard. I heard scampering footsteps around us as we came to a stop.

"Who's there?" called a boy's voice.

"Mr Hawkins and Mr Meares," replied Hugo.

The buildings around us formed grey silhouettes in the fog. I heard the slam of a door or shutter, and then another voice rang out from behind us.

"Waddya want?"

"We've come to see the Earl of York," said Hugo.

"Why?"

"I wish to interview him for a newspaper," I called out.

"Is that a woman?" asked a boy's voice.

"No women allowed!" shouted another.

There were more running footsteps and then further slamming of doors.

"This isn't promising," said David quietly. "Usually we'd have been invited in by now."

"Hello?" Hugo called out. "Mr Hawkins here! What's keeping you?"

Everything fell silent and I saw a flickering light in the

fog, but when I looked directly at the flame it disappeared. I sensed there were people hiding in the gloom around us, watching us. My heartbeat began to pound in my ears.

"Hello?" said Hugo again, in a quieter tone this time.

Another door slammed.

"Show the woman in!" came a voice. "Jus' the woman, no one else!"

I stepped forward, unsure as to where I was going. The missionaries walked with me and I saw a dark doorway up ahead of us. A boy stepped out with a tallow candle in his hand.

"We said *just the woman!*" His face was twisted into an expression befitting someone far beyond his years.

"We should accompany her," said David.

"No yer don't."

"Then you mustn't harm her!" he ordered.

The boy grinned. "I won't do nuffink to 'er, mister."

"Please be careful, Miss Green," said Hugo.

Nervously, I followed the boy through the dark doorway.

CHAPTER 25

I remained a few paces behind the boy as we walked along a wooden corridor lit only by the candle in his hand. We entered a high-ceilinged brick and timber room with a large fire at the centre of it.

The walls were lined with boys dressed in ill-fitting clothing. Some of them removed their pipes from their mouths to whistle or to make crude remarks about me. I stopped and looked around for Edward Keller. My mouth felt dry and there were prickles of perspiration on my forehead and under my arms. I felt as though I were about to be preyed upon.

My spectacles misted up from the warmth of the fire, and I wiped them with my trembling, gloved fingers. I had thought my decision a brave one, but now I began to consider it foolhardy. If these boys decided to harm me I would be entirely defenceless.

"Miss Green!" called out a voice from somewhere above me.

I looked up to see Ed Keller climbing down a ladder from a gallery I hadn't noticed until that very moment. Once he had descended, he strode up to the fire and gave a short whistle. A small terrier wearing a silk neckerchief trotted out from the shadows to join him.

I stood taller than Ed, but I had no doubt that he was my superior in strength. He had a wispy moustache and his face appeared younger than I guessed he was. He wore a top hat and a dark frock coat over a colourfully striped velvet waistcoat. The gold of his tie pin and watch chain glittered in the firelight.

"You know my name?" I asked in surprise.

My voice sounded timorous in the large room and I was uncomfortably aware of all the eyes fixed upon me.

"Hev'ryone knows who the reporter is." He grinned at me, displaying two rows of crooked yellow teeth. "Where's your mate the inspector today?"

"I don't know."

"Ain't he your friend?"

"He's investigating the murders and I am working on the news stories surrounding them."

"So 'e ain't your friend?"

"We are colleagues, nothing more."

Ed laughed. "I get it." Then he winked. "I wouldn't of let yer in if yer'd been with 'im. The coppers ain't welcome round 'ere. He ain't waitin' outside, is 'e?"

"He doesn't know that I'm here."

"Don't he?"

Ed sat himself on a stool by the fire, spread his legs wide and ran his tongue along his upper lip as he looked me up and down. "Yer didn't tell 'im yer were comin' ter see me? This 'ere's a dangerous place for ladies. We don't usually allow women in 'ere, do we boys?"

There was a murmur of agreement from the rest of the room. The dog lay down next to the stool and licked itself.

"Can I offer yer some 'ot gin, Miss Green?"

"No, thank you."

"Go on, I insist. I'll tek offence if yer refuse."

He clicked his fingers and a boy with a large birthmark on one cheek approached me with a clay flask in his hand. I reluctantly took it from him and the sharp smell immediately struck my nose.

"Go on, Miss Green!" Ed cajoled.

Although I didn't want to drink a single drop of it, I felt too afraid not to. I took a quick sip and tried not to choke as the gin burned my throat. Once the burning sensation had gone, I was left with a warm, pleasant feeling in my forehead and I finally understood why so many people found comfort in this particular drink.

The boy with the birthmark retrieved the flask from me.

"There you go. Ain't too bad, is it?" said Ed with a wink.

"Why do they call you the Earl of York?" I asked.

"I calls meself it. And I calls me dog Prince Regent. Will all this be goin' in yer newspaper, Miss Green?"

"Not all of it. I thought I could ask you a few questions about Jack and the other terrible murders. Then I will write up your answers and it will be published."

"I like the sound o' that. I ain't never been in a newspaper before!"

I removed my notebook and pencil from my handbag and noticed that my hands were shaking as I did so.

Ed had also noticed.

"Give 'er a bit more gin, Pie Face."

I took another obligatory sip and couldn't help but gasp as it burned my throat again.

Ed laughed. "Good stuff, ain't it, Miss Green? Now you sees why hev'ryone's drinkin' it day and night. What questions yer gonna ask me, then?"

I held the notebook in my weak right hand and prepared to write with my left.

"Tell me about Jack."

Ed scratched his chin.

"He lived here with you, I understand? Where did he come from?"

"I dunno where he comed from. I found 'im shinin' shoes on Shaf'sb'ry Avenue. I had words with 'im 'cause my boys was shinin' shoes there 'n' all. But he were good at what he done, so I told 'im if he come and lived and worked 'ere and gived me a cut that would do us all jus' fine."

"How long ago was that?"

"Abaht two years, I reckons. He were a good 'ard worker, but he 'ad an 'abit o' not always doin' what he were told. There's certain rules what we all got ter stick to 'ere. It's all abaht survival. Yer must understand that, Miss Green. The boys 'ere 'as 'ard lives."

"I can imagine they do." I glanced around at their watchful faces. "What did Jack do wrong, exactly?"

"He didn't do nuffink wrong in the usual sense o' the word, but if I told him to go a-cadgin' then he'd go a-thievin', and if I told him ter go a-shinin' e'd go a-cadgin'. See what I means?"

"I think so." I began to relax as I took down my notes. Perhaps it was the effect of the gin, or perhaps I had begun to feel reassured because Ed was being so co-operative. "Did Jack ever mention his family?"

Keller shook his head. "That's one o' the rules. We don't talk abaht fam'ly 'ere. Why d'ya think we're all 'ere? This is our fam'ly. Ain't no use in talkin' abaht the people what's let us down."

"Is that what happened to you?"

"I ain't talkin' nuffink abaht that." His jaw tightened and he inhaled deeply as he sucked on his pipe.

"May I ask how old you are?"

"Twenny-seven."

"And how long have you lived here?"

"Since I were eleven or twelve."

"And you get by through begging and stealing?"

"The boys do shinin', carryin', sellin', sweepin' and they takes messages from one place to anuvver. Then we gots a few crippled boys and they do the cadgin', 'cause there's nuffink else they can do, is there? And people takes pity on the cripples. Them lot earns more money than the rest of us! I trains the stronger boys to box. We makes money off o' some of the boxin', depending on whether we wins or loses. And we looks after fings fer people."

"Such as?"

"Pubs 'n' shops. If the landlord o' The Three Feathers don't want no stones thrown at 'is windows, 'e's gotta pay a few of our boys to keep a lookout, like."

"The boys threaten to throw stones if he doesn't pay them?"

"Nah, Miss Green!" Ed laughed. "You got me wrong, you 'ave. All wrong. And when we does thievin' we only thieves from the rich people 'cause they can spare a bit, can't they?"

"Jack took my bag. Do I look like a rich person?"

"Yer got proper togs on and yer got food to eat and someplace ter live."

"But I'm not rich."

"Nah, but that's what were wrong wiv Jack, weren't it? He weren't s'posed to go nickin' yer bag like that. I never asked 'im ter do it."

"So he did something wrong?"

"Yeah. He were one o' me best, but he done things wrong 'n' all."

"Did you punish him?"

"Yeah, now 'n' then like. 'E's gotta stick ter the rules like ev'ryone else."

"How did you punish him?"

"I ain't sayin'. That's private."

"Did you tell him that if he kept on doing things wrong he would have his throat cut?"

"Now, that ain't right, Miss Green." Ed got up from his stool and walked towards me with his jaw pushed out. Prince Regent followed behind him, emitting a low growl.

"You take that right back! Yer can't say nuffink o' that sort. I punished 'im when I 'ad ter, but I never laid no finger on 'im. That ain't 'ow I do fings. Ain't I right, boys?"

There were mutters of agreement from all directions as Ed stared me in the eye, unblinking.

"I'm sorry," I said. "I don't wish to upset you. I just want to find out who killed Jack."

"We all wanna find out who killed 'im," said Ed. "You fink I don't miss 'im? He reminded me of meself when I were younger. I were right fond of 'im. What's 'appened is he strayed onto the Daly Boys' patch and they've got all upset abaht it. I've got some of me own boys lookin' into it."

"You think he was killed by a rival gang?"

"Yeah, so it won't do yer no good tryin' a blame me fer it. Watch what yer sayin', 'cause you can be dealt wiv if needs be."

He tapped his foot on the ground, and when I looked down I noticed a trapdoor beneath him. My breath quickened as I thought about the miserable cellar it almost certainly led down to.

"Have you ever seen the man in the mask?" I asked.

"Yeah, I seen 'im. What of it?"

"Do you know who he is?"

"A lunatic, proberly."

"Do you think he could be the killer?"

Keller shrugged. "How'd I know?"

"How many times have you seen him?"

"Dunno. Three, four p'r'aps. Some of the boys 'ave seen 'im 'n' all."

"Doing what exactly?"

"Just walkin'. I've 'eard 'e only comes out night-times."

"Did you see him on the evening of Jack's murder, or the night when Mr Larcombe was murdered?"

"Nah." Ed returned to his stool and I began to relax once again.

"You did some work for Mr Larcombe, I believe?"

"Yeah, and I were one of 'is best customers. A lotta the jewellery in that pop-shop's mine by rights."

"*Actually* yours?"

"Yeah, from people what 'ave paid me wiv jewellery for favours."

"I've heard that Mr Larcombe was ruining himself with drink."

"Who ain't?" Ed laughed.

"Did you have a good relationship with Mr Larcombe?"

"A *good relationship*?" Ed repeated, mocking my accent. "What's that mean, Miss Green?"

"Did you get on well?"

"Sometimes. The drink got to 'im, as yer say. It ain't easy doin' business wiv someone when they've bin drinkin' a lot, like."

"Were you still doing business with him up until the day of his death?"

"Not so much. Some o' me stuff 'ad gone missin', and I weren't too trustin' of 'im after all that."

"What stuff?"

"Things what yer don't need to worry about. He were killed by one of 'is customers."

"Which one?"

"How would I know? It's obvious, ain't it? The drink took a hold of 'im and 'e 'ad a fallin' out with just about hev'ryone what knows 'im."

"So you think Jack and Mr Larcombe were murdered by

two different people? What about Mrs O'Brien and Mr Yeomans? What do you know about them?"

"Enough now, Miss Green. Time to ask you a few questions o' me own."

He ran his tongue along his upper lip once again.

CHAPTER 26

"I don't need to answer any questions. I'm a news reporter." My voice still sounded weak.

"My place, my rules. Where d'ya live, Miss Green?"

"Cripplegate."

"And you ain't married?"

"No."

"Fancy marryin' the finest yer can find in St Giles?"

He emptied his pipe onto the floor before getting up from his stool and taking off his frock coat. He walked over to me with his hands on his hips.

"I have no desire to be married, Mr Keller."

"Yer don't?" He loosened his necktie. "Well then, yer don't know what yer missin', do yer, Miss Green?"

He was close enough for me to smell the tobacco and gin on his breath.

"Who do you think killed Jack and Mr Larcombe?"

I fixed his eyes with mine in the hope that I could bring him back to the conversation in hand.

"Put yer pencil and notebook down, Miss Green. We've finished wiv all that."

His hand gripped my left wrist, and I noticed that his fingernails were yellow and dirty. I pulled my arm away and quickly put my notebook and pencil in my bag, my heart thudding against the wall of my chest.

I had to get out of there as soon as possible.

"Thank you for agreeing to speak to me, Mr Keller. I'll take my leave now."

"There's no need ter leave quite so quick, Miss Green. 'Ows about some more gin?"

"I must go."

I glanced behind me, hurriedly looking for the door through which I had entered.

Pie Face appeared at my side with the clay flask.

"That's a nice jacket yer wearin', Miss Green," said Ed. "Does it unbutton easy?"

He grabbed the hem of my jacket and tugged at it.

"Get off me!"

I felt a swell of anger. I would do my best to fight him off if I had to, but I knew that he was stronger, and he had all his boys to help him. A few of them had gathered closer to us, surrounding me.

"'Ave some gin. That'll 'elp."

He took the flask and pushed it up to my face. I turned away and tried to walk towards the door, but he still had hold of my jacket.

"I told yer this were a dangerous place for ladies, but yer didn't listen, did yer? Get 'old of 'er skirts, Pie Face."

"No!" I cried out as loudly as I possibly could in the vain hope that the missionaries were still waiting for me in the courtyard.

Ed laughed as the boy grabbed at my skirts. I kicked out with my foot and caught him squarely on the shin.

"Ow!" he shouted, cursing loudly.

"Bring a candle over 'ere!" Ed called out. "I wanna be able

ter see what I'm doin'."

Then he gave me such a violent shove that I fell backwards onto the floor. I held my breath and screwed my eyes up tight.

Was there any use in me fighting when I was so heavily outnumbered?

I opened my eyes again to see Ed fumbling with his belt.

"Get off me!" I yelled, kicking out my feet with as much strength as I could muster.

Ed skipped back a few steps and laughed.

"She's a fighter," he said. "I'll 'ave ter knock 'er out."

He raised his fist threateningly.

I covered my head with my bag, cowering beneath it. As I did so, I heard a loud crashing, splintering sound.

"Leave her alone!" came a man's voice.

I remained where I was, waiting for the inevitable blow to come.

"Mr 'Awkins," said Ed in a calm voice. "And Mr Meares. Good mornin' to yer both."

Tears of relief sprung into my eyes. I lowered my bag to see the missionaries' concerned faces staring down at me.

"No, Ed," Hugo said, glaring at the gang leader.

Ed backed away.

"She were willin'," he said. "She just needed a bit more persuadin'."

"Are you all right, Miss Green?" David bent down and helped me to my feet. "We heard you cry out. We should never have let you come in here alone."

My entire body was trembling. "It's all my fault. I shouldn't have come. I made a mistake. I didn't realise what it would be like."

I didn't look back at Ed. Instead, I stumbled as quickly as I could through the door, along the dark corridor and out into the cold, murky courtyard.

CHAPTER 27

The foyer of St James's Hall was filled with the bright colours of evening gowns and the glossy shine of silk top hats. Polite chatter and perfume mingled in the air.

"I read your interview with the gang leader," said Eliza.

She wore a turquoise satin dress, which was unfashionably loose fitting. My sister had stopped wearing her corset the previous year and no longer had any desire to strap herself into a tight bodice.

"Tell me more about him," she said. "Was he frightening?"

"A little. He was unpleasant."

"I think you're extremely brave, Father would be proud of you."

"Mr Sherman is delighted with the interview and sales of the *Morning Express* were brisk yesterday."

I was trying desperately hard not to dwell on what had almost happened to me in King's Head Yard.

"How marvellous! And it's so pleasing to see you in such a pretty dress."

My gown was of russet-coloured satin with fringing

around the hips, a small bustle and a buttoned bodice. I wore a fur-lined cape over the top, which was beginning to make me overheat.

"And you've lost your sling too, I see. Is your arm feeling fully recovered?"

"Almost. It still feels weak, but I shall practise writing with my right hand again and that will soon strengthen it. How was your meeting with the London Society for Women's Suffrage?"

"Quite enlightening. There was a wonderful speech given by Miss Annie Hodgkins of the Isle of Man, where women landowners are permitted to vote. England really must do a lot more to catch up. The good news is that support is increasing within Parliament, particularly among the Liberal members. You must come along to the next meeting of the West London Women's Society. There is so much more you could write about our work in your paper. On second thoughts, I suppose you're quite busy reporting on these horrific murders these days. Will there be no end to them?"

I sighed. "The funeral of Mr Larcombe was held today, and you should have seen the crowds. I feel so sorry for the people living down in St Giles. It must be terrifying for them to know that the killer is stalking their streets!"

"Look at you, Penelope! Your face is all creased up with worry. You'll start to look older than your years if you're not careful."

"I can't help but worry."

"Dreadful things are happening in that slum, and it may sound awful to say it, but thank goodness it has been confined to that area alone. I have great confidence that they'll catch the man. Your friend Inspector Blakely is working on it, isn't he?"

My stomach flipped uncomfortably at the mention of his name.

"Are you blushing, Penelope?"

"No, I'm just rather warm in this cape."

"Come, it's time to take our seats." Eliza glanced at the piece of paper in her hand. "It's a miscellaneous programme tonight. I'm so looking forward to the piano recital by Madame von Belloc."

We took our seats on the green horse-hair benches in the magnificent concert hall inspired by the Moorish palace of Alhambra.

Three violinists and two cellists were seated on the stage. I gazed up at the colourful arches and carved geometric patterns on the ceiling, lost for a moment in their beauty until the leering face of Ed Keller loomed into my mind. I was grateful for the loud applause that interrupted my thoughts as the conductor strode onto the stage and took a short bow.

"String Quintet in B Flat," whispered Eliza. "One of my favourite Mendelssohn pieces."

The music was pleasingly light, rising and falling in a smooth rhythm. I found I could listen to it more clearly when I closed my eyes. I imagined it washing away all of the unwelcome thoughts in my head and resolved that I would protect myself from making any further mistakes. Although Mr Sherman had been overjoyed to read my interview with Ed Keller, I wasn't sure that the risk I had taken was really worth it. Hugo Hawkins and David Meares were the only other people who knew what had happened to me at the hands of Ed Keller, and I had sworn them to secrecy, embarrassed that I had ignored everyone's warnings so flagrantly. I had behaved foolishly.

Could Ed be the murderer?

The rumours had begun as soon as my interview with him was published. He had admitted to falling out with both Jack and Mr Larcombe, and when I asked him about the other murders, he hadn't answered my question. Instead, he had attempted to attack me.

Had he tried to silence me?

I wondered whether James had read the interview. I watched the conductor nod, dip and sway on the stage and struggled to imagine how I could ever face James again without a deep sense of shame.

"That was marvellous," said Eliza as we left the auditorium. "I do enjoy our concerts. I can't bear to take George with me because he always falls asleep and snores dreadfully. Would you like to join me at the ballad concert in aid of the London Orphan Asylum? I think it's in May."

"I'd love to, Ellie."

"What were we talking about before that pleasant interlude? Ah, yes, the inspector. I noticed you blushing."

I had hoped she would have forgotten.

"Do you have feelings for him?" she probed.

"No!"

"The vehemence of your reply suggests that my guess was correct." She surveyed me as if she were a doctor trying to ascertain what was wrong with her patient. "Is he not engaged to be married?"

"Yes, he is. To a lady named Charlotte."

"Oh Penelope, how awful."

"Awful? There's nothing awful about it. I have no romantic feelings toward him. I've only been working with him because the boy who snatched my bag fell victim to the St Giles killer."

Eliza shook her head sadly. "Of all the people you would choose, Penelope. A man who is to be married."

"I haven't chosen him," I hissed. "I don't care for him at all. In fact, he is rather dull. Police officers often are."

Eliza laughed, which angered me even further.

"It's no use pretending to me, Penelope. I'm your sister and I know you too well."

"Let us suppose for a moment that I do appreciate the inspector's company. And I'm speaking theoretically, of course."

My sister gave a solemn nod.

"I would suggest that spending a number of years living alone may sometimes make another person – who would ordinarily be of no consequence at all – seem rather more appealing than they might be under other circumstances."

"My goodness, Penelope, you don't half mince your words when talking about your feelings! You're almost as bad as my husband. You're lonely and have been for some time, and now a dashing detective has entered your life and you have fallen for him."

"I'm not lonely and he is *not* dashing!"

"But you've fallen for him?"

"And not that either!"

I pulled out my handkerchief and wiped my brow. I refused to believe that I could be attracted to James. For one thing, he was younger than me, and for another he was engaged to be married. The incident in the cab had been nothing but a moment of weakness. Perhaps a moment of loneliness. It would never happen again.

"I must return home now, Ellie. I plan to do some work on Father's papers this evening."

"Of course."

"I bought a tin of Peek Freans biscuits, did I tell you? I've eaten all the biscuits, but I keep the tin on my writing desk. It gives me something new to remember him by. This is more than just writing a book, isn't it?"

"Is it?"

"Each evening I sit down to read something he's written

or look at one of his sketches and I feel closer to him. Closer perhaps than I ever did when he was with us. Reading his words gives me a sense of how much he adored his plants and his travels."

"I have no doubt that he did. More than his own wife and daughters, I should say."

"Oh no, I don't agree. I'm sure he loved us and Mother even more so. But when I read his work I find his enthusiasm and excitement almost enchanting."

"Have you read *everything* he wrote Penelope?"

"No, not yet. He wrote so much, didn't he?"

"Yes indeed. I haven't read everything yet either, but a few of his diary entries are not quite so enchanting."

"I'm sure you're right. Father must have experienced dull days just like the rest of us."

"That's not quite what I meant, Penelope."

"What did you mean?"

"I'll let you continue with your reading and you will discover it for yourself."

"To what are you referring, Ellie?"

"Just continue reading, Penelope. Read everything and then tell me what you think."

Back at my lodgings, I made myself a cup of cocoa, sat by the fire and read some more of my father's diary entries. I read them more thoroughly this time, searching the words for any clues to what Eliza had alluded to earlier that evening.

I travelled by mule from the Lebrija River to Bucaramanga, and from thence along a pleasant valley of sugar cane, coffee and tobacco to the small town of Piedecuesta, where the local people make cigars and straw hats. I collected some specimens of Epidendrum Atropur-

pureum, which grows plentifully here, and continued my journey along a narrow mule track up to La Mesa de Los Santos, a plain 6,000 feet above the level of the sea.

Here the mighty condor can be seen, the span of its wings reaching up to ten feet. I observed one soaring without a beat of its wings for the best part of half an hour. Cattleya Mendelii is to be found on the vertiginous rock faces which descend from this great plain. I have heard of orchid hunters dangling natives on ropes over these precipices in order to retrieve the beautiful specimens.

Unwilling to risk the life or limb of myself or any other man, I rode on to Los Santos and then Curiti, where the last portion of my journey was completed on foot. Before long, I came across a profusion of rose-coloured Cattleya Mendelii among the ferns and bromeliads. After constructing a makeshift basket out of twigs, I collected as many plants as I could and prayed that at least a dozen would survive the heat of the journey back to the river.

I still felt certain that my father's final visit had been to the falls of Tequendama. His diaries and drawings had been discovered by a search party in a hut not far from the falls.

I would need to return to the reading room and once again examine the map which Mr Edwards had found for me. La Mesa de Los Santos sounded like a magical place to me and I pictured my father there watching the soaring condor. I closed my eyes and wished I could have been there to share the sight with him.

What had Eliza meant? And why had she refused to tell me?

CHAPTER 28

"We need to continue with our reporting on St Giles' Rookery." Mr Sherman strode around the newsroom as he talked. "The interview with the Earl of York – what a wonderful name! – was extremely popular with our readers. The men were even talking about it in the Turkish baths yesterday evening."

"High praise indeed," said Edgar.

"I detect a fashion for slum stories," continued Mr Sherman. "I suppose it began with *The Bitter Cry of Outcast London* last year, and the public's appetite for such tales shows no sign of waning. I have heard tell that some journalist is disguising himself as a slum dweller and going to the trouble of spending nights in the dosshouses."

"Slummers," piped up Frederick.

"What?"

"That's what they call people who go sightseeing in the slums. They wear common clothes and mingle with the inhabitants. A rather grimy experience, I suspect."

"Slummers. So that's what they call them, eh? There is great interest in these abysmal places these days."

"I've come across a lady who organises tours of St Giles," I added. "I saw her showing people around and I'm told that she charges quite a bit for the experience."

"A friend of mine is a regular slummer," said Frederick. "So much so that he has fathered a child with a gingerbread seller in Whitechapel."

"Is that so?" Mr Sherman raised an eyebrow.

"A chap from Magdalene College, Cambridge! Who would have thought it? Don't tell his father."

"There's no danger of that, Potter. I have no idea who the chap's father is." Mr Sherman turned to face me. "Miss Green, I need an article now which details the daily hell these people are living in. I want to read of dirt, disease and drunkenness. And we need to mention dead infants."

"Dead infants?"

"Have you read *The Bitter Cry*? There are tales of numerous families sharing one room and a dead infant lying in the midst of them."

"And pigs," added Frederick. "They keep pigs in the rooms as well."

"Yes, I've read it," I said. "And some of the living conditions described are more horrendous than I could ever have imagined. But I haven't encountered anything quite as terrible as that in St Giles so far."

Although articles on conditions in the slums had informed the public about the plight of people living there, I couldn't help but think there was an element of gleeful exploitation of their misery on the part of some writers.

"Keep on looking, Miss Green. I wouldn't wish for you to be distressed, of course, but if you can write about something which instils horror in our readers then your article will be all the better for it. Mr Fish, I will need you to work undercover."

Edgar's brow furrowed. "Me?"

"Yes. Do what this other chap is doing and disguise your-self. You must drink in some of the public houses there and sleep in some of the lodging houses."

"I'm not sure that—"

"Mr Fish, as your editor I am ordering you to do so. It needn't be for long; just long enough to get a good story out of it. See if you can get talking to a gang. I like the sound of this rival gang the Earl of York mentions in his interview. Remind me what they're called, Miss Green."

"The Daly Boys."

Edgar looked at me then back at Mr Sherman, his mouth opening and closing several times. "But I'm not sure I'm suitable—"

"Of course you are, man! You're a news reporter!"

"But I'm supposed to be working on the General Gordon story."

"Hand it over to Purves."

"The gangs are dangerous, Mr Sherman," I said.

"Well you managed to speak to one of them without any problems, Miss Green. I'm sure Mr Fish can do the same."

"Ed Keller is unpleasant."

"I can imagine he is, but you made it out of there alive, didn't you? You got the story and that's all that matters."

Mr Sherman was interrupted by a knock at the newsroom door.

"Come in!" he exclaimed. "Why, Inspector Blakely! What brings you here?"

I hadn't seen James since the mortifying incident in the cab. My heart began to thud furiously and I bent my head over the typewriter, trying to hide my face as best I could.

"Good morning, Mr Sherman," said James. "I have more news on the St Giles killer."

I felt him glance at me and knew that it would be churlish to ignore him. I looked up and gave him a meek smile. He took off his hat and smoothed his hair. He appeared more handsome to me than he ever had before. His suit was grey with a subtle check and he was wearing the star-shaped tie pin once again.

I cursed myself silently and busied myself with pressing the keys on the typewriter.

"Not another murder?" said Mr Sherman.

"No, but a rather odd letter. It mentions someone whom Miss Green may know. Please may I ask her about it?"

"Of course," Mr Sherman replied.

A messenger boy barged into the room with a telegram and thrust it into the editor's hand.

"Thank you, boy. My apologies, Inspector, I must deal with this. Please discuss the letter with Miss Green and I shall return shortly."

As Mr Sherman left the room, James cleared his throat, pulled up a chair next to mine and sat down. The scent of his cologne reminded me of the moment in the cab when I had kissed him. I sat stiffly in my seat and wished I could have been anywhere but there.

"Hello Penny. How are you?"

"I'm very well thank you, Inspector."

I steeled myself to look at him, then grinned widely, aware that my expression was far from genuine.

"The sling has finally gone!" he said with a smile.

"Yes. Hurrah!"

"I read your interview with Ed Keller. You took a big risk speaking to him, but the article was very insightful. How was he with you?"

I felt my stomach turn. "He relished the idea of being interviewed."

"I'm sure he did. He thinks rather highly of himself."

"I think you should treat him as a suspect."

"Did he let anything slip?"

"Not overtly, but he ignored my questions about Mrs O'Brien and Mr Yeomans. He is adamant that Jack was killed by a rival gang and that Mr Larcombe was killed by a customer with whom he had argued. But by suggesting that other people are responsible, he could be trying to deflect attention from himself."

"It's possible."

"It's more than possible. I think it's extremely likely. He admitted that he'd fallen out with both Jack and Mr Larcombe in the past."

"Is that a motive, do you think?"

"Of course it is. I've given it a lot of thought since I met him and I'm certain he must be responsible for the murders. He's an objectionable man." I felt a bitter taste in my mouth.

"He is indeed. I know E Division have had a number of dealings with him. I'll investigate further."

"You must! Will you speak to him today?"

I gave him an imploring look and his expression was puzzled, as if he were wondering what I hadn't told him about Keller.

"I'll try to. In the meantime, here's the letter I mentioned." He unfolded it and smoothed it out on the desk next to the typewriter. "It arrived at Scotland Yard this morning and is signed Adam D.V. again."

What a turnout for the funeral, and all because of me! It's flattering to finally have everyone's attention. It is also rather pleasing to see Mrs Baxter learning her lesson.

Adam D.V.

"He was at Mr Larcombe's funeral?" My heart felt as though it had leapt up into my throat. "But how strange! Why would he do that? That's peculiar behaviour. Anyone could have seen him. I might have seen him! I didn't attend the service, but I mingled with the crowds outside the church before Mr Larcombe's burial at Kensal Green. I didn't notice anyone acting suspiciously."

"Why would you? I think our man might be quite adept at blending in with the crowd. And this letter cannot be construed as firm evidence that he attended the funeral. He may have simply heard that many people turned up."

"The name Mrs Baxter is familiar," I said.

"She is Mr Larcombe's sister. Have you come across her?"

"Yes, I think I saw her at the inquest, and she's the same lady who organises the slum tours, isn't she?"

I recalled the wide-faced woman with copper eyes whom Martha and I had encountered. "I didn't realise she was Mr Larcombe's sister; no one had told me that. What does Adam mean when he says that she's *learning her lesson*? Does he feel that she is deserving of her grief?"

"It's possible. I was hoping that if you knew her you might have some idea. This letter may be a hoax, but I'll go and show it to Mrs Baxter all the same and find out if she knows who this Adam is. Perhaps she spoke to him at the funeral or can tell us about an argument she's had with him. He appears to bear some animosity towards her. She lives in Clerkenwell and I've already alerted G Division, who are sending officers to her home. I should get over there now. If this letter is from the murderer, it seems that Mrs Baxter is familiar with him. And it's a fair bet that Mr Larcombe also knew him."

"Why's he doing this?"

"I wish I knew."

James stood up and put his hat on.

"I wonder if Ed Keller was at Mr Larcombe's funeral," I said. "He must have been."

"I'll find out."

We held each other's gaze for a moment and I wanted to apologise to him for my behaviour in the cab. I wanted to reassure him that it would never happen again, but with Edgar and Frederick in the room it was impossible to say anything of the sort.

"Good luck, James."

CHAPTER 29

I worked in the reading room that afternoon and asked Mr Edwards for the map of Colombia once again.

"Is your friend missing the library?" he whispered as he unrolled the map across my desk.

"I don't think so. I've had to do some of his work for him, which he's rather happy about. And he isn't a personal friend of mine. We just happen to work for the same newspaper." I felt the need to distance my association with Edgar and the altercation that had happened there a few weeks previously. "Hopefully his reading ticket will be reissued soon."

"I doubt it," said Mr Edwards, pushing his spectacles up his nose. "The Head Librarian doesn't like fighting in the reading room."

"Do you think La Mesa de Los Santos would be marked on this map?"

We spent a moment looking for it.

"I think it's near Bucaramanga," I added.

Mr Edwards wafted his forefinger over the map as he searched it. "There's Bucaramanga." He planted his finger on it and I noticed that his nails were neatly manicured.

"Ah yes, it's a number of miles northeast of Bogota. Quite far from the Tequendama Falls, then, which are just south-west of Bogota. I'm finding it quite difficult to track my father's movements during his final journey."

"What was the name of the first place you were looking for? Santos something?"

"La Mesa de Los Santos. Apparently, it's beautiful there and I should like to know where it is."

"I should think that much of Colombia is beautiful. The name has such an agreeable sound to it."

I began to feel reassured that Mr Edwards had forgiven me for associating with the type of men who got themselves into fights in the reading room.

"Would you like me to find out more about Mesa, La Mesa, Santos la Mesa – however it's said – for you?"

"Let me write it down for you." I tore a page from my notebook and spelt out the name. "And thank you, Mr Edwards. If you could find a mention of it in any of the books on Colombia that would be extremely helpful. Oh, and the Tequendama Falls. Let me write that name down as well."

"My pleasure, Miss Green." He took the piece of paper from me and smiled.

Loud muttering from the other side of the room distracted us and we both turned to see what was happening. Readers were supposed to remain quiet and, although some whispering was sometimes tolerated, any noise above that level was prohibited, as I had already discovered.

I could see people getting up and going over to speak to others. A few people left the room abruptly.

"Something's happened," I said.

"I shall go and ask them to lower their voices."

He walked off and I watched him speaking to the group for a moment. But instead of returning to their desks, a number of people entered into conversation with Mr

Edwards. My curiosity got the better of me, so I stood up from my seat and walked over to join them.

"Is everything all right?" I asked.

"Another murder," said Mr Edwards with a grim expression on his face.

I felt a heavy sensation in my stomach.

"Not again. In St Giles?"

"Not this time. It happened near King's Cross," said a man with bushy whiskers and a bald head.

"I must go." I cried.

I dashed back to my desk, packed away my papers as quickly as I could, left the museum and hailed a cab on Great Russell Street.

"Not 'eard nothin' abaht a murder," said the cab driver.

"Can you take me to King's Cross?"

He nodded and I climbed into the cab. I pulled the collar of my jacket up to keep warm and reminded myself not to be too hasty in making any assumptions about this murder.

Perhaps it had been committed by a separate perpetrator under altogether different circumstances. Perhaps someone had met with an accident which had been mistakenly reported as murder.

I prayed that the man who called himself Adam hadn't struck again.

The cab made good progress until Gray's Inn Road, where the traffic was blocked by a brewer's cart unloading barrels.

I could hear the cab driver hollering at him: "Why don't yer block up the 'ole road while yer at it?"

The man unloading the barrels replied with a derogatory comment about the cabbie's parentage and a torrent of profanity was hurled back at him.

All around me, horses, carts and carriages were at standstill. Even the horse-drawn tram couldn't get through and its driver knew curse words I had never heard before and almost drew a blush from my cheeks. I lifted up the hatch in the roof and handed the cabbie my fare.

"I'll walk from here."

I walked up Gray's Inn Road and it soon became apparent that it wasn't just the brewer's cart that was stopping the traffic. Ahead of me, I saw people standing in the road as more impatient drivers tried to make their way round them. People were gathered around the junction with Acton Street and I pushed my way through to see what was happening.

"Press!" I called out, waving my card in the air. "Let me through!"

It made little difference, but it did give me an excuse to push and shove. At the end of Acton Street, I reached a line of bobbies who were trying to keep people back.

"Miss Green from the *Morning Express*." I showed one of the constables my card. "Is Inspector Blakely here?"

He turned his nose up, clearly reluctant to allow a reporter through his barricade, but his reaction reassured me that James was already on the scene.

"Is he expecting you?"

"Yes."

The lie allowed me to walk past him and up the hilly street to Percy Circus: a circle of well-to-do townhouses arranged around a pleasant, wooded rotunda. Five streets radiated out from the circus and I could see that each had been blocked off by the police to prevent public access. The rotunda was encircled by railings with a small gap forming an entrance. The presence of a constable at the entrance suggested that the murder had taken place within the wooded rotunda.

I shuddered and took my pencil and notebook from my bag to demonstrate that I was there on press business. A number of constables stood speaking to people in the doorways of their homes and press reporters were busy scribbling away in their notebooks. The sound of sobbing drifted towards me and I saw two women sitting on the steps leading up to a house, one comforting the other.

I walked up to the entrance of the rotunda.

"Can I help you?" asked the young, chubby-faced constable.

"I'm looking for Inspector Blakely."

"He's in there."

I stepped forward, but he blocked my way.

"No, you ain't goin' in. Wait for 'im 'ere."

I tried to peer through the railings and between the trees, but all I could see were a few men in dark coats.

The weak sunshine found its way through the clouds and the street was eerily quiet apart from the sound of the woman's sobbing.

"Penny."

I turned to see James walking out from the rotunda. His face was pale and solemn. He passed the constable and joined me.

"How are you?" I asked. I felt no embarrassment seeing him now that there was something far more serious for us to work on.

"I've been better. We came here to speak to Mrs Baxter, but it seems someone else got here before us."

"She's the victim?" My knees felt weak. "It's *him* again, isn't it?"

"Sadly, yes." James rubbed his brow. "I should have come here as soon as I received that letter. I was foolish not to. It was obvious she was to be the next victim, wasn't it?"

"No, I don't think it was obvious. There was a strong possibility that the letter might have been a hoax."

"It wasn't a hoax though, was it? I should have treated it more seriously." His face was flushed with colour and he spoke through clenched teeth.

"Don't blame yourself, James."

"At the moment I do, I'm afraid. The killer gave us fair warning and now he's vanished again and we have no hope of finding him."

"You'll find him."

"We had better do so. You don't want to see what he's done to that poor woman in there."

He pointed back at the trees and I felt a lurch of nausea as I thought of Mrs Baxter with her copper-coloured eyes, wearing a colourful feathered hat and talking to the slummers in St Giles.

How could she be dead?

"No one should suffer in that way," said James.

He took his handkerchief out of his pocket and wiped his face. I reached out and touched his arm. I wanted to reassure and comfort him, but briefly touching his arm was all I could do. I withdrew my hand and readied myself with my notebook and pencil.

"What have you found out so far?"

"Mrs Baxter lived in Holford Place, about fifty yards from here. Her husband says she left the house to go on a shopping trip and was walking down to King's Cross Road, where she planned to take the tram. It was something she did every Friday. Somehow, our man apprehended her between her home and Percy Circus, and has taken her into the trees, where he has cut her throat. He may have forcibly taken her there, but I'm inclined to think she willingly went with him because no one heard any cries for help.

"The police surgeon has estimated her time of death at between midday and half after one o'clock. She was found by a neighbour, who noticed what she thought was a bundle of clothing left among the trees. The killer has left a blood-stained coat and pair of gloves at the scene, presumably because he didn't want to be seen wearing them after he left.

This is a brazen attack in the middle of a pleasant place such as this, and just around the corner from King's Cross police station!"

"In daylight. This is the first murder in daylight, isn't it? He's taking more chances. Someone must have seen something."

"They will have. We're getting as many witness statements as we possibly can."

"Where did he go? Where is he now?" I shivered.

"Probably as far away from here as he could get."

I thought about the killer's most recent letter.

"If he attended Mr Larcombe's funeral, he might also attend the next one," I said.

"That's a good point. I'll ensure that there's a good police presence at Mrs Baxter's funeral in case he decides to put in an appearance. It's a strange thought that the killer should attend the funeral of his victim, but I suppose we already know we're dealing with a strange man."

"It could be Ed Keller, couldn't it? Someone must have seen the killer around here. If the description of him is even remotely similar to that of Ed then he must be arrested. Did you manage to discover what Winston Nicholls told Tom Clifford about having seen the murderer after Mr Larcombe was killed?"

"I found Tom to be rather nebulous on the matter."

"Does that mean Winston didn't see the murderer? One of them must have made the story up. I wonder which."

"And look who's approaching now," said James, looking over my shoulder. "Speak of the devil and he will appear."

I turned to see Tom Clifford and Winston Nicholls approaching us.

"Nicholls has an unusually keen interest in the case, doesn't he?" said James. "I've lost count of all the letters he's sent to Scotland Yard."

Tom strode up and greeted us. "Inspector Blakely and Miss Green. One rarely seen without the other." He cackled. "And Larcombe's sister, eh? Someone's clearly got a grudge against the family."

"What does this mean for the investigation, Inspector?" asked Winston, the brim of his black felt hat shielding his eyes.

"It means G Division is now involved in the case, along with E Division and the Yard. We have a lot of men working on this now."

"And still no idea who did it?"

"We're gathering as much information as we can."

"I'm convinced enough of one man's guilt, that's for sure. What are you doing about Reuben O'Donoghue? I put it in a letter to you detailing his involvement."

"He was arrested, as you know, Mr Nicholls, but we have witnesses who saw him at the time of Jack Burton's murder and he cannot have been in two places at the same time."

"You have witnesses who saw him and yet no witnesses who saw what happened to the boy? It makes no sense to me, Inspector. I think you're protecting him."

"I have no interest in protecting Mr O'Donoghue. My only interest is in catching this killer before he strikes again."

"Clifford tells me you have received letters," said Winston.

"We have quite a number now, including those from yourself, Mr Nicholls."

"Letters from the killer as well?"

"Given the nature of what has happened here today, I have no wish to make the contents of the letters public. They form an important part of our investigation."

"Does *she* get to see them?" asked Winston, nodding in my direction without actually looking at me.

"I am not prepared to divulge any more, Mr Nicholls."

"Of course she's read them!" scoffed Tom. "Inspector Blakely and Miss Green have a *close* friendship."

He gave me an unpleasant leer as his jaw worked on a piece of tobacco.

"Please excuse me, gentlemen, but I need to continue with my work. Today is certain to be a long one, as you can imagine."

"Same goes for us all, Inspector," said Winston.

"What do you mean?"

"I'm investigating this case myself."

"Thank you for your offer of assistance, Mr Nicholls, but this is a matter for the police."

"I'm now working as a private detective."

"Are you indeed? I thought you were a clerk. Where did you gain your credentials to become a detective?"

Winston removed his hat and prodded a finger into his damp hair. "My credentials are in here. Sleuthing is an innate skill."

"If you say so, Mr Nicholls."

On an easier day, James would probably have been amused by the man's delusions.

"I wish you the best of luck with your detective work," he continued.

Then his expression turned stormy and he pointed his finger at Winston. "However, let me warn you now that misleading, obstructing or otherwise interfering with a police investigation is a punishable offence. For the benefit of the poor victims, I suggest you leave well alone. And if you, Tom Clifford, print anything else fallacious, such as questionable sightings of the murderer, the Yard will not hesitate to speak directly to the editor of *The Holborn Gazette*."

"That's happened before, hasn't it, Miss Green? Didn't the Commissioner of the Yard once have you removed from your job?" goaded Tom.

"That was a long time ago, and he made a mistake," I replied. "This is different, Tom. James is warning that the pair of you could endanger the investigation."

"We could *endanger* it, could we?" Tom laughed. "How nice to have such power! Don't you agree, Winston?"

I felt my heart pound with anger.

Winston placed his hat back on his head. "I shall keep you informed of my investigations, Inspector."

"Which is more than the inspector will do in return!" added Tom.

The two men turned and walked away.

CHAPTER 30

"'A man of five feet and eleven inches in height with a black moustache, black silk hat, a black coat, and speckled trousers,'" read Mr Sherman from a copy of *The Holborn Gazette*. "'His eyes were wide, green and unblinking.'"

He paused and glanced at me. "He sounds a tall fellow, and with those eyes you'd think he would be easy for the police to find, wouldn't you?"

"I don't know where Tom Clifford got such a description from," I replied. "It's rather different from the ones we've published."

"Tom's description sounds more intriguing." He put his pipe in his mouth.

"Of course it does. He's making up facts to sell newspapers."

"And he's working closely with a private detective, I hear."

"He's not a private detective," I scoffed. "It's Winston Nicholls, son of Martha Nicholls, who lives in St Giles. When I first met him, he claimed to be working as a clerk, but now he says he's a detective. He's been sending Inspector Blakely letters about the case."

"As has the murderer, although frustratingly the Yard won't let us print them."

"James is worried in case they cause too much upset. Once people learn that the murderer has attended the funeral of one of his victims and identified the next victim in advance, there'll be pandemonium. Some people will stay away from the next funeral, fearing for their lives, while many more who had never known Mrs Baxter might descend on it in the hope that they will be able to spot the murderer."

"That's understandable, although it's still rather frustrating that we can't print them. The letters must give some clue to the murderer's identity, surely?"

"Not a great deal. He calls himself Adam D.V., but the police don't yet know what the D and the V stand for. The postmarks on his letters are all from the Chapel Place post office on Oxford Street."

"So the staff at that post office need to look out for a man who matches the description we've published, is that right?"

"Yes. The description we've printed is hopefully reliable. It's based on the statements of the witnesses Inspector Blakely spoke to."

Mr Sherman picked up a copy of *The Morning Express* and turned to my article on Mrs Baxter's murder. "'Jeanette Barnett, who resides at number twelve Holford Place, says she saw a young man walking with Mrs Baxter at ten minutes to midday. He was respectably dressed and five feet nine inches tall. He wore a black top hat and a dark overcoat. Harry McCarthy, who is a milk delivery boy for Armitage Dairies, says he saw a tall man speaking to Mrs Baxter at midday. The man wore a brown woollen coat and had fair-coloured whiskers.' We do know that this chap's called Adam though, don't we?"

"It's unlikely to be his real name. But whoever he is, we can be sure that he knew Mrs Baxter because he identified her in his letter and she seems to have willingly spent time in his company. Not only was she seen talking to him, but she appears to have entered the rotunda in Percy Circus without putting up any resistance. No one reported hearing or seeing signs of an argument or struggle between them."

Had Mrs Baxter known Ed Keller? Would she have walked into the wooded area alongside him without concern?

I wondered if he had been arrested yet.

Mr Sherman sighed and folded up the newspaper. "I don't envy the police in this case. It's a hard nut to crack, but there hasn't been a great deal of progress, has there? This Adam fellow must be amused by the force's lacklustre efforts so far."

"They're doing their best. Have you read what Winston Nicholls has said about the police in *The Holborn Gazette*?"

I picked up the newspaper, turned to the article and read out: ""Once again, Londoners have been left reeling by another horrific attack," said private detective, Mr Winston Nicholls. "There is no telling where the killer might strike next and people cannot sleep in their beds at night until this man is caught." Frustrated by the lack of police progress with the investigation, Mr Nicholls believes he will soon have the killer snared. Perhaps our gratitude will not be due to the Metropolitan Police, but to the singular efforts of one brave man in tracking down this murderous brute.'"

"Oh dear," said Mr Sherman. "I wonder whether Inspector Blakely has read that yet."

"I hope not."

"Good luck to this private detective fellow," Frederick piped up. "Hopefully he'll be the next victim!"

"Let's stop short of ill will against the man, shall we?" said Mr Sherman, puffing out a cloud of pipe smoke. "This article angers me as much as it does you, and Clifford's only written it because he feels excluded from the investigation. Why else would he team up with a lunatic who, out of nowhere, considers himself an expert sleuth? It would be funny if it wasn't so damn worrying. We're losing readers to the *Gazette* and I'm worried this trickle will become a stream and then a river if we don't do something about it. Miss Green, I want you to interview the husband, Mr Baxter, about the loss of his wife and brother-in-law."

"I can't imagine he will want to speak to me at this time."

"Of course he won't, but I need you to be insistent with him, Miss Green! Don't take no for an answer!"

"He will no doubt be at Mrs Baxter's funeral. I could try and find a way to speak to him there rather than calling at his home."

"When is the funeral?"

"Tomorrow."

"Do it tomorrow, then. I know the man is upset, but tell him that a few words from him in our newspaper will remind people to be on the lookout for the killer."

"As if anyone needs reminding," said Frederick.

Mr Sherman left the newsroom with a familiar slam of the door.

"By the expression on your face, Miss Green, I'd say you're less than enamoured with the prospect of interviewing a grieving man at his wife's funeral!" Frederick laughed.

"Have you heard from Edgar? How's he finding his undercover work?"

"He's thoroughly miserable!" Frederick laughed again. "He's been bitten by rats and fleas, and had to rid himself of an infestation of lice. Those lodging houses are crawling with vermin."

"Why did we choose this profession, Frederick?"

"I don't know, Miss Green. I really don't know."

CHAPTER 31

A large crowd gathered for Mrs Baxter's funeral in foggy Myddelton Square. The tower of St Mark's Church loomed above us, ghostlike, and I felt uneasy as I walked among the mourners, surveying them through the black veil of my mourning hat.

Could the murderer really be among these people?

It was easy to spot Martha Nicholls among the crowd in her wide-brimmed hat covered with black ribbons and bows. She was accompanied by her son.

"I've told Winston that I don't want none of 'is sleuthing while we're 'ere. We're mournin' Mrs Baxter and that's it. Once 'e's got an idea in 'is 'ead, yer can't stop 'im!"

Martha laughed affectionately, while Winston looked straight past me.

"'E's chattin' to all the reporters now. 'Ave you spoke to 'im?"

"I have. We saw each other in Percy Circus."

"Winston's workin' all hours on it, ain't you Winston?"

He gave a weak smile by way of reply and said nothing.

"'Ow did yer get on with the Earl o' York?" she asked.

"I managed to interview him."

"Did yer? Well, I must say I'm impressed. 'E didn't try nuffink, did 'e?"

"Such as what?"

"Yer know what I mean. 'E tries it on wiv the ladies, or so I've 'eard. I tried to warn yer abaht 'im, but yer got outta there alright, so 'e must've gone easy on yer."

"I was fine, thank you Martha."

My skin prickled and I glanced around at the crowd, worried that Ed might appear among the sea of faces.

Inside the church, I found James standing next to the font. He wore a black suit and had dark circles under his eyes.

"You look tired," I said.

"I am, rather. This case is consuming such a lot of my time, and unfortunately it's coincided with my grandfather's ill health."

"How is he?"

"Frail. Does anyone here rouse your suspicions?"

I watched the mourners as they took their places in the pews and recognised a number of them from St Giles. They were easy to identify as their clothing was so threadbare.

"Everyone looks rather similar when they're dressed in mourning clothes don't they? And it's difficult to recognise the women when they wear veils over their faces. Is Ed Keller here?"

"No, he's in the cells at Bow Street."

"He's been arrested?" A grin spread across my face.

James smiled in return. "I knew that would please you. E Division are currently holding six men, including Ed Keller, and G Division are holding another four. The Home Secretary is taking a keen interest in our progress now and we're rounding up anyone with the faintest whiff of suspicion about them.

"Ed Keller's no stranger to Bow Street station, of course, and they can always find a number of petty charges to hold him on. The crucial business will be finding evidence to connect him to the murders, if there is any. I doubt that he's literate enough to write the letters."

"He may have had someone write them for him."

"It's possible, but it would be risky to have an accomplice who might betray him. He has a habit of falling out with people."

I couldn't help but smile at the fact that Ed Keller was behind bars for the time being.

"So the murderer may not be here at all?"

"He may be, and he may not be." James stifled a yawn. "All we can do for now is observe and remain vigilant."

Mrs Baxter was buried in the churchyard of St Mark's. As the mourners gathered by the graveside, I surveyed the crowd once again, looking for someone who didn't appear to fit in. I couldn't see everyone clearly in the fog, and I wasn't exactly sure who or what I was looking for.

Someone with a strange stare or a sinister way about them? Perhaps someone who didn't appear particularly upset about Mrs Baxter's death?

Although my veil obscured my vision slightly, it was a useful means of concealing my prying eyes.

I saw Reuben O'Donoghue standing a head taller than the mourners around him as we listened to the committal. I had forgotten that he was quite handsome, and as I watched him I struggled to believe the stories I had been told about his violent past.

Could Winston Nicholls be right about him?

As the mourners began to depart, I introduced myself to Mr Baxter, a pale-faced, bewildered-looking man with a quivering grey moustache. He didn't refuse to speak to me; instead, he appeared to be locked in his own grief, indifferent to my presence. He gave brief answers to my questions about his wife and brother-in-law, pausing to wipe his face with a sodden handkerchief a number of times.

"I'm going to stay with my sister in Weymouth," he said at the end of our conversation. "I need to leave London and I shan't be sorry if I never return."

"Let's 'ope there ain't no more," said Martha Nicholls as she came to say goodbye to me, accompanied by her son and the missionaries. "I don't want there ter be no more."

"All they need to do is arrest O'Donoghue, Ma," said Winston. "That'll put an end to this awful business. It's an outrage that he's been allowed to attend his victim's funeral, and looking so pleased with himself at that. I dread to think what he's planning to do next."

"How are you, Miss Green?" asked David Meares.

It was the first I had seen him and Hugo Hawkins since they had rescued me from Ed Keller.

"Very well, thank you."

I smiled broadly, as if to demonstrate that I was fully recovered from my ordeal.

"That is good news indeed," said Hugo kindly. I felt relieved that the missionaries were keeping to their word and had not mentioned the attack to anyone else. "Are you ready, Mrs Nicholls? The carriages are waiting out in the square."

"They brought us out 'ere. Ain't that kind of 'em?" said Martha. "Saves me shoe leather, that does."

"We try to help where we can," said Hugo. "Would you like to join us for prayers in the chapel, Miss Green?"

"Thank you, but I must get back to Fleet Street if I'm to meet my deadline."

I watched the small group leave and felt worried for Martha returning to her cold, dilapidated home in the slum. She deserved better. They all did.

I was one of the last to leave the churchyard. As I did, I found James standing by the gate smoking a pipe.

"Tobacco?" I said. "A pipe? Doesn't the future Mrs Blakely abhor pipe smoke?"

"Much needed, I'm afraid," replied James.

"But doesn't the odour linger?"

"It can linger all it likes. Quite frankly, the tobacco will help steady the ship."

"Are you all right, James?"

"No, I'm not all right." He glowered. "I hoped I would pick up some clues from the funeral today. This is a damned frustrating business. Mrs Baxter shouldn't have lost her life. I should have stopped him! He sent a letter to the Yard practically telling us what he was about to do! And if he sends another letter saying he was at the funeral today I will find it exceedingly difficult to keep a calm head."

"Perhaps he wasn't here. Perhaps he's one of the men who's been arrested."

"I hope so, but what if he isn't? What if he writes another letter taunting us and then murders again? I don't like this pattern, not one little bit." He thumped his gloved fist against the gatepost. "I'm supposed to be stopping him! And yet I am no closer to the man than I was when this sorry business first began!"

CHAPTER 32

The *News of the World* was the first newspaper to print Adam's letters, but the rest of Fleet Street quickly followed suit. I knew James hadn't wanted the letters published and suspected that CID in E or G Division had shared them with the reporters. The murders had also made the news on the continent and in America. The murder of a middle-class woman in a pleasant district of London had caused many to fear that just about anyone might become the next victim.

I managed to distract myself for an evening by continuing my work on Father's letters and diaries. The stove in my lodgings was only small, so I wore an old, thick shawl over my shoulders for warmth. Mr Edwards had kindly found me a book in the reading room that contained some information about La Mesa de Los Santos, and I had made brief notes on its environment and topography.

Now Tiger was sitting on them atop my writing desk, next to the empty tin of biscuits. 'Peek, Frean & Co Biscuits, London' was written beneath a picture of an elephant frolicking in the jungle with a brightly coloured howdah on its back.

Had the tins my father saw in Bogota carried the same picture? I wondered.

I read a letter which he had written to my mother in March 1875.

The jaguars are a particular nuisance during the month of March, when the turtles lay their eggs. A jaguar can scoop a turtle out from its shell without even opening it! The natives must keep their cattle in enclosures at night, but even then a jaguar has been known to break in and steal a calf or goat. In a village here, I found six well-armed men willing to take a canoe up from the Santo Domingo wetlands in the direction of the San Lucas mountains, where there are great deposits of gold.

I was interrupted by a knock at my door. Tiger dashed under my bed as I opened it to find my sister and Mrs Garnett standing there, deeply engaged in conversation.

"Be on the lookout for foreign gentlemen," said my landlady to Eliza. "Everyone's saying that only a foreigner could be capable of such murderous behaviour."

"What about the man in the mask?"

"He's what everyone was talking about a week or so ago, but now they're saying that he's a foreigner."

"What sort? From Europe or India or Africa?"

Mrs Garnett shrugged. "I don't know. He might be a Jew for all we know; perhaps a Polish Jew. Lots of them have a look about them, don't they? It's best to avoid any foreign-looking men, wouldn't you agree, Miss Green? And you would help yourselves, ladies, by not staying out after dark."

Her dark eyes were wide and fearful.

"But Mrs Baxter was murdered in the middle of the day!" said Eliza. "And I arrived here on my bicycle. No man is likely to accost me while I'm on my bicycle, is he?"

"I should think he would stay well away from your bicycle, Mrs Billington-Grieg."

Mrs Garnett sucked her lip disapprovingly as she looked down at Eliza's divided woollen grey skirt.

"Hello Penelope," said Eliza. "I found myself bicycling along Fore Street and thought I would pay you a quick visit. We were just discussing these terrible murders."

She removed her bonnet, which, like her jacket, was damp with rain.

"So I heard."

"Any further news on the culprit? What's the latest from the Yard?"

"A number of men are under arrest at the moment. Each police department has been rounding up all the petty thieves, drunkards and lunatics in their divisions. I'm sure our streets are safer now than they have been for a long time!"

I smiled in an attempt to lighten the mood.

"A friend of my neighbour knew Mrs Baxter. Isn't it dreadful?" said Eliza. "Especially when you consider that she could have been saved. The killer actually wrote to the police telling them he was about to murder her next!"

"Disgraceful," added Mrs Garnett.

"He didn't quite say that," I said. "He mentioned her in the letter, but when the police received it they weren't sure whether it was a hoax or not."

"One can't take risks with such a letter. He actually wrote her name down! They knew about her!" said Eliza.

"The police have received a great many letters about the murders," I replied.

"They're overwhelmed, aren't they? They need more constables to cope with it."

"They have so much to do. James is rather frustrated with the lack of progress at the moment, but he's working as efficiently as possible."

"I'm sure he is. But they're no closer to catching the man, are they? How many people have been killed now? Four? Five?"

"Mrs Baxter was the fifth victim."

"And a respectable lady, too! It's extremely frightening," said Mrs Garnett. "Until now, I've always slept well at night, safe in the knowledge that murder has a higher incidence among the lower classes. But things have changed now! It could be any of us! There, but for the grace of God, goes Mrs Garnett."

She tucked a steel grey curl under her white, cotton bonnet.

"I wonder whether it's worth leaving London until he's caught," said Eliza.

"I would go at the drop of a hat," replied my landlady. "But we have to stay here and make a living, don't we?"

"There's no need to leave London. He'll be caught very soon," I said hopefully. "Would you like some sherry, ladies?"

"I never touch the stuff but I'll make an exception tonight for medicinal purposes," said Mrs Garnett, bustling past me into my room.

Eliza followed, removing her damp tweed jacket. "I think that shawl you're wearing once belonged to Grandmother, Penelope," she said. "How it's survived the moths over the years, I'll never know."

I retrieved the bottle from beneath my bed and poured a measure of sherry out into three tin cups.

"You haven't bought yourself any glassware yet?" asked Mrs Garnett, examining a dent in her cup.

Eliza hung her jacket up by the stove and sat in the chair at my writing desk while Mrs Garnett sat on my bed, wiping her brow with her apron. I knew that there were thousands of people like Mrs Garnett in London worrying about the murderer and where he would strike next. I felt a twinge of anger that one man had been the cause of such anxiety for so many.

"The chances of any of us becoming victims are extremely slim," I said, feeling the need to reassure my visitors, even though I felt worried myself. "And although these deaths are regrettable, we can't allow ourselves to become hysterical about them. Instead, we must focus on catching the man responsible. That's what Inspector Blakely is working on, along with many other police officers. We must trust in them to do their job."

"But it's taking them a while, isn't it?" said Eliza, gulping back most of her sherry.

"What's your inspector doing about it?" Mrs Garnett asked me.

"He's not *my* inspector."

I could see Eliza smiling out of the corner of my eye, but I chose not to look at her.

"He was in this room once," said Mrs Garnett.

"Is that so?" said Eliza.

"That was not a social visit. It was an important meeting about the Lizzie Dixie case," I retorted. "And the door was kept open all the time, wasn't it, Mrs Garnett? And you remained close enough to hear our conversation, did you not?"

"But what's he doing about this murderer?"

"Everything he possibly can: examining the scene of each crime, talking to witnesses, pursuing every new lead, writing reports and all the rest of it."

"I like a man who works hard," said Mrs Garnett wistfully. I noticed that her cup was already empty. "Hercules was always inclined towards lethargy."

"Hercules?" Eliza said.

"My husband. He died twenty years ago and not from overwork, I can assure you. I don't think the man did twelve labours in his entire lifetime, despite his name!"

She cackled at her own joke and put her cup to her lips, appearing disappointed when she realised there was nothing left in it.

"Would you like a drop more sherry, Mrs Garnett?"

"No, no. That's quite enough for me." She stood up slowly. "It's made me get to thinking about Hercules, and I don't want to go thinking about him too much."

She sucked her lip again and walked over to the door. "No visitors after nine o'clock, Miss Green, remember? Good-night Mrs Billington-Grieg."

Once Mrs Garnett had left the room, Eliza surveyed the papers on my desk. "I see you're working on Father's letters," she said.

"Yes, I didn't realise a jaguar could eat a turtle without even opening its shell. In fact, I didn't realise jaguars ate turtles at all."

I poured some more sherry into our cups.

"Fascinating, isn't it?"

"I think I've read most of Father's diaries now and I haven't yet come across the entries you alluded to."

"Which ones?"

"The ones which you said weren't as enchanting as the others. I'm still not sure what you could have meant by that."

"It's not worth dwelling on that too much," she said with a dismissive wave of her hand. "You'll know what I'm talking about as soon as you read it. Do you know which publishers you plan to approach?"

"Yes, I've drawn up a list. We need a publisher who can print Father's drawings in full colour plates. Wouldn't that look good? And some maps would be useful too. I find I often need to refer to a map so that I can picture the routes he took. And to think he was doing all this and we had no idea how fascinating his life was. If only he had taken us with him!"

"If only. It would have been far too dangerous for us, of course."

"Perhaps not as dangerous as London with a killer wandering the streets."

"Oh, Penelope, stop frightening me! You said yourself that there was little chance of us falling victim to this man. I should go before it gets too late and I find myself being chased by a strange foreigner with a knife."

She finished her sherry, stood up and put her jacket on. "This hasn't dried out at all. Oh well, it will have to do."

"Ellie, I can't help thinking that you're being evasive."

"About what?"

"About the event I haven't yet encountered in Father's diaries."

She sighed. "I've told you to read it for yourself and then tell me what you think about it. If I describe it to you, there's a danger that I will colour it with my own opinion on the matter. I'd like to find out what you think of it first."

"Can't you give me a clue?"

"It's when he canoes up a river, and I can't remember which river it is, I'm afraid."

She put on her gloves.

"Father wasn't perfect. You realise that, don't you, Penelope?"

"Of course. No one's perfect."

"Good." She pulled on her bonnet and tied it firmly under her chin. The bow on her bonnet was limp and wet. "Because I have a growing concern that you think he might have been."

"I think he went on some wonderful adventures, and that

he was the first person to bring certain varieties of plant to Britain."

"Yes, he did some admirable things, but it's important that we try to remember him for the person he was and not as some idealised individual. When one spends quite a lot of time alone it's easy to develop a strong attachment to someone."

"Ellie, he was our father! Of course I have a strong attachment to him!"

"Yes, and so do I. Perhaps I'm not explaining this very well. Father is probably dead. You know that, don't you?"

"Yes."

My throat tightened and I saw that my sister's eyes were damp.

"Don't become too attached to him, Penelope. Remember it's likely that he spent the best times in his life without us."

"How can you say that?" My voice cracked and I felt a hot tear roll down my cheek. "We were his daughters. He loved us and Mother very much. Why are you saying such things, Ellie?"

She took a handkerchief from her pocket and dabbed at each eye.

"I'm just trying to give some perspective on matters. I'm very happy that you're writing this book about Father, but while you're doing so, don't forget to live in the present. You spend a lot of time on your own. Don't forget that there are people here with you now to whom you can also be attached."

She opened the door and looked back at me. Her brown eyes looked just like Mother's.

"You don't have to be alone, Penelope."

CHAPTER 33

"Turner? I think I've 'eard the name round 'ere, but can't fink who it is," said Martha.

James and I stood with her in the cold, breezy courtyard, with laundry billowing over our heads.

"Is 'e a suspect?"

"Not necessarily," replied James. "We believe he was at Mrs Baxter's funeral. You don't recall seeing anyone you know as Mr Turner being there?"

She screwed up her face in thought. "I'm gonna 'ave ter think on it. Keep askin' round 'ere, though. There'll be someone what knows 'im. Common name 'n' all. There must be a fair few Turners in these parts."

"Thank you, Mrs Nicholls."

James's reply was curt. I could see the tension in his jaw and his brow was more furrowed than usual. What we hadn't told Martha was that Mr Turner had been mentioned in the latest letter Adam D.V. had sent to Scotland Yard. James was certain it could only mean one thing: that Mr Turner was to be the next victim.

"What do we do now?" James had asked after showing me

the letter. "Tell everyone with the name of Turner to stay in their homes?"

I saw you looking for me when Mrs Baxter was laid to rest. You could have reached her in time, but I think you know that by now. I had a pleasant conversation with Mr Turner, who was polite to me for once.

Adam D.V.

"It's nice of yer ter visit me, though," continued Martha. "Hev'ryone's forgot about St Giles since Mrs Baxter got murdered. We ain't 'ardly seen no bobbies round 'ere, nor reporters neither. I'm 'opin' that murderer ain't botherin' wiv us no more and 'e's moved on ter ovver parts o' London."

"Did anyone at Mrs Baxter's funeral look suspicious to you?" I asked.

"Nah, didn't see no one what looked out o' place. Apart from all the police and reporters, of course. They proberly started suspecting each other! Hev'ryone else looked normal to me. D'yer think the murderer were there?"

"Anything is possible," said James.

"Reuben O'Donoghue were there. P'r'aps it's 'im? Police ain't come up with no one better, 'ave they? Yer needs ter arrest 'im again, Inspector, and ask 'im some proper questions."

"We'll speak to him again, Mrs Nicholls," said James. "If you can think of anyone who might harbour a grudge against Mr Larcombe and his sister, you'll let me know, won't you? Perhaps someone had an argument with them?"

"Oh, lotsa people 'ad arguments wiv 'em alright."

"Such as who?"

"I'm gonna 'ave ter think on that one 'n' all."

"Well please do, Mrs Nicholls, and let me know. Please excuse us, we must continue our search for Mr Turner. If you recall anyone with that name, will you please let a constable know or tell them down at Bow Street station?"

"Will do, Inspector."

"Do you think Winston might know a Mr Turner?" I asked Martha.

"'E might."

"Do you know where he is this morning?"

"I dunno. 'E's doin' 'is detective work now, ain't 'e?"

"If you see your son, Mrs Nicholls, please can you ask him to speak to us?" said James. "He may well have come across this Mr Turner in the course of his, er, detective work."

"Course I will. Oh, I almost forgot." Martha rummaged in the pocket of her apron and pulled out a small piece of card. "I found this blowin' across the yard this mornin'."

She handed the card to James.

"It's dirty, like someone's trod on it. But I ain't got no idea who 'e is. Weren't the letters from someone called Adam?"

I looked over James' shoulder at the crumpled card, which read:

Mr Adam de Vries
23 Leinster Gardens
London W2

I felt my heart miss a beat.

"Thank you, Mrs Nicholls," said James. "This is extremely interesting. Do you know this man?"

"Never 'eard of 'im."

We left the courtyard and turned into the street which led to Seven Dials.

"*It could be him!*" I exclaimed in a loud whisper. "*Adam D.V.! Adam de Vries!*"

"Let's not leap to conclusions, Penny," replied James as a broad grin spread across his face, "but this is an encouraging find, indeed. It seems Adam has been rather careless. Oh, look at this."

Ahead of us, the cobblestones were covered with little rectangles of white card. I stooped to pick one up.

"Here are more of them. He's accidentally dropped them, hasn't he?"

James bent down and began to gather them up. "I suspect so. The card case must have fallen out of his pocket, but there's no sign of it here. It's likely someone has made off with it, especially if it was a good one and made of silver."

We continued gathering up the cards.

"Or perhaps the card case was picked from his pocket?"

"Yes! You could be right. The thief could well have taken the case from him and then run along this street emptying the cards as he ran. These ones aren't particularly muddy or damp, so I shouldn't think they've been on the ground for long. Maybe they were dropped during the night or early this morning. We're onto him now!"

We got to our feet and James put the cards in his pocket.

"I think we need to get to Leinster Gardens now, don't we?" he said. "Every police division is searching for people by the name of Turner and if we're quick we might get to Adam before he can reach him."

He looked at me, his blue eyes twinkling and his face flushed with excitement. "Are you ready, Penny?"

My heart began to pound faster still. "I think so!"

CHAPTER 34

"The name Leinster Gardens sounds familiar," I said as the cab made its way through Leicester Square. "I think it's near where my sister lives in Bayswater."

"I should imagine it's an affluent street," said James.

He took one of the cards out of his pocket and examined it. "And a man with a card such as this is likely to be well-to-do. I've no idea why someone who lives in such a place would be travelling to St Giles and murdering people."

"Perhaps he's a slummer."

"You mean one of those people who likes to visit the slums for the sake of enjoyment?"

"Yes, and Mrs Baxter organised tours of St Giles, didn't she? Another of the victims, Mrs O'Brien, used to allow the visitors to look inside her home. Mrs Baxter paid her a tuppence for each visit, Martha told me."

"You think the pastime of slumming could provide an explanation? There might be something in that."

"Perhaps we can ask Adam de Vries when we see him? I wonder how he'll receive us."

"One can never tell. If the rest of the Metropolitan police force wasn't so busy looking for Mr Turner, I would have asked a few of the constables to accompany us. With a bit of luck, he'll come quietly down to the police station at Paddington."

"And if he doesn't?"

"Well, we've faced a rather sticky situation together before, haven't we?"

"And we were both shot."

"Yes, that was rather unfortunate. There's always a risk when confronting these people, but with a bit of luck there will be house staff present when we call. Possibly even a wife and family. I doubt that he would want to create a scene in front of others. I think it would be best if you were to remain in the cab while I go and see him. I don't want to put you in danger again."

"I won't be in danger if I'm with you."

"Penny, you were shot last time."

"The chances of that happening again are rather slim, don't you think?"

"I wish I knew."

Regent Street was busy and James was growing impatient. He opened the hatch in the roof and called out to the driver: "We're in a hurry, can't you take a shortcut? How about going through Berkeley Square and then Grosvenor Square? You'll get to Park Lane quicker that way, and then we'll be at Marble Arch before we know it."

"You fink I don't know where I'm goin'?"

"I have every confidence that you know where you're going, but I'd like to get there a little quicker if possible. This is urgent police business."

I heard the cab driver grumbling as James shut the hatch. We lurched left into a side street and the horse broke out into a trot.

"Cabmen can't bear a passenger suggesting another route, can they?" he said. "They always think they know best."

James sat back in his seat, so that my shoulder was resting just inches away from his upper arm. Sitting with him in a cab again reminded me of the evening when I had embarrassed myself. The current pause in the conversation finally gave me the opportunity to say something I had been wanting to say for the previous two weeks.

"James, I haven't found the chance to apologise."

I fixed my eyes on the horse in front of us, too ashamed to look at him. From the corner of my eye, I saw his face turn toward mine.

"For what?"

"That evening. In the cab after we'd been to Ye Olde Cheshire Cheese."

"Oh that!"

He chuckled and I finally turned to look at him.

"What's so amusing?"

"I saw a different side to you, Penny."

He smiled and his eyes lingered on my face. I turned my attention back towards the horse.

"You won't see that side of me again; it was a mistake. It was all a mistake. I want to make that clear."

"It sounds as though you've been worrying about it. Please don't. You did nothing wrong."

"Did nothing wrong?" I looked at him again. "Of course I did! My behaviour was unladylike, inconsiderate and inappropriate."

"I think you're being rather hard on yourself. You have nothing to apologise for, Penny."

"You are engaged to be married and I am a spinster. There are rules regarding how a lady should behave. In fact, I'm not sure it is wholly appropriate for the two of us to be sharing a cab at this moment."

"We're working, Penny!" James laughed. "As I've already said, please don't worry or apologise for your behaviour."

"So the embarrassing incident is forgotten about?"

"If that's what you wish."

The smile left James' face and I looked back at the horse again.

The hatch in the roof opened and the cabman yelled down to us: "There's an 'orse down on Grosv'nor Square. We can sit 'ere 'n' wait, or 'ave you got any wise ideas about another way ter go?"

"You're the cabbie," replied James curtly. "Can't you come up with an alternative route?"

"I would, but I ain't sure it's one yer'll be 'appy with, sir, seein' as yer know these roads better 'an I do."

He slammed the hatch shut and James rolled his eyes.

After passing along the edge of Hyde Park, we turned right into Leinster Terrace and James asked the cabman to stop.

"I'll walk from here up to Leinster Gardens," he said to me. "I'd like to approach the address quietly on foot. Wait here and ask the driver to continue up to Leinster Gardens in about five minutes or so. That should give me enough time."

He climbed out of the cab.

"I'll come with you."

"No, Penny, it's not safe."

"But I might know him from St Giles. The name on his card is likely to be false and he might be someone I've spoken to before. I can help you."

James checked his watch and sighed. "I don't think you should come with me, but I also know that there is no use in my trying to argue with you."

"Thank you."

We asked the cabman to wait for us and walked up the

street, which was lined with trees and large, cream, stuccoed houses with elaborate porches. A cold wind whipped around us and I heard the rumble and whistle of a train, although I couldn't see where the railway line was.

"The trains must come through here between Praed Street and Bayswater stations," said James. "I suspect there is an uncovered piece of track between the houses somewhere in order for us to have heard the engine that clearly."

We walked only a short distance further before I stopped. There was a heavy, sinking sensation in my chest.

"Of course," I said. "That is why I've heard of this street before."

"Why?"

We had reached number twenty Leinster Gardens.

"We're almost there. Someone is playing a trick on us."

"A trick? Penny, what are you talking about?"

"Come and look at the number which Adam claims to live at."

We reached the house and looked up at its smart front door with cream painted columns either side of it.

"A trick? I don't see what you mean. This is Mr de Vries' house, isn't it?"

"No, it's not. No one lives here. Look at the windows."

"You can't see into them, they're blackened out."

"Exactly, and the same with number twenty-four next door. Look. And there are no steps down to the basement. These houses are just a façade."

The porches, windows, balustrade and railings were exactly the same as those adorning the other houses on the street, but I remembered now that these were not proper homes.

James looked down at the card again. "Twenty-three Leinster Gardens. Yes, this is the right place. Just a façade, you say. But why?"

"For the railway line. That train we heard passed through a tunnel beneath our feet here, and there's a cutting on the other side of this façade."

"Well, I'm staggered."

"I remember reading about it. When the railway line was built, numbers twenty-three and twenty-four of Leinster Gardens had to be demolished to make way for it. It was decided that they would retain the façade of the demolished houses so as not to spoil the whole street."

James stood staring at the counterfeit houses in front of us, his shoulders slumped. "I'll be blowed. We've been fooled! Mr de Vries is playing games with us. He purposefully sent us out on a wild goose chase to Bayswater. He dropped those cards on purpose, and we fell for it!" James pulled one of the cards from his pocket and scrunched it up in his fist. "I should have known it wasn't a proper address on the card!"

"How could you have known?"

"I work for the Metropolitan Police. I should know these things about London! And I should have been suspicious the moment he left a card lying around with his address on. He obviously wasn't going to lead us to his home, was he?"

"We weren't to know. We had to come and investigate the address, didn't we?"

"I don't like being played for a fool!" James spun round angrily and called out to the street: "Mr de Vries! Are you here, Mr de Vries? Are you watching us? Come out of hiding, you coward!"

Everything was silent except for the whipping of bare tree branches in the wind.

CHAPTER 35

"So who are we looking for?" snarled James as the cab took us back along Bayswater Road. "It's unlikely that his name is truly Adam, and he certainly doesn't live in Leinster Gardens. He could be five feet and nine inches tall or five feet and eleven inches tall. Or somewhere in-between. He wears dark clothing and a dark hat. Most witnesses say he's fair-haired, although some say he's dark-haired. He may have a moustache and he may not. Does he wear a mask? Or is someone entirely unconnected wearing the mask? I'm feeling lost, Penny, truly I am. Do you mind if I smoke?"

I shook my head and he took out his pipe.

"Witnesses seem rather tricky to rely on," I said. "If you see a man briefly and are then asked to recall some hours later how tall he was, how do you decide by how much five feet eight inches differs from five feet nine? And if it's dark, how is it possible to discern the colour of a man's hair? I think we should concern ourselves less with what the man looks like and consider instead why he has targeted the victims he has targeted. He must have known Mr Larcombe and Mrs Baxter because he planned for both their murders. So what was it that made him behave so violently toward them? Was it an act of revenge?"

"They may have upset him in some way."

"They must have done. I think it would pay to undertake some more rigorous questioning of the victims' families and friends to find out who each might have made an enemy of before their deaths."

"In theory, E and G Division are doing just that. The trouble is that Mr Larcombe, in particular, made an enemy of so many people."

James lit his pipe and inhaled deeply.

"But we must already know the killer, don't you think?" I said. "He has a good knowledge of St Giles and he must be good at blending in with the crowd as he's been able to attend the funerals of several victims without arousing any suspicion. He's literate, because he is able to write letters, and the quality of his writing suggests a good level of education, unless he has someone else to write the letters for him."

"We shouldn't rule it out, I suppose. He clearly enjoys taunting us and seems to enjoy the hysteria he has created across the city. Are those three bobbies I see running?"

He leant forward out of the cab door to get a closer look at the three constables in their distinctive blue uniforms running from Bayswater Road into Hyde Park. James sat back and lifted the roof hatch.

"Driver, follow those police officers! I want to find out what the commotion is."

"Perhaps they're chasing a thief?" I suggested.

"It's quite unusual to see three officers running in that manner. And look at this traffic!"

The cab waited for a gap in the long procession of horses and carriages so that we could turn right onto the carriageway that ran through the park.

"We're going to lose sight of them if we have to sit here much longer!" I said.

The cab eventually found space to turn into Hyde Park and James opened the roof hatch again.

"Faster!" he ordered. "I need to catch up with them!"

The driver flicked the horse with his whip and it broke out into a fast trot.

James leant over the door of the cab, trying to catch sight of the constables.

"There they are! On the path over there! And it looks like they've been joined by some officers from the Royal Parks Constabulary now. Once we've got ahead of them I'll ask the driver to stop and then I'll speak to them."

"And what if it's nothing?"

"How can it be nothing?" James snapped. "Something isn't right."

"James, I know you're angry that Adam keeps evading you, but don't you think chasing these police officers is a step too far? I don't see how they can be of any help to us."

James turned to face me and I didn't like the glimmer of rage in his eyes.

"Have you any idea what it feels like to have the weight of this case on your shoulders, Penny? Five people are dead and I'm no closer to finding the brute than I was four weeks ago. And to worsen matters, he is determined to taunt us by sending us letters and leaving his visiting card, which has directed us to a false address. He's playing games with us and he's winning. The public is terrified and the press is full of nothing but disdain. Yes, that's *your* lot."

He pointed a finger at me and I shrank back from him. This was not the man I knew. He was talking to me as if I were someone else entirely.

"It's very easy for the press to point out where we're going wrong, but I defy anyone to get this right. *Anyone!*"

"I saw what he did," I said quietly. "I saw the boy murdered."

I could feel tears building behind my eyes and tried my best to keep them back.

"So you've seen what we're dealing with. This man is a monster. He needs to be caught. Therefore, don't question me about why I should want to speak to a group of police officers I see running through Hyde Park!"

He opened the hatch. "Stop here, driver! That'll do. Open the doors for me."

I watched James as he ran from the cab. Then I removed my spectacles and wiped my eyes with my handkerchief.

I didn't have long to wait before James returned. He strolled briskly up to the cab with a firm scowl on his face. I heard him speak to the driver and then he leapt back into the seat beside me.

"Another murder," he said breathlessly, "and I'll bet you it's our poor friend Mr Turner."

The horse broke into a trot again as we drove across the bridge over The Serpentine.

I felt my stomach churn. "Where?"

"Royal Avenue in Chelsea. B Division has sent a telegram to the neighbouring divisions requesting help. Apparently, the crowds are getting out of control down there."

CHAPTER 36

On reaching Chelsea, we found King's Road blocked by people, so we made the remainder of our journey on foot. A line of bobbies had been tasked with keeping the crowds out of Royal Avenue, an attractive broad street with smart houses overlooking a strip of lime and plane trees. The constables let James and me pass, and at the far end of the avenue I could see the distant portico of the Royal Hospital.

"Is Ed Keller still being held by E Division?" I asked.

"I believe so."

"If he is, then he can be ruled out as a suspect, I suppose."

The wind blew up the avenue as we walked towards a group of constables gathered about halfway down. The victim was someone of reasonable wealth judging by the appearance of the house, which stood four storeys high with a balcony, window boxes on each sill and a shiny black door. A horse and covered carriage stood outside the property and I guessed that it was waiting to take the victim's body to the mortuary.

A wide man with red whiskers and wearing a dark grey

suit introduced himself as Inspector Dunleath of B Division CID.

James shook his hand. "Inspector Dunleath, this is Miss Green from the *Morning Express*. You don't mind a reporter being here, do you?"

Inspector Dunleath shrugged. "No escaping them really, is there?"

He gave me a smile then blew his nose into a large blue handkerchief.

"Who's the victim?" asked James.

"Mr Albert Turner. Forty-seven years of age. A lawyer. He lived here with his wife, although she wasn't present at the time of the murder. He had his throat cut in the drawing room."

"Who did it?"

"A guest."

The inspector handed James a visiting card, which looked painfully familiar.

"I knew it," said James. "Penny, look at this."

"Adam de Vries again," I said. "Inspector, you must have a good description of him from the person who admitted him to the house. Who answered the door?"

"The parlour maid," he replied. "She's speaking to my colleague at this present moment. She's rather distressed, as you can imagine. All the staff are extremely upset."

I took my notebook and pencil from my bag and began to take notes.

"Mr Turner's throat was cut?" asked James.

"Yes, and it made a terrible mess."

"Was Adam de Vries known to him?"

"That's what we're trying to establish. He must have had a justifiable reason for agreeing to see the man when he called round. We'll find out from the maid on what business Mr de Vries was attending."

"Has she given a description of Mr de Vries?"

"So far we know that he was about five feet ten inches tall and had fair hair. He was twenty-eight years of age or thereabouts."

"Whiskers?" I probed.

"The maid hasn't mentioned any."

Inspector Dunleath paused to sneeze, before blowing his nose again. "The butler also saw Mr de Vries, so we are interviewing him as well."

"And none of the staff were able to apprehend the attacker?" James interjected.

"They tell us it all happened too quickly. Mr Turner was attacked within minutes of Mr de Vries being admitted into the drawing room. The parlour maid had gone to the kitchen to fetch tea and she discovered Mr Turner on the floor of the room when she returned with the tea tray. Mr de Vries had already left the room and she found him in the hallway. She hurried after him, but he dashed off out of the front door. He left his hat behind on the hallway table."

"Ah, interesting! Has it any distinguishing features which could help us identify its owner?" I asked.

"Not that we've established so far. It's an inexpensive top hat, but we know little more than that."

"Any idea in which direction the assailant ran?"

"Up that way." The inspector pointed towards the portico of the Royal Hospital. "He scarpered across Burton's Court and that would have taken him up to Queen's Road. From there, he could have turned left and run towards the barracks, or he might have turned right and got as far as the river. For all we know, he's hopped onto a steamboat. The butler chased him but only got halfway across Burton's Court. He's not a young man, and he didn't see which direction Mr de Vries took from there. Some officers have been sent to the address in Bayswater to apprehend him. He may not be there at present, of course, but they can wait for him to return."

The inspector sniffed as he tried to find a clean portion of his handkerchief on which to blow his nose.

"They'll have rather a long wait," replied James. "It's not a proper address. We've just come from there. Mr de Vries left his calling cards scattered about the place in St Giles. I think you'll also find that his name is a pseudonym. I've been chasing after this man for weeks now and am getting no closer to apprehending him. To make matters worse, he's sending me letters like this."

James pulled the most recent letter out of his coat pocket and handed it to the inspector.

"Good Lord," said Dunleath. "He named Mr Turner in his letter?"

"We received it at Scotland Yard this morning and have been searching for a Mr Turner ever since. We were unable to reach him in time."

Inspector Dunleath sighed and handed the letter back to James. "Well, you'd better come inside and speak to the staff. You'll want to see the scene of the murder, I'm sure. Your colleague, Chief Inspector Cullen, is already here."

"Yes indeed." James turned to me. "My apologies, Penny, but we can't allow the press inside the house as yet."

"That's quite all right," I replied. "I can't say I want to go inside in any case."

"Do you have everything you need for your report?"

"I do. I need to get to the office now in time to meet my deadline. Good luck, James."

He gave me a smile, but I could see sadness in his eyes.

CHAPTER 37

An unpleasant odour greeted me as I arrived into the newsroom that afternoon, a filthy man in ragged clothes sat at Edgar's desk.

"Miss Green! Have you missed me?"

"Edgar?"

He scratched at his neck, which already looked red raw.

"Don't come too close," he replied. "I'm playing host to a fine crowd of creatures."

"Fleas?" I asked.

"And lice," said Frederick, wrinkling his nose.

"How was St Giles?" I asked.

"It has some hospitable gin shops, but I can't say I recommend the dosshouses. I'm lucky not to have been struck down by an infectious disease."

"Did anyone suspect that you were a news reporter?"

"Some chaps thought I was a bit fishy, but most of them were too drunk to care. As long as I bought them a drink, that is. I hope I'll be reimbursed by Mr Sherman in due course. I was an extremely popular chap when I was buying the beer and gin. And look, here's something that will cheer you up."

He handed me a letter, which I took carefully from his grimy hand.

I read it out: "'The Director of the British Museum begs to inform Mr Edgar Fish that a reading ticket will be delivered to him on presenting this note to the Clerk in the Reading Room within six months of the above date.'"

I paused and then said, "Well done, Edgar. You got your reading ticket back!"

"Father pulled a few strings. I finally managed to find him sober at his gentleman's club. Thank you for your help with all the Sudan work."

The door to the newsroom opened and slammed shut as Mr Sherman strode in. "Our wanderer returns, eh, Miss Green? Are you pleased to see him?"

"Of course. I'm always pleased to see Edgar."

"He's written pages of notes on his experiences, so we have many good stories to publish. He's back here now because I want him to work with you on the murders. There's almost too much to keep up with after today's terrible events in Chelsea. I take it you've got everything you could get your hands on so far?"

"Just the circumstances of the murder. I didn't have time to interview any witnesses before the deadline."

"Super. Get it all written down and I'll have a look at it later this evening. I want you and Edgar back in Chelsea early tomorrow morning. Before he does anything else, however, I'm taking him down to the Turkish Baths, where he can get a proper wash and scrub from Ahmet, my favourite tellak."

Edgar was clean-shaven and well-groomed when I met him

outside Sloane Square station early the following morning. The ornate buildings around us were bathed in pale sunlight and there was birdsong in the trees. I took in the scene and reminded myself that there was beauty in this city, even in winter.

"How nice it is to be in a pleasant part of town again," said Edgar as we walked along King's Road. "Wide streets, respectable stores such as Peter Jones and a well-bred class of people."

"But it seems that murderers are venturing into Chelsea after all."

"Shocking, isn't it? You come to expect it in a place like St Giles, but Chelsea?"

"We need to find out what the connection might have been between Mr Turner and St Giles."

"You think there is one?"

"There has to be. He was specifically targeted by the killer."

"But does the link have to be St Giles? The killer may have known him by other means."

"It's possible, I suppose. I hope we can interview some of Mr Turner's servants."

"The police may not allow us to."

"I'll ask James."

"Ah yes, there's always your schoolboy inspector." Edgar smiled.

We reached Royal Avenue, which was still blocked by a blue line of police constables.

I asked for Inspector Blakely and Inspector Dunleath.

"No press allowed down there today," came the reply.

"But you let us through yesterday."

"Not today."

"Why not?"

"No press today."

"Can we see Inspector Blakely from Scotland Yard, please?"

"No press today."

"No press!" came a voice from behind us. I turned to see Tom Clifford grinning, his tobacco-stained teeth on display. "Mr Fish and Miss Green! Looking for a story?"

"We're already working on it, thank you."

"So am I. I'm assisting the private detective."

"Where is he?" I asked, looking around for Winston Nicholls.

"Not here."

"He's investigating this murder as well, is he?"

"It's the same man again, isn't it? Adam de Vries."

"What do you know about Adam de Vries?"

"Same as you, most probably."

"Inspector Blakely only found out his name yesterday."

"Did he? Well, Winston Nicholls came across his calling card the day before that."

"Perhaps he should have shared his find with the police!"

"He's tried a number of times to share information with the police, but they don't appear to be interested in what he has to say. That's their loss. Fortunately for him, we print all of his findings in *The Holborn Gazette*."

"And what are his findings?"

"You mean to tell me you haven't been reading our superior pages?"

"I have, but I don't recall any of his findings leaping out at me."

"You wait, Miss Green. Just you wait. Your inspector's on the back foot. And what a surprise to see you here, Fish. Finally out and about on a story?"

"Out of our way, Clifford, we've work to do."

"Well, that's a first!" Tom laughed again.

"Where can we find Winston Nicholls?" I asked.

"What do you want with him? Finally beginning to believe he's onto something, are you?"

"I'm keeping my mind open."

"There you go, you are indeed! Given up on the inspector now?"

"Where's Nicholls?"

"How do I know? Try his home or his mother. You know his mother, don't you? Go and find him yourself."

Tom sauntered off and Edgar sighed.

"I regret stealing his story. Tom and I used to be such good friends."

"I don't think that friendship is any great loss."

"It helps to be able to work together. We used to share a good deal of information. Oh well, I suppose the best thing to do now is make my way down to The Coopers Arms. Heard of it? You can get a nice drop of porter in there."

"I suppose a public house could be a good source of news. You're likely to find someone in there who might be able to tell us more about Mr Turner."

"I get most of my stories from pubs, as you well know. Care to join me?"

"The last time I went to the pub with you, Edgar, I suffered a bout of intemperance."

He laughed.

"I'll knock on some doors instead and try to find some witnesses that way," I said. "Good luck."

❦

"A masked man running through the streets of Chelsea shortly after Mr Turner's murder?" said Mr Sherman with delight. "What a capital story!"

He rubbed his hands together excitedly. "What sort of mask was he wearing?"

"A coal porter in The Coopers Arms told me it was a dark mask which covered the upper part of his face; certainly his eyes and nose," said Edgar. "The landlord of the pub told me that a number of customers had seen the same man running away from Royal Avenue."

"It has to be the murderer! Don't you agree, Miss Green?"

"He matches the description of the masked man seen in St Giles around the times of Jack and Mr Larcombe's murders," I said.

"He went into Mr Turner's home, cut his throat and ran off in disguise! The masked man is back!" said Mr Sherman, clapping his hands together with glee. "Have any of the other reporters got hold of this news?"

"Not that I know of," said Edgar.

"Good, good. Get it all written down as quickly as you can, but ensure that I can read your handwriting, Fish. Did you come across any witnesses who saw the masked man, Miss Green?"

"I didn't, sir. I was trying to find someone who could enlighten me in regard to Mr Turner's connection with St Giles. I found out that he considered himself a philanthropist and liked to help fallen women in the slums."

"Did you find anyone who saw the murderer?"

"No. I'm waiting to speak to one of Mr Turner's servants about that."

"Good, and when will you do that?"

"When I can persuade Inspector Blakely to permit me to do so."

"You didn't manage to do that today?"

My editor's expression had swiftly changed from one of jubilance to one of exasperation.

"No, the police wouldn't allow us anywhere near the crime scene."

"Shame."

Mr Sherman turned away and I felt a sinking sense of disappointment. The large grin on Edgar's face did nothing to improve my mood.

However, there was something I had gleaned from my interviews that day which I hoped would prove useful. Neighbours of Mr Turner had told me he had been a short man with greying-orange hair and a thick moustache. The description matched the appearance of the man with whom I had seen Reuben O'Donoghue arguing on the foggy day when I had ventured to speak to Ed Keller accompanied by the missionaries.

Had Mr Turner and Reuben argued? If so, what about?

I felt certain that an important clue lay within their conversation, but I didn't know how to discover it.

CHAPTER 38

My room felt cold that evening and my mood was rather despondent. After a day in Chelsea, Edgar had managed to find the best story about Mr Turner's murder and my efforts had afforded me very little. I put on an old overcoat of my sister's and cuddled Tiger on my lap as I sat by the little stove and sipped a cup of cocoa.

I had discovered that Mr Turner had visited St Giles as a philanthropist and I had seen him arguing with Reuben O'Donoghue, but this did not help to explain why the man who called himself Adam de Vries had killed him.

Could Reuben be Adam de Vries?

With little more than wild theories in my mind, I put Tiger on the floor, stood up from my chair and went over to my writing desk. I had almost finished reading Father's diaries. I opened the one from 1875.

Fallen trees are making our navigation of the Opon troublesome and my companions and I have been obliged to lift our canoe out of the water at regular intervals as we try to scramble our way along the riverbank, carrying it above our heads.

I call it a canoe, but it is little more than a hollowed-out tree trunk. Notwithstanding, it is a capacious tree trunk and accommodates six men reasonably comfortably. I have collected a number of pretty oncidiums from the banks, and their sprays of profuse blooms are quite a sight to behold.

Despite the beauty of this land, its dangers are not to be underestimated. We regularly encounter alligators enjoying their repose on sandbanks, and the deadly coral snake and the colossal boa are enough to petrify the hardiest of natives. At night, we camp on the sandbanks and take turns to keep watch, our firearms loaded and poised.

The most concerning source of danger is the red men who inhabit the forests here. Twice today, arrows have whistled across the river, just narrowly missing our heads. The vegetation on the riverbank is so thick and luxuriant that I have yet to catch sight of our foes hiding among it.

Mrs Garnett hammered on my door and startled me.

"The inspector is here to see you, Miss Green!"

I jumped out of my chair, removed my sister's overcoat and tried to re-pin my hair and smooth out my burgundy print dress as I walked over to my door. I prayed that James wasn't visiting me to bring news of yet another murder.

"He's waiting for you in the hallway," said my landlady.

I followed her down the narrow wooden staircase, then descended the wide carpeted stairs.

"James! Is everything all right?"

He stood in the hallway with his hat in his hand.

"Everything is very well, thank you, Penny."

We exchanged a smile and James glanced over my shoulder at Mrs Garnett, who had decided to remain in the hallway with us, dusting the table vigorously as a pretext for her lingering.

"There's nothing to worry about," he said. "I was just passing."

He glanced at Mrs Garnett again and she hummed a tuneless song as if she wasn't listening to our conversation.

"You've heard about the man in the mask seen running away from Mr Turner's house?" I asked.

"I have. It's extremely interesting."

He fidgeted with the brim of his hat.

"A neighbour told me he was a philanthropist in St Giles."

"It's good to establish the connection, isn't it? I've heard he discovered the place on one of Mrs Baxter's slum tours and subsequently visited the pubs in the area and enjoyed the company of..." He paused to clear his throat. "The company of *certain ladies*," he added quietly.

I could sense Mrs Garnett behind me still, almost leaning in to hear more.

"Now it's beginning to make sense," I said.

"Do you think so?" said James. "I'm finding it all rather baffling."

"I meant Mr Turner's connection with St Giles."

"Ah yes, I see what you mean. Yes, it's a useful development."

He scratched the back of his neck and I guessed that this topic of conversation had not been what James had come to talk about.

"I shall go to St Giles tomorrow and found out more about what Mr Turner did there," I said.

"Good idea. You'll let me know what you discover?"

"Of course."

"And have you seen Winston Nicholls recently?"

"No. Edgar and I saw Tom Clifford in Chelsea today, but he refused to tell us where Winston was."

"Ah. E Division have been on the lookout for him for a couple of days now and there has been no sign of the fellow anywhere."

"Is he a suspect?"

"He's one of the men they would like to speak to."

"I'll ask Martha where Winston is."

"Thank you. Be careful how you go about it, though. If you drop a hint that the police wish to speak to him, she's unlikely to tell you his whereabouts."

"I'll try to be as tactful as possible."

"Well, it's late and I should be going," announced James loudly, looking over at Mrs Garnett.

His brief visit felt rather unfulfilling with the presence of my landlady constraining our conversation. I opened the front door for him and he went out but paused on the top step.

"I wish to apologise for my short temper yesterday," he whispered. "I was rather angry about that trick de Vries had played on us. I shouldn't have spoken to you in that way."

"Please don't worry. You have a lot of work to do and it's only normal that you should feel the strain of it sometimes."

"And I don't want you to feel embarrassed," he whispered even more softly.

"About what?"

"We didn't manage to finish our conversation in the cab on the way to Bayswater, did we?"

"Oh that." I glanced back at Mrs Garnett, who was dusting the picture above the hallway table and looking over at me.

I turned back to James. "I'm no longer embarrassed about it," I whispered. "I've forgotten about the whole incident."

"Of course." He put his hat on and scratched his chin. I heard the faint sound of stubble rubbing against his fingernails. "It's probably inappropriate for me to say this, but I haven't."

"Haven't?" I felt puzzled. "You're telling me you *haven't* forgotten about it?"

"Indeed I haven't. I am happy to remember it."

He smiled and I felt a skip of excitement in my chest.

"But I shouldn't say any more than that. Goodnight, Penny."

He disappeared down the steps and into the darkness before I had the chance to bid him goodnight in return.

CHAPTER 39

I drank some coffee at a stall in Long Acre the following morning in the hope that it would clear my head. Weak sunlight emerged between the grey clouds and I watched a shopkeeper open his draper's store for the day. I had slept little that night; instead, I had repeated the conversation with James in my mind so frequently that I felt perplexed.

If I had understood him correctly, he had told me that he was happy to remember the incident in the cab. It would have been a flattering comment to hear if he wasn't engaged to be married, and I felt sure that his future wife would not approve if she knew he had said it.

His words had both buoyed and saddened me at the same time. And I also felt angry. Why would he say such a thing when he knew that nothing could ever develop between us? It was almost irresponsible. A word from him explaining that he held no affection for me would have been hurtful, but it would have been preferable because it might have removed the *what if?* question from my mind. *What if James had never met his fiancée?* I disliked myself for thinking it, but I wished that he had never met her. I returned my coffee cup to the stall and walked up Langley Street, between the looming brewery buildings.

"I'd say spring's in the air," said Martha, looking up at the blue patch of sky above the courtyard. "What are we now? Middle of Feb'ry?"

"Hopefully it won't be long before the weather warms up," I said as Martha pegged a shirt onto the washing line.

"So 'e's got 'imself another one. And in Chelsea this time," said Martha. "Mr Turner. I've bin reminded on who 'e was now. I couldn't think of 'im when the inspector was 'ere askin' after 'im the other day."

"I heard he was a philanthropist."

"That's a fancy name for drinkin' down the pub, is it?"

"I heard he liked to help fallen women."

Martha laughed. "That's 'ow yer describes it, is it?"

"And somehow he upset the man who calls himself Adam. Did Mr Turner know Mr Larcombe and Mrs Baxter?"

"Yeah, I think 'e first started comin' down 'ere on one o' them toff tours what Mrs Baxter arranged." Martha picked up the end of a rope that was coiled up on the ground and pulled on it to winch the line of laundry high up over our heads.

"It seems that each of the victims knew at least one of the other victims," I said loudly over the squeaking of pulleys.

"That's what you gets round 'ere."

"But neither Mrs Baxter or Mr Turner lived here, and both had good reason to come here. I'm sure that reason is linked to their murders somehow, but I can't understand how exactly."

"It ain't yer job to understand it. Leave that ter the police. They bin makin' a nuisance of themselves."

"What are they doing?"

"One o' the bobbies went and started askin' Winston about Mrs Baxter. They was askin' 'im as if 'e done it!"

She looped the end of the rope around a large iron peg on the wall.

"I'm sure they don't think that he could have done anything to Mrs Baxter. They're asking all the men in this area about the murders."

"But 'e don't even live 'ere. 'E lives in Red Lion Square! Why'd they wanna go askin' 'im questions?"

"I suppose everyone's a suspect at the moment because they have no idea who's behind the murders."

"My son ain't a murderer!"

"Of course not, Martha." I realised it was going to be difficult for me to ask her where Winston was without antagonising her.

"I haven't seen Winston for a few days," I said tentatively, avoiding any eye contact.

"Yeah, well, if truth be told 'e's lyin' low."

"So where is he now?"

"Stayin' wiv a friend."

"Where though?"

"I ain't at liberty ter say. 'E's sworn me ter secrecy."

"But if he's innocent, then surely he has nothing to hide?"

"Of course 'e's innocent! What are yer tryin' ter suggest?" Martha put her hands on her hips and glared at me.

"I'm not suggesting anything, Martha. What I mean is that he's an innocent man, so there's no need for him to hide. Besides, that might look like he's guilty after all."

"'E just wants to be left alone."

"Left alone where?"

"Why yer so keen to know where 'e is? It ain't nothin' ter you, is it?" She gave me a sharp look.

"Martha, please don't be angry. Winston is most definitely innocent, as you say, but by hiding away he's likely to make the police suspicious. I know Inspector Blakely is interested in talking to him about the investigation work he's been doing. He may have come across something which the inspector has missed."

"That's more 'an likely."

"So if Inspector Blakely can meet with him they can discuss the case."

Martha eyed me for a moment, then shook her head. "Nah, there's summink goin' on 'ere. The police ain't never been interested in nothin' Winston's got to say abaht the case. So why's they so int'rested now? Yer workin' for the police, ain't yer?"

She jabbed a finger at me. "They've sent yer 'ere in the 'opes I'll be stupid enough to tell yer where 'e is. That's a real shame, Miss Green, a real damn shame 'cause I always thought you was a nice lady. You told me you was a news reporter, not the police. And now it turns out yer the same as the rest of 'em and yer must think I were born yesterday and be 'appy to tell yer where me son's 'idin' just so's yer can go back and tell the police and get 'im arrested. Well, it ain't 'appenin', I can tell yer! I may be poor, but I ain't stupid, Miss Green. Got that? I ain't stupid!"

I sighed, desperate to reverse the tone of the conversation. "Martha, it's not what you think. I'm not working for the police. I just want to help them find the man who's doing these terrible things. We need to get him off the streets."

"Course we do. But that man ain't my son!"

Martha stared at me forlornly and I noticed that her lower lip quivered slightly as she turned from me and strode back toward her home.

"Martha!" I called out after her, but my voice wavered.

She felt as though I had betrayed her.

A friendship had been lost.

I left Martha's courtyard cursing myself over my clumsy attempt to find out where Winston was. I thought the conversation over again in my mind, trying to understand how I could have phrased my words to better effect, but the damage had been done.

With a heavy heart, I walked down the narrow lane toward Seven Dials, sunshine illuminating the crooked rooftops and rags fluttering in the windows.

A man swaggered towards me, accompanied by two boys. He wore a top hat and long velvet overcoat, and a small dog trotted by his side. My heart began to pound all the way up to my throat as I realised the man was Ed Keller. E Division must have released him again.

But when?

"Mornin', Miss Green."

He stopped when he reached me and grinned widely, exposing his crooked yellow teeth. "Why 'aven't you come a'visitin' me lately?"

"I heard you had been arrested." I gripped my bag tightly to stop my hands from shaking.

"I'm always gettin' harrested." He laughed as he looked me up and down.

"What do you know about Mr Turner?"

"Another drunkard, like Yeomans and Larcombe."

"He was a lawyer."

"That don't mean he weren't a drunk."

Ed stepped closer to me and ran his tongue along his upper lip. "I enjoyed you a'visitin' me," he said in a soft voice. "Fancy interviewin' me again? I got lots I can tell yer."

"No, thank you." I took a step backwards. "Do you know anyone who would want to kill Mr Turner?"

"I might do. I'll tell yer if you come back wiv me now."

"Goodbye, Mr Keller,"

I continued on my way, my whole body trembling

violently. I heard him mutter something crude to the boys and they laughed. I hated how he had made me so fearful of him. It had been foolishness on my part to try to interview him. I should have heeded the warnings and stayed away.

I was supposed to be finding out if someone in St Giles could tell me more about Mr Turner, but with Martha angry at me and the danger of Ed Keller ever present, I wished that I could be anywhere but here.

CHAPTER 40

We were making slow progress up the river this afternoon when we heard the unmistakable twang of bows. In the duration of less than a minute, countless arrows flew at us and I ducked my head as they whistled around me. In return, I fired several shots into the vegetation on the riverbank, but there was no sign that I had succeeded in hitting my intended targets.

Once the attack had subsided, we realised that our companion in the stern of the canoe had two arrows firmly embedded in his chest. We pulled the canoe onto the nearest sandbank, but he suffered terribly during his last moments. He died swiftly from his injuries.

We made camp on the riverbank and dug a resting place for our dead companion. Not one of us rested at nightfall; instead, we all remained awake with our firearms at the ready. The red men had resolved to finish us off and we didn't have long to wait.

We kept completely silent as we sheltered under some trees at the edge of our camp clearing. Before long, we heard the vegetation rustling around us and, although there was little moonlight to see by, I could discern the dark forms of our foe gathering in the clearing.

On my command, we opened fire and such was the blaze from our *rifles that the flailing limbs and gaping mouths of our insurgents were briefly lit up in the darkness. Their shrieks and howls curdled my blood, but it wasn't long before an eerie silence descended.*

When we were certain that they were all dead, we lit our lamps and surveyed the tangled bodies of the men who had attacked us. They were young men with strong physical forms, each wearing no more than a cloth around their loins. We will bury them at first light.

"Why didn't you tell me about the massacre, Ellie?"

I was seated on an easy chair in my sister's drawing room, with sherry almost spilling over the edge of my glass. I had visited her as soon as I had finished reading this diary entry.

"I didn't know what to make of it. I still don't. I prefer to think that it never happened." My sister was seated on the other side of the fireplace from me, rummaging through the work basket on her lap.

"I can understand why you would like to forget about it, but it happened. Father killed those men."

"He was defending himself."

"I suppose so." I sighed. "And I suppose that if he hadn't done it they would certainly have killed him. They had already killed one of his companions."

"It's difficult to understand when you live in a civilised country such as ours. Life in South America is rather different, it would seem. The rules are different."

"Are they different? I'm not sure they are. Presumably the men who attacked Father did so for a reason. Was it because he was trespassing on their land?"

"But is it their land? It once belonged to the Spanish."

I took a gulp of sherry and enjoyed the warm, comforting sensation in my chest. I had begun to realise that I knew little of the circumstances surrounding Father's plant hunting. I had always assumed that his work had been honourable.

"I don't see how a meaningful pursuit of orchids can degenerate into a massacre," I said. "It seems that such a high price was paid for all those beautiful plants he brought back to England."

"Yes, and Father paid the ultimate price. He lost his life to those endeavours."

"I'm beginning to wonder if he was killed in revenge for what he did to those men."

"We can speculate for a long time, Penelope, but even if we reached a conclusion we would be unable to bring him back. Conflict such as this is commonplace in any part of the world where the European sets foot outside his own domain. Occasional resistance from natives is natural, although it usually subsides when they realise that we mean them no harm."

She took a piece of embroidery out of her work basket and began to stitch.

"On the contrary, it does them good," said George, Eliza's husband, as he marched into the room. "It won't be long until civilisation is brought to all four corners of the globe, and what a marvellous day that will be."

My brother-in-law was a tall man with wavy brown hair swept to one side. He had thick mutton-chop whiskers and the buttons on his waistcoat were strained around his stomach. The buttons pulled even more as he sat down on the settee and opened up his newspaper.

"How can a globe have four corners?" Eliza asked her husband.

"Why must women always pick holes in a fellow's words?" he said from behind the *Morning Express*.

"As I was saying, Penelope," continued Eliza. "There is no need to document any acts of violence in Father's book. It wouldn't improve the reputation of Frederick Brinsley Green. Even though people understand that these unfortunate incidents occur in the name of exploration—"

"Commerce, Christianity and civilisation," George piped up.

"Thank you, but that's a rather old-fashioned phrase now," she said.

"It is still relevant."

"Thank you, George." Eliza rolled her eyes. "You know what I'm trying to say, Penelope. Let's forget about this horrible incident. We both find it upsetting to dwell on and neither of us can imagine our own father doing such a thing. But life is what it is."

I gazed into the bottom of my glass and tried to remember what my father had looked like. I could still picture his kindly dark brown eyes, which creased at the corners when he smiled, and I also recalled his light brown whiskers. He hadn't looked like a man who would commit murder.

A friend of his had given my mother a sketch of my father, which was a good likeness. I wanted to see it again to remind myself what he had looked like and to somehow find some reassurance in it that he had been a good person.

"You've escaped the masked man so far then, Penelope?" I looked up to see that George had lowered his newspaper and was regarding me with his cool blue eyes.

"Fortunately, I have, and it shan't be long before he's caught now."

I thought of Winston Nicholls and wondered whether James had been able to locate him.

"I haven't told you yet, Penelope, that I'm taking the children to Mother's," said Eliza. "I can't bear the thought of this killer roaming around. I'll bring them back to London once the police have caught him. George has suggested I stay up there with them, but I'm helping to organise the women's suffrage demonstration, which will take place in Hyde Park next month."

"How will Mother cope with looking after the children?"

"The nurse and the governess will also be staying there."

I tried to picture Eliza's six children, along with two members of her staff, residing in Mother's little cottage in Derbyshire.

"It will be rather a tight squeeze," I said.

"It will indeed! But they will rub along just fine up there, I'm sure. And it is far better than their being murdered!"

"The children aren't in danger, Ellie."

"How can you be sure of that? Anyone could be targeted next, absolutely anyone. No one is safe. I don't understand how all this started in the slums and then spread to Clerkenwell and now Chelsea. Chelsea of all places! What are the police doing about it? Every so often I read that some fellow's been arrested and then he's let go again, and all the while I have no idea what the police are up to. What does your friend the inspector make of it all?"

"He's working extremely hard."

I thought of how tired and despondent James had appeared recently. I didn't want to let slip that he was struggling to find the man responsible.

"He must have an inkling of who's behind it, has he not?" said George.

"He has a good description of the man now, and we know that the killer is using a pseudonym in his letters. James is finding the case a challenging one, but he's the most capable man for the job. And he's not doing all the work by himself, of course. There are many officers from each of the divisions working on this."

"And a private detective," said George.

"Which one?"

"Some chap whom I saw mentioned in *The Holborn Gazette*."

"George, you shouldn't be reading *The Gazette*. It's the bad newspaper, remember?" said Eliza with a smile.

"Winston Nicholls?" I said.

"I can't recall his name," replied George. "Anyway, I thought it was an interesting development that the Yard has decided to bring in a private detective to sort this business out."

"The Yard didn't bring him in. He has appointed himself as a private detective. In fact, I'm not sure he has any investigating credentials at all."

"Is that so? Well in that case, this thing's even more of a mess than I first thought."

"Anyone can decide to become a private detective if they so wish. I'm not sure why *The Holborn Gazette* thinks that Nicholls's findings are worthy of anyone's attention."

"Desperation, I suppose. The police are doing such a dreadful job of it all."

"It's a difficult job," I said, gritting my teeth.

"It certainly is," added Eliza. "Don't forget, George, that Penelope knows the Scotland Yard inspector *extremely well*."

"This is why I cannot allow you to have a profession, Eliza," said George. "I won't have you knowing your male work associates *extremely well*. I'm afraid this is what happens when men and women are forced to work together. Keep 'em separate, I say. Like doctors and nurses."

"Don't forget that we have women doctors now, George," said Eliza.

"Women doctors!" George almost spat out the phrase. "What a ridiculous notion. Can you imagine a chap visiting his doctor on Harley Street and finding a *woman* sitting behind the desk? How is a chap expected to discuss matters of a personal nature with a member of the female sex? What if she should be required to carry out a physical examination? I pray that I make it to my deathbed without encountering a woman doctor."

"You've finished your sherry, Penelope. Would you like some more?" asked Eliza.

"Yes, I'd like a large glassful. Thank you."

CHAPTER 41

'L amplough's Effervescing Pyretic Saline. Provides Instant Relief in Headaches and Sickness, and Cures the Worst Form of Skin Complaints.'

I read the advertisement a number of times as the omnibus took me to Fleet Street the following morning. Two men sitting opposite me were browsing *The Holborn Gazette*.

I sighed and wondered if my father's reputation would be damaged if the massacre he had been involved in became public knowledge.

Was Eliza right when she said that conflict such as this was commonplace when Europeans travelled in remote parts of the world? How had my father been able to write so calmly about the event in his diary?

I understood that he had been defending himself, but there had been no hint of remorse in his account. *Surely he had felt saddened by the deaths of these men?* The revelation had changed the way I now thought about him. *Did I want to feel close to a man who was responsible for bloodshed? Could I ever feel proud again to be his daughter?*

I could feel my enthusiasm for the book about his life

waning. It would be a struggle to write if I was unsure about how I should remember him. I hadn't seen him for nine years and I had long since accepted that he was probably dead, but this didn't prevent me from feeling a new sense of loss. I had lost the man I thought he had been, and it left me with an overwhelming feeling of loneliness.

I arrived in the newsroom to find my desk already occupied.

"James?"

The surprise lifted my despondent mood.

James was clean-shaven and wore a smart crimson silk tie I hadn't seen before. I recalled what he had said to me on Mrs Garnett's doorstep and my face flushed.

"Penny!"

He stood up from my chair and I tried to dampen my smile, aware that Edgar and Frederick were watching us.

"Meet our new reporter, Miss Green," laughed Edgar. "He's given up on his detective work having decided this murder case will be the death of him!"

James gave a hollow laugh. "Indeed."

I sat down at my desk. "There hasn't been another—"

"Thankfully, no. No more murders, nor even another letter. I came here to check with you about the location of Winston Nicholls. You haven't seen him, I presume?"

"No. So he's still missing? I think his mother knows where he is, but she refused to tell me. It sounds as though he has already been scared off. She said that a constable from E Division was asking him too many questions."

"E Division have been keeping watch outside his home, but there have been no sightings of him for several days."

"Probably because the police are loitering outside it," said Edgar. "Why don't you just break into his house? If you find a mask and a knife in there, you'll know you've got your man."

"That may be our next step," said James. "Mr Turner's maid and butler were both able to give us a good description of the man who calls himself Adam de Vries. And although he doesn't have any distinguishing features, the murderer does seem to bear something of a resemblance to Mr Nicholls. I should like to arrest him."

"You think he and Adam might be one and the same?" Edgar asked.

"I can't be certain, but he's a pretty likely candidate. And his disappearance is rather suspicious, don't you think?"

"What's the evidence against him?" Edgar persisted.

"Apart from a physical resemblance, he has also taken a keen interest in our investigations, possibly because he wants to know how close we are to catching him. By presenting himself as someone interested in the case, he could be hoping that we will automatically exclude him from our investigations. Why would a murderer appear to investigate his own crimes? It makes no sense, which is why I believe he may be doing it to put us off the scent. And he's found a decent platform via *The Holborn Gazette*. Can you see how he's trying to manipulate us? Another manipulation, of course, is the creation of this Adam de Vries character; a man who we know doesn't exist. However, like Mr Nicholls, he does like to write letters."

"But the handwriting on the letters doesn't appear to be a match," I said.

"No, but that's to be expected, isn't it? Obviously, if he were to use the same handwriting he would incriminate himself immediately."

"Do you see now, Miss Green?" said Edgar. "That's why you're not a detective."

"Thank you for that, Edgar. We do know that Winston Nicholls attended the funerals of both Mr Larcombe and Mrs Baxter. The more you put the pieces together, the more it makes sense. I've never liked the man and he has always struck me as odd in his manner. He struggles to look people in the eye, which is just the sort of thing you would expect from someone who has committed such terrible crimes. Oh goodness, poor Martha."

The forlorn look she had given me came back to my mind. "This will be too upsetting for her. It may be too much for her to bear."

"If Nicholls has attended each funeral, then presumably he'll be at Mr Turner's funeral," said Edgar.

"Yes, I've already given that some thought," said James. "Mr Turner is to be buried at Brookwood Cemetery out in Surrey tomorrow. The funeral party will be taken there on the Necropolis Railway. I'll make sure that myself and a number of police officers are among the mourners."

"And press," said Edgar. "We're going too, aren't we, Miss Green? I want to be there when this Nicholls chap is arrested. It's going to make a first-rate news story."

Cemetery Station, the terminus for the Necropolis Railway, was tucked away down a narrow street behind Waterloo Station. James and I met outside the ticket office next to the wrought-iron gates through which coffins were brought to be loaded onto the funeral train. There was a constant rumble from the archway above our heads as trains arrived into and departed from Waterloo.

James wore a black overcoat and bowler hat, and I was also dressed in black mourning attire. Our breath hung in the cold, grey air, and I lifted my black veil so that we could see each other more clearly. The confusion I had felt about the conversation on Mrs Garnett's doorstep had thankfully passed and instead I felt happy that we were united in our goal to find Winston Nicholls.

"You must be subtle about this arrest, James. You must try to avoid upsetting Mr Turner's family and friends at his funeral."

"Of course I will. You can trust me with that much, can't you, Penny?" He grinned. "I know most of your colleagues down in Fleet Street think the police have been entirely incompetent with regard to this case, but we're about to prove them wrong. Shall we go in?"

We went into the ticket office and purchased a second-class coffin ticket before making our way toward the waiting room, where the mourners were beginning to gather.

"There are to be constables from L Division disguised as mourners in first-class and third-class," whispered James. "If they find him in their carriage, they have orders to wave a handkerchief from the window so that we know where to find him when the train arrives at Brookwood."

"That sounds like a good plan. Look, there's Martha Nicholls."

Martha was talking to another woman and the missionaries, and appeared conspicuous in her wide-brimmed hat.

"And there's Winston, look!" I whispered. "He's standing just behind her."

"Excellent."

"Don't arrest him now," I pleaded with James. "Not in front of all the other mourners, it would be too disruptive and Martha would be ashamed."

"Don't worry, I'll wait until he's on the train."

We were ushered out onto the platform, where plumes of steam from the waiting funeral train hissed into the air. It comprised three passenger carriages and one windowless coffin carriage at the rear.

"I know that some of the people here may recognise me,"

muttered James, "but it's important that I look like one of the mourners. If anyone asks us any questions, we're to tell them we're brother and sister."

"There you are!" said Edgar, his loud voice drawing inquisitive stares from the people standing around us.

"Shush, we're trying not to be noticed," whispered James. "My sister and I are here to mourn our departed friend, Albert Turner."

"Your *sister?*" said Edgar, eying me incredulously. I watched his face as the realisation finally dawned on him. "Oh yes, your *sister.*"

"Inspector Blakely! Miss Green!" said Hugo Hawkins as he and David Meares joined us.

"Shush!" said James. "We don't want the mourners to know about the police presence here."

"I'm sure yours is a familiar face to many of the people from St Giles by now," said Hugo with a puzzled expression.

"Yes, I suppose it is, but I'm trying to remain inconspicuous. I don't wish to alarm anyone."

"It's because he's planning to arrest someone here," Edgar chipped in. "That's the reason for all the hugger-mugger."

"Edgar!" snapped James. "No one is supposed to know!"

"Please don't worry, Inspector Blakely, your secret's safe with us," said Hugo. "Who's the suspect?"

"I'm not at liberty to say."

"Winston Nicholls," said Edgar.

"Shush!"

"It's not going to be such an enormous secret when he's arrested, is it?" retorted Edgar.

"Can you be sworn to secrecy, gentlemen?" James asked the missionaries.

"Yes, of course," replied David.

"Thank you. Please don't mention this to anyone else

here. If he gets wind of what's happening he'll likely skedaddle again."

"You have our word," said Hugo.

"Good mornin', Miss Green," said a man passing behind us, and I instantly recognised his Irish accent.

"Mr O'Donoghue. How are you?"

"As well as can be, thank you." He glanced at James and the missionaries before swiftly moving on.

"It seems Reuben O'Donoghue is in no mood to be amicable this morning," said Hugo.

We boarded the train and took our seats in a second-class compartment. James and Edgar sat side-by-side, while I sat in the seat opposite them.

"It seems I'm a wonder at disguise," said Edgar. "Neither of those missionaries recognised me! I came across them while I was undercover in St Giles."

"You were rather filthy-looking. I didn't even recognise you when you were sitting at your own desk," I said.

"It's a shame the missionaries now know why we're here," said James. "I didn't want anyone else knowing of our plans."

"You can trust the missionaries. They helped me out of a tight spot," I said.

"When?" asked James. "What happened?"

"Nothing much. It was a while ago now."

I felt his concerned eyes on me as two elderly women in wide black dresses and long veils entered the compartment. They were joined by a thin man, who was suffering from a persistent cough.

"Seeing Reuben O'Donoghue just then has reminded me of something," I said. "A few weeks ago, I saw him arguing with a man who I'm sure was Albert Turner."

"What were they arguing about?" asked James.

"I don't know. Mr Turner said something about how he was trying to help a woman and then he and Reuben saw us and they both scarpered. I don't think they wanted anyone to overhear them."

"I believe he's a rather argumentative man," said Edgar. "When I was undercover in St Giles, I saw him arguing with one of the missionaries. That Hawkins chap, I think it was. He's the older, shorter one, isn't he?"

"Why would he argue with a missionary?"

"Perhaps arguing with people is a favourite pastime of his."

"It's funny," I said, "because Reuben has never struck me as argumentative. I've heard stories of him having a violent manner, but he's always been perfectly civil to me."

"You're a lady," said Edgar. "That's why he behaves differently towards you."

"Do you know what caused the argument between Reuben and Hugo Hawkins?" James asked Edgar.

"I overheard them talking about money. Reuben seemed to be accusing the missionary of some sort of financial misdemeanour. I saw them when I was leaving The Three Feathers one evening and would have hung about to listen in, but I was accompanied by a large, one-legged soldier who had unfortunately befriended me for the evening."

The carriage jolted as the train pulled out of the station, a trail of steam and smoke billowed past the window.

"So when do we go looking for this Winston chap?" asked Edgar, rubbing his hands together in expectation.

"I suppose we should do it now," said James.

"Do you know what he looks like, Edgar?" I asked.

"That's a very good question, Miss Green. No, I don't. I've never clapped eyes on the fellow."

We walked along the corridor stealing careful glances into each compartment, I looked out for Martha in her wide-brimmed hat in the hope that Winston would be seated with her. Groups of passengers dressed entirely in black stared back at us.

"We look as though we're up to no good," I said to James.

"We do rather, don't we? Still, this has to be done. As soon as we have eyes on him I shall wave my handkerchief from the window."

In the last compartment, I spotted a familiar-looking man in a black top hat. Perhaps he sensed that I was looking at him, because he quickly lifted his head and returned my gaze.

It was Ed Keller.

The breath seemed to leave my chest for a moment. He gave me a wink and I hurriedly looked away, my mouth suddenly dry.

"Well that's one traverse done with no sign of Nicholls or his mother," said James. "Are you all right, Penny? You look rather pale."

"I'm fine."

"Right. Let's try again." We walked back along the corridor, rocked by the motion of the train as we went. As I looked into each compartment, I saw that we were attracting stony glances and someone pulled a curtain across the window of his compartment so that we couldn't see inside.

"This Nicholls chap is not in second-class, is he?" said Edgar once we had checked each compartment a second time.

"They must be in third-class," I added.

We stood at the end of the carriage and James removed his hat, pulled a window down and pushed his head out to look around.

"No handkerchiefs from the other carriages," he said once he had pulled his head back in. He smoothed his ruffled hair.

"You want to be careful sticking your bonce out like that,"

said Edgar. "A passing train or obstacle could take a chap's head clean off."

"The lack of handkerchiefs concerns me," said James, replacing his hat. "I'd have thought the other officers would have had plenty of time to check their carriages by now. Where's the chap got to? We saw him at Cemetery Station."

"I'll go through second-class again," I said.

I walked up and down the carriage, averting my eyes from Ed Keller's compartment and wishing that James wouldn't keep pushing his head out of the window to look for handkerchiefs. Edgar's warning had given me cause for concern.

The countryside raced past the windows and the quantity of green unsettled my eyes. I had become so accustomed to the grey of London that I had almost forgotten what rolling fields looked like. After a while, I felt rather knowledgeable about the occupants of each compartment, who no doubt thought I had lost my mind as I persisted in repeatedly walking along the corridor.

"He's not here," I said.

James sighed. "And he's not in the other carriages either. There's only one other place that I can think of."

"The coffin carriage?" asked Edgar.

James responded with a sombre nod.

CHAPTER 42

"W e'll have to wait until the train arrives at Brookwood Cemetery," said Edgar.

"But that's when the coffin's removed from the carriage. We can't simply dive in there just before the ceremony takes place," replied James. "The carriage will have to be searched before then."

"It can't be," I said. "You can only get in there once the train has stopped. And if Winston Nicholls is in there, he'll have time to escape. Besides, I don't believe he can be in there. How could he have got inside it?"

"Perhaps he slipped in unnoticed at Cemetery Station," replied James. "We can't have him finding the opportunity to escape once we arrive at Brookwood. I can get inside the coffin carriage while the train is moving. All I have to do is hope that the doors at the end of each carriage are unlocked."

"You can't, James! It's not safe! You'd have to jump over the couplings while the train is moving. Just one lurch of the train and you'd be thrown down onto the track! Please don't attempt it," I implored.

"And how can you be sure that there'll even be a door at

the end of each carriage? Sometimes they're just dead ends," added Edgar.

"This carriage has a door at either end," said James walking towards the one nearest us. "All I need to do is hope that third-class has the same."

"But the funeral carriage won't, surely?" said Edgar.

"There's only one way for me to find out."

"James, you'll get yourself killed!" I entreated. "This is nonsense, Winston Nicholls is not in the coffin carriage."

"Then where is he?" asked James. He took off his bowler hat and gave it to me. "I think the wind will take this as soon as I leave the carriage. Would you mind looking after it for me?"

"But James!" I clasped his hat in my hands.

"Penny, I've been on this train before." He rested his hand reassuringly on my arm. "I know that it will slow down to crawling pace when we near the cemetery, and we're almost there. Please don't worry."

He turned and tried the handle of the door at the end of the carriage. To my great disappointment, it opened. The noise of wind and the rattle of the wheels filled my ears.

"Go careful, old chap," said Edgar.

"See you in Brookwood," said James.

He stepped through the door, gave me a brief smile and then closed it behind him. The carriage fell silent.

"Edgar, I feel faint."

I staggered back against the side of the carriage and he held my arm as I slowly sank to the floor.

"Why would he risk his life?" I said in a weak voice.

"He's desperate to catch his man. I didn't realise the schoolboy inspector could be such a daredevil."

Within minutes, the train began to slow down. I stood by the window, gripping James' hat in my hands and praying that he would return safely. The train stopped at Brookwood

Station and there was a brief pause before we continued slowly down the branch line, which ran through the cemetery. A flat expanse of green peppered with trees and headstones stretched out on either side of us. I lowered the window and peered out with one hand resting on my hat to keep it in place.

"You shouldn't be doing that, Miss Green!" scolded Edgar.

I looked ahead at the first-class carriage and the engine, and then back towards the third-class and coffin carriages behind us.

"There's no sign of him," I said, bringing my head back inside the carriage. "Surely we must almost be there? The train is moving so slowly."

Waiting to find out what had happened to James was quite intolerable.

We seemed to be travelling only marginally faster than walking pace. I looked down at the lawn beside the tracks and a thought sprang to mind. I pushed the window down so that I could reach the handle on the other side of the door.

"Miss Green," Edgar said with a warning tone to his voice. "What are you doing?"

"Please can you look after James' hat?" I handed him the bowler. "And my bag."

"Miss Green, you're as foolhardy as the inspector! Don't be getting any ideas about leaping from this train before it reaches the station!"

"I want to see if James is all right. And if he's got into the coffin carriage and found Nicholls, I'll be ready to help as soon as the train stops."

"There's no need! You're sure to break your limbs doing such a thing!"

"Please can you close the door after me?" I put one hand on my hat, checked that the ground was clear ahead of me and pushed down on the handle. The door swung open and I leapt forward, hoping to hit the ground at running pace.

It turned out to be a faster pace than I could match. I immediately stumbled and rolled several times over on the grass. The surprise took my breath away and my black skirts and petticoats billowed out and tumbled around me. I felt my spectacles fly off. As I willed myself to stop, I caught a glimpse of Edgar leaning out of the open door, calling out to me. The train rumbled past as I lay still, the air knocked from my chest. People stared open-mouthed from the windows and then I saw another face staring at me, this time from the gap between third-class and the coffin carriage.

"James!" My breath had returned. "James!"

I stumbled to my feet as the train rolled on ahead of me. James was clinging to the door at the end of third-class and I surmised that there was no door leading into the coffin carriage. I picked up my hat and cracked spectacles and ran after the train. I could see a building and platform ahead of me and, as the train slowed down, I was able to match its speed by lifting my skirts and running as swiftly as my attire allowed. The heels of my boots dug into the grass and I knew that it wouldn't be long before my corset began to restrict my breathing.

"Penny!"

James' voice was almost lost amid the noise of the train. He was shouting something to me, but I couldn't hear what it was. I was fatigued from running but relieved that James hadn't yet perished between the carriages. It looked to me as though he would be stuck where he was until the train came to a halt.

The train reached the platform and I climbed up onto it, my lungs almost fit to burst. My hair had lost most of its pins and fallen down around my shoulders. As the train slowed to a standstill, James jumped out onto the platform and almost fell over, as I had done.

"Penny!" he said breathlessly. "It turns out there's no way into that coffin carriage from third-class, and I couldn't get back into the third-class carriage. The door seemed to be stuck!"

He looked down at the spectacles in my hand. "Oh dear! Your glasses are broken."

"They can be repaired. I'm so pleased to see that you are safe," I said.

His eyes moved between my long, unpinned hair and my face, and I realised that he hadn't seen me without my spectacles on many occasions.

"You took quite a tumble," he said softly.

"I couldn't bear the wait to find out whether you were safe."

We held each other's gaze.

"I'm sorry," I said, "I'm in a complete mess. I need to smarten myself up. And Edgar's got your hat, by the way."

I glanced over James' shoulder and saw someone walking towards us.

"We're in trouble," I said, watching the scowling station master as he approached us.

"I'm Inspector Blakely of Scotland Yard!" James announced before the station master could reach us. "I'm here on police business. I believe there to be a fugitive inside that coffin carriage."

I hoped he was right, otherwise our actions would seem rather foolish.

A door in the coffin carriage opened and a railway man stepped out. James pushed past him and clambered inside. Meanwhile, several men gathered close by and I realised they were the undercover constables. The other mourners disembarked from the train and made their way into the refreshment room on the platform. I hoped they would be undisturbed by the arrest of Nicholls.

Two men in dark suits began unbolting the main doors of the carriage to bring the coffin out.

"Stop that man!" cried James.

Someone had jumped down from the door by which James had entered. Winston Nicholls had been flushed out. He paused on the platform, glanced at the crowd by the refreshment rooms, then took off in the opposite direction along the platform towards the open green of the cemetery.

James and the constables followed and I was impressed to see the missionaries, Hugo and David, join them. As I watched the men recede, I became aware of another man stepping out of the coffin carriage. He was unmistakable in his pork pie hat.

It was Tom Clifford.

He looked at me and then ran towards the refreshment room.

"Stop!" I called out.

I chased after him and managed to grab at the tail of his jacket. He spun round angrily and tried to pull away.

"What on earth do you think you're doing, Miss Green? And why do you look like some sort of harpy?"

"What are you doing consorting with a criminal?"

"Get off my jacket!"

"Not until you tell me what you're up to!"

I hung on as tightly as I possibly could.

"In a stew, Miss Green?" said a voice that made my skin crawl.

Ed Keller grabbed Tom by the arm.

"We'll 'old 'im 'ere till the coppers get back with 'is mate, shall we? What allurin' 'air yer 'ave, Miss Green."

Tom tried to pull his arm away from Ed, but he didn't try

too hard. By the look in the reporter's eye, he also was fearful of the Earl.

I stepped back from Ed Keller and tried to find the loose pins in my hair. "What were you doing in the coffin carriage with Winston Nicholls, Tom?" I asked as I tidied my hair.

"None of your business," said Tom. "And I'm not getting arrested because I've done nothing wrong!"

Despite James' wish to not disturb the mourners, a crowd had gathered on the platform to watch the proceedings. Among them I could see Martha's large hat, but I didn't dare catch her eye.

We didn't have long to wait before James returned with the constables, the missionaries and a slump-shouldered Winston Nicholls wearing handcuffs.

"Well done, Penny," said James breathlessly. There were beads of perspiration on his forehead. "I didn't expect to find the two of them in there!"

"You should thank Ed as well," I said reluctantly.

"Glad I could be of hassistance," said Ed, handing Tom into James's custody before striding off.

"Well done for catching hold of Winston," I said to James.

"I've got David Meares to thank for that. Turns out he's quite accomplished at running," said James. "He tackled him to the ground!"

"I'm very proud of him," said Hugo with a wide smile.

A large woman in a flowing black dress and an elaborate hat and veil approached us. "Do you think we can proceed with my husband's funeral now please, Inspector?"

"Of course, Mrs Turner. Please accept my deepest regrets and most sincere condolences."

CHAPTER 43

"This was all carefully planned, of course! Your reporters conspired with Scotland Yard to have my man arrested! This is how you react to falling circulation numbers, is it?" barked Charles Cropper, editor of *The Holborn Gazette*. He was a tall, hairless man with gold-rimmed spectacles and his long face was red with anger.

"Our circulation isn't falling!" Mr Sherman said defensively.

"Well ours had been nicely increasing until your reporters had mine arrested!"

"Mr Cropper, you will need to take this up with the Yard," Mr Sherman replied.

"Oh, I will, don't you worry about that. But this is a set-up and I am going to make sure the entire world knows about it!"

"Mr Cropper, may I ask you to pause for one moment and explain what exactly your reporter was doing in the coffin carriage with a murderer?"

"He was under the impression that Mr Nicholls was a private detective and the two had been working closely together as you're well aware. Nicholls told him they had to hide in the carriage because the police were trying to arrest him. It is only now that I, and Mr Clifford, have realised that Nicholls himself was the killer and was attending the funeral of his victim for some macabre reason only he can account for."

"It's an extremely odd thing to do," said Mr Sherman.

'I accept it was. But there was no need for my man to be arrested too! I blame your staff."

"The man brought it upon himself."

"He did not!"

"He was assisting Mr Nicholls in evading arrest," I said.

Mr Cropper spun round and glared at me. "You keep out of this!"

"I'm unable to, I'm afraid. You seem to think I had something to do with it," I replied.

Mr Cropper turned back to face Mr Sherman. "The relationship your woman reporter has with that deplorable Blakely character at Scotland Yard is inappropriate! He has given her information about the case which should not be shared outside the police force. You're no doubt aware that Scotland Yard has a stringent code on how the police conduct themselves with members of the press? I will certainly be reminding the Commissioner about it and requesting that both are dismissed from their posts!"

"Let's not forget that the St Giles killer has now been caught," said Edgar. "Surely you should feel relieved that Londoners can now sleep safely in their beds."

"That's enough from you!" shouted Mr Cropper. "You started all this by stealing my reporter's story!"

"It was only about a man selling his fat wife's corpse."

"It doesn't matter what it was about! You stole it! The *Morning Express* has flouted every rule of journalism in the book!"

"That is going a step rather too far," said Mr Sherman.

"You don't deserve to be in business!"

"Mr Cropper, have you asked yourself what your best reporter was doing consorting with a killer?"

"He didn't know the man was a killer, did he?"

"Didn't he?"

"No! Winston Nicholls had proved himself to be a very useful source to my man."

"There's no doubt he had more knowledge about the murders than anyone else."

"Exactly! And Clifford wasn't getting much from the Yard, was he? Everything Blakely knew was being passed on to your woman reporter here."

"My involvement began due to a personal incident," I said. "The boy who stole my bag was one of Winston Nicholls' victims."

"That must have been set up as well! It was all planned!"

"How?" I asked incredulously.

"You have ways and means!" He pointed at me. "You're a woman. Women are manipulative creatures."

Mr Sherman got to his feet and frowned so hard that his bushy eyebrows met.

"Mr Cropper, you will not stand in my office and insult my staff."

"I speak only the truth!"

"Tom Clifford is the biggest toad there is," Edgar chipped in.

"There you go, you see?" Cropper pointed at Edgar this time. "Another example of how unprofessional your journalists are!"

"Mr Fish, let's not resort to name-calling," said Mr Sherman, "it doesn't help our cause. Mr Cropper, I've heard all you have to say. Now, will you please leave my office?"

"Your newspaper is on the way out, Sherman! It's had its

day. Your readers will desert you when they hear of the manner in which your reporters conduct themselves."

"Mr Cropper, please go and discuss Clifford's arrest with Scotland Yard. My reporters and I have work to do."

"Oh, I will all right. Blakely and Green will never work again. I shall see to that!"

As Mr Cropper marched out of the office, Mr Sherman sighed and sank his head down into his hands.

"Get out of here, you two, and stay out of trouble. I don't want to hear any more tales of you jumping out of funeral trains, Miss Green. It's unbecoming of a lady, and quite frankly it's embarrassing. I want a report from you as soon as Mr Nicholls appears in front of the magistrates. Fish, I want you back on the General Gordon story again. He's expected in Khartoum any day now."

He dismissed us with a wave of his hand.

"That was a bit rough from Cropper," muttered Edgar as we returned to the newsroom. "Cropper's going to come a cropper himself if he carries on in that manner!"

He laughed, but I struggled to raise a smile. I hadn't been able to stop thinking about the moment at Brookwood Cemetery when Martha had realised that her son was under arrest. She had become unsteady on her feet and had been taken into the refreshment room for a reviving brandy. I felt worried for her; the news had come as a severe blow. She had believed that her son was innocent and I couldn't imagine how she must be feeling now that he had been taken into custody. I prayed that Martha wouldn't be targeted by others because her son was a murderer.

I sought the quiet of the reading room that afternoon. I should have felt happy that the St Giles killer had been caught, but there were too many unanswered questions for me to be fully content that Winston was the murderer.

What motive did he have for killing each of the victims? Had he really been the man in the mask?

"How is the book progressing, Miss Green?"

I looked up to see Mr Edwards smiling down at me. He pushed his sandy hair back out of his eyes.

"It's progressing rather slowly. I've been somewhat busy in recent days."

"Of course! I expect you've been reporting on these terrible murders. Isn't it wonderful news that the man has finally been captured?"

"It is indeed."

"And you're wearing new spectacles, I see."

"Oh, these are old things. I broke my usual pair."

"Oh no! How did that happen?"

I was reluctant to tell him that I had jumped from a moving train. Mr Edwards seemed a sensible type who would be shocked by unladylike behaviour.

"I sat on them!"

"Whoops!" He chuckled. "I have done a similar thing myself. Fragile things aren't they, spectacles? Now, with the St Giles murderer caught, you'll have more time to work on your father's book, no doubt."

"I suppose I will, yes."

"I'm looking forward to reading all about your father."

I felt a knot in my stomach. "Oh, it'll be some time yet before it's published."

"He was clearly a very interesting man. I remember you telling me that some of the specimens he collected are on display in the Natural History department in South Kensington. I visited them last week."

"Did you really?"

"Yes. And he was quite an artist as well, wasn't he? What

beautiful sketches and paintings he made of the plants he had collected. Did you ever watch him while he was painting?"

"Once or twice. If truth be told, he was away rather a lot."

"He must have spent a lot of time travelling, but it was all truly worthwhile. If it hadn't been for him, we would have no knowledge of the beautiful plants he brought back to England."

"He made mistakes as well. He didn't do everything perfectly."

I still hadn't been able to look at Father's diaries since I had read his account of the massacre.

"I'm quite sure he didn't do everything perfectly. No one's perfect, are they?" said Mr Edwards.

"No, they're not."

"Except you, Miss Green."

"Me?"

He gave me a swift bow and walked quickly away.

I looked back at the book in front of me, but the words seemed to swim on the page and a wave of bashfulness washed over me.

CHAPTER 44

"**M**artha!" I called up to her window.

No washing hung from the ropes strung across the courtyard and the washtub remained empty.

"Martha!"

"She ain't comin'," said Susan, who was stacking up a pile of sorry-looking furs by the privies.

"Have you seen her recently?" I asked.

"She ain't talkin' to no one."

"Martha! Can you hear me?" I called out again.

A woman's face appeared at the window below Martha's.

"Shut yer noise!"

"I'm sorry, I'm looking for Martha. Is she here?"

A man appeared at the woman's shoulder and stared down at me.

"Can you tell Martha that Penny Green came looking for her? I want her to know that I'm thinking of her. Will you tell her for me?"

There was no reply from the couple. I watched Martha's window for a moment longer and fancied that I saw one of the rags move slightly, but perhaps it had been nothing more than a draught.

❦

"There you go, you see. You have a modicum of speed now! I told you it would be better on a hill."

Eliza jogged along the pavement, her three eldest children running alongside her.

"Go faster, Auntie Penelope!" they shouted.

Eliza's bicycle juddered over the bumps on Kensington Park Road as I perched uncomfortably on a small seat between one large wheel and two smaller wheels, each hand clutching tightly to a steering grip. It was probably unsafe to travel at this speed in the fog, and my fears were confirmed when I suddenly noticed a carriage on the road ahead.

"How do you stop it?" I called out.

"No need to stop! You can move past the carriage without any problems!" said Eliza.

"But I want to stop!"

"Then slow your pedalling."

The pedals seemed to be moving of their own accord and there was enough momentum in them to resist any attempt on the part of my feet to stop their motion. Fortunately, I was wearing one of Eliza's divided skirts as my knees see-sawed up and down.

"Slow your pedalling!" said Eliza again, growing breathless as her pace quickened.

"I'm trying!"

The rear of the carriage was drawing ever closer.

"Ellie, it's not stopping!"

The carriage was almost upon me and its wheel axle was level with my head. I pictured a dreadful decapitation as Eliza shouted at me.

"Turn to the right!" she cried.

I twisted the steering grips to the right with all the strength I could muster and the bicycle swerved to one side of the carriage. I almost lurched into the spinning spokes of the large wheel to my left.

"Help!" I cried as the bicycle veered across the road and into the path of a man trotting up the road on a large horse. It reared up in fright and the bicycle hit the kerb. There was nothing I could do as I was launched forward onto the pavement.

"Good gracious!" exclaimed a woman close by as the paving stones came up to meet me. I narrowly avoided hitting the ground with my chin as my hands and arms absorbed the main impact of the fall.

"That machine shouldn't be allowed on the road!" shouted the horseman, trying to calm his steed.

Within a few moments, Eliza and her children had gathered around me.

"Penelope, you haven't damaged your arm again, have you?"

"No, Ellie, I'm fine, thank you. Just a few bruises." I got up and dusted myself off. "What fun! It's about time I bought myself one of these marvellous contraptions."

I recovered from the excitement of the bicycle ride with a cup of tea back in Eliza's drawing room.

"Mother's disappointed that she didn't get to see her grandchildren," said my sister. "We were all packed and ready to depart for Derbyshire the following day when the news spread that the killer had been arrested. Excellent work on the part of your inspector!"

"I think everyone's extremely relieved."

"Of course they are! It was a terribly worrying business. Has James worked out why the man chose to murder so many people?"

"The theory is that he argued with each of them over one thing or another, and he carried out the murders as some form of revenge. In fact, the more I think about Winston Nicholls the more I struggle to understand what his real motive for murder might be. If the reason stemmed from an argument, I can think of plenty of people in St Giles who have fallen out with one another. Reuben O'Donoghue, for example. He helped me when Jack took my bag, but I saw him arguing with Mr Turner and Edgar told me that he had also argued with the missionary Hugo Hawkins. And even though he had an alibi at the time of Jack's murder, there is still a chance that he could have attacked the boy and persuaded someone to lie for him. He's a charming man, but by all accounts he's capable of violence. The more I think about it, the more I am persuaded that he's a more likely suspect than Winston Nicholls."

"No, don't say that!" said Eliza, her eyes wide. "I can't bear to think that the killer may still be out there!"

"I'm probably overthinking it a little. Nicholls is probably the right man," I said hurriedly, feeling the need to reassure her.

"There's rather a lot of chatter coming from downstairs. Cook has a loud voice," said Eliza.

She got up and rang the bell for the maid.

"Did I tell you, Penelope, that my neighbour Mrs Kershaw attended Mr Turner's funeral and said that it was a scene of chaos with the two men getting arrested just before the ceremony!"

"It can't have been pleasant for Mr Turner's widow, and Winston's mother Martha is particularly upset."

"She would be, wouldn't she? Nobody wants their son to be going around murdering people. It must be extremely difficult to accept."

"How did your neighbour know Mr Turner?"

"She's a philanthropist and so was he, by all accounts. He took a keen interest in helping fallen women in the slums."

"Yes, I heard that his interests lay in that area."

"Where has the maid got to? They're not usually chattering like this. Do help yourself to another cake. Have you finished reading all of Father's papers yet?"

"Not quite. I'm worried about what else I might discover about him."

"I shouldn't think there is anything else upsetting in there. You must remind yourself of the circumstances in which he found himself. It was perhaps the only option left open to him when the natives had been firing arrows at him day after day."

"He could have left and gone somewhere else."

"Perhaps, but he could hardly have got out of there quickly when the only means of transport was either by canoe, by mule or on foot. You forget how spoilt we are with our roads and railways."

I sighed. "I suppose I shall return to the work before long. Although my research in the reading room will be rather tricky from this point onwards as the clerk who was helping me paid me a compliment and now the situation between us feels rather awkward."

"He propositioned you in the reading room?" Eliza's cup stalled between her saucer and mouth.

"Not quite. It was merely a small compliment, and then he ran off afterwards as if he were embarrassed."

"You must be extremely flattered, Penelope. It has been a long time since anyone propositioned me."

"You should come and work in the reading room with me."

"I should! And what is the reading room clerk like?"

"He's quite pleasant."

"Perhaps you should find the opportunity to get to know

him a little better. He may even distract you from the inspector!"

"I don't require any distractions from Inspector Blakely. He is now very busy preparing for the trial of a notorious murderer and I am very busy with my work. In fact, I haven't seen him for some time. About four days, in fact."

Eliza laughed. "Of course! So long now that you've probably almost forgotten about him."

The maid came into the room.

"Ah, there you are Florrie. What's all the noise in aid of? Has something happened with Cook?"

The girl fidgeted with her apron.

"It's terrible news again, Mrs Billington-Grieg. There's been another murder in St Giles' Rookery."

CHAPTER 45

Tower Street was filled with people and fog. I battled my way through the crowd and found myself at a junction with a narrow street.

"What's this place called?" I asked a girl in a shabby shawl.

"Lumber Court."

"Press!" I called out. "Let me through please!" I squeezed along the street, which was a row of tumbledown rag shops and second-hand furniture stores. Old garments had been hung outside the windows and piled up on lop-sided tables. I made my way to the first constable I could see and introduced myself as a reporter.

"Who's the victim?" I asked.

"Mr O'Donoghue. He was found inside his shop with his throat cut."

"Reuben?"

I stared at the constable's young face, unable to believe what he had just told me.

"Reuben O'Donoghue? The tall Irishman?"

"You knew him?"

"Yes." For a moment, the noise of the crowd receded. I stood rooted to the spot as people bustled around me.

"*How?*" I said to myself.

The door of a shop opened nearby and out stepped Chief Inspector Basil Cullen, James' superior at Scotland Yard.

"Inspector Cullen!" I called out.

"Miss Green." He gave me a solemn nod.

He was a tall, wide man with a thick grey moustache and a bulbous nose. The two of us had disagreed in the past, most recently during the Lizzie Dixie case.

"Inspector Blakely is delayed," he added, pre-empting my question.

"That's unlike James."

I took my notebook and pencil from my bag and wondered what could have happened to him.

Did he know yet that Reuben had been murdered?

A reporter from the *News of the World* joined us.

"What can you tell us, Inspector?" he barked.

"It's an exact copy of the pawnbroker's murder," said Cullen. "Chloroform has been used once again. We found a rag soaked in it next to Reuben's body. He was a large man, and our killer seems to have lain in wait for him and used chloroform to subdue him before cutting his throat."

I felt nauseous.

"The police surgeon thinks the time of death was at about eight o'clock yesterday evening," continued Cullen. "The shopkeepers in Lumber Court became aware that something was wrong when Mr O'Donoghue failed to open his shop this morning. We gained entry to the premises at two o'clock this afternoon. E Division is speaking to neighbouring shop-keepers and people who were in the area at the time."

"So Winston Nicholls is innocent?" asked the reporter.

"It is too early to speculate."

I removed my gloves, took down some notes and tried to

think of more questions to ask Cullen while I had his attention. My mind felt exhausted as I tried to accept what had
happened.

*Why Reuben? And if neither he nor Winston Nicholls was the
murderer, then who was?*

"Who do you think Adam de Vries is, Inspector Cullen?
How is he getting away with this?" I asked.

"If I knew that I wouldn't be standing here now," the
inspector retorted with an exasperated sigh.

"We've received more witness accounts describing the
masked man," said Inspector Fenton, who had just arrived
with Inspector Pilkington.

"He's got nothing to do with it!" came an irate shout from
someone behind me.

I turned to see the angry face of a reporter from
The Times.

"The masked man is a figment of the imagination!" he
bellowed. "It's about time you stopped looking for him and
did something useful! How many more murders can we
endure? If the Home Secretary has an ounce of common
sense, he'll have every detective in Scotland Yard summarily
dismissed! The investigation into this case has been an act of
folly from start to finish!"

"What are you actually doing to catch this killer, Inspector?" called out the reporter from the *News of the World*.

I put my notebook in my bag and slipped away to avoid
the shouting.

I had almost battled my way out of Lumber Court when I
heard someone calling my name. Looking around me, I
caught sight of James in his bowler hat. I stayed where I was
as he pushed past people to reach me. His suit and tie
were black.

"How are you, Penny?"

"Not very well. Did you know that it's Reuben this time?"

Something about the caring glance James gave me caused the tears to spill down my cheeks. Flustered, I rummaged about in my bag for a handkerchief, but I could barely see a thing through my tears.

"Here, have mine," said James, taking off his gloves and handing me a pale blue silk handkerchief. "I brought a spare with me."

I thanked him, removed my spectacles and wiped my face. The handkerchief was scented with his cologne.

"You're wearing black," I said. "You look like you've been to another funeral."

"I have. My grandfather's."

"Oh dear." Fresh tears sprung into my eyes. "I'm so sorry, James."

He took my hand gently in his. "Please don't be sad, Penny. He led a long and happy life. He was prepared for his death and, although his passing has left us desolate, we were also prepared for it, which is far more than can be said for the poor unfortunate souls who have had their lives taken by this dreadful killer."

"I've just spoken to Cullen. He's at the shop with Fenton and Pilkington."

"Well, it sounds as though there are enough detectives there for the time being. Let's get out of this crowd and find a more peaceful spot where we can give this terrible business some thought."

He let go of my hand and I followed him out of Lumber Court and Tower Street. We crossed the road and came to a standstill outside Aldridge's Horse Bazaar.

"I was beginning to believe that Reuben was the murderer," I said as we watched a gingerbread seller making a brisk trade among the onlookers. "People had spoken of him being behind the murders for so long. And the more thought I gave to Nicholls, the more I struggled to understand what his motive might have been."

"I've had a difficult time trying to gather evidence for Nicholls' trial."

"But it wasn't Reuben, was it? It must be Ed Keller, mustn't it?"

James took a folded piece of paper from his pocket and gave it to me.

"This arrived at the Yard yesterday," he said, "but it sat unnoticed for the rest of the day. Nobody was on the lookout for any more letters as we thought we already had our man."

I unfolded the letter and read the now familiar handwriting.

Poor Mr Turner. Couldn't his loved ones have been allowed to grieve in peace? For all your hasty work, inspector, it seems you have the wrong man. Wasn't Mr O'Donoghue also a suspect once? I think another visit to St Giles is in order.

Adam D.V.

"Who *is* he?" I heard anger in my voice.

"I don't think Ed Keller is literate enough to write letters like these. We're looking for an educated man and I think it's time we visited Hugo Hawkins," said James. "An uneasy glance passed between him and Reuben O'Donoghue at Mr Turner's funeral. Did you notice it when you said a brief hello to Reuben? You were the only person among us whom he greeted. He glared at me and the look he gave Hawkins was one of utter contempt."

CHAPTER 46

Away from Lumber Court, the foggy streets were eerily quiet as James and I walked toward the chapel on Neal Street. We saw constables making enquiries at doors, but few other people were milling about.

"Hugo can't be the murderer, can he? I can't imagine him murdering anyone," I said.

"Because he's a missionary?"

"It's partly that, I suppose. But he helps people around here. He serves them soup on a cold day and he saved me from trouble once."

"You mentioned that on the funeral train, Penny, but you didn't elaborate. In what way did he help?"

"It's nothing."

"I don't believe it's nothing, because you have mentioned it twice now. What happened?"

"It was when I went to see Ed Keller. He tried to attack me."

James stopped and stared at me. "What did he do?"

"I don't like to dwell on the details."

"Did he hurt you?"

"No, I was completely unharmed, and that was because the missionaries heard me shout out and came to rescue me."

"I'll have him arrested again."

"There's no need. It was entirely my fault. I shouldn't have put myself at risk like that."

"It's not your fault! Have you been blaming yourself ever since the incident happened?"

"No."

"You have, haven't you?" James' eyes searched mine.

"Perhaps I have."

"I'll get him once we've finished with Hugo. Presumably there were witnesses?"

"Yes, the missionaries. And all those boys he has down there at King's Head Yard."

"I could wring his neck," he said through clenched teeth.

"Shall we go and speak to Hugo now?"

We walked on and reached the door of the chapel a few moments later.

"I picked up my revolver on the way here," said James, patting where it sat in the holster beneath his overcoat and jacket.

He pulled open the door of the chapel and we stepped into the candlelit gloom. Tendrils of fog had found their way inside and snaked around the legs of the chairs arranged neatly before the altar.

"There's no one here," I whispered.

"Hello!" James called out. "Mr Hawkins?"

The silence made me uneasy. Having visited the place before, I had grown accustomed to being greeted by the missionaries and seeing other people here. It was the first time I had seen the chapel empty.

"I suppose they're all in Lumber Court," I said, feeling a growing sense of unease.

"I think there's someone over there," said James.

"Where?" My breathing was quick and shallow.

"He's sitting in front of the altar."

I looked in the direction James was pointing toward and saw the figure of a man seated in one of the chairs.

"If there's someone here, why didn't he answer us?"

James withdrew his revolver from its holster and together we walked down the aisle toward the altar. The figure in the chair didn't stir. He was wearing a dark hat and dark clothing.

"Hello?" James said softly as we drew level with him.

The man turned his head slowly towards us.

"Hugo?"

The missionary gave us a weak smile.

"I wondered when you'd come." He glanced at the revolver in James' hand. "There's no need for the gun, Inspector. I won't do you any harm."

I could see that James was considering whether to put the revolver back into its holster. He decided to keep it in his hand.

"Why didn't you answer us, Hugo?" I asked. "We called out for you when we came in."

"Did you? I didn't hear you." His close-set eyes were languorous and his head nodded slightly, as if he were sleepy.

"What do you know about Reuben O'Donoghue?" James asked.

"I know he thinks I stole some money."

"And did you?"

"No, of course not."

"You do realise that Reuben is dead?"

"Is he? Oh dear."

He turned to look at the altar, an odd half-smile lit up by the flickering candles. His lack of remorse surprised me.

"He's not usually like this," I whispered to James. "Perhaps he's drunk, or maybe he's taken opium."

"It's all rather strange," he whispered to me.

Then he spoke to Hugo. "Were you in Lumber Court last night, Mr Hawkins?"

The missionary looked up at us again, sleepy-eyed. "No."

Then he winced slightly and drew a hand up to his chest. I looked down at his hand and had to stifle a shriek.

"Look!" I hissed. "Look at his hand!"

It was covered in blood.

Then I looked down and saw that his trouser leg appeared wet. All around his right boot was a dark pool of blood, which was slowly spreading across the stone floor.

"Mr Hawkins, you're hurt!" exclaimed James, putting his revolver back in its holster. He bent down next to him. "You're bleeding! What happened?"

"Leave me, I'm fine."

"We're not going anywhere."

James parted the missionary's jacket. His dark shirt was soaked with blood and the fabric was torn where I guessed a knife had struck him. His chest heaved with laboured, uneven breaths.

"We need something we can use as a bandage," said James.

"Have my scarf," I said, pulling it off and handing it over to him.

Hugo's eyelids were heavy as James tried to wrap my scarf around his chest. It wasn't long enough to be of any great use.

"Who did this to you, Hugo?" asked James.

"It was a mistake. He didn't mean to."

"Who?"

"He only did it because he loves me."

"I'll go and find a doctor," I said.

I ran out of the chapel and began calling at doors along Neal Street. Eventually, I found a woman who knew where a doctor lived and told me she would summon him. I ran back to the chapel, where a few people had gathered as word spread about the injured man.

Inside the chapel, James had placed his overcoat on the stone floor and helped Hugo lie down on it. My scarf was soaked with blood and I wasn't sure that a doctor would be able to do anything to save the missionary.

"Has he told you who attacked him?" I asked James.

"No, and I think we're losing him. Can you hear me, Hugo?"

The missionary's face was pale and his eyes were closed. Bubbles of blood were collecting across his lips.

"Hugo?" I knelt down by his head. "Hugo, who attacked you? Where's David? Did David hurt you?"

At the mention of David's name, the missionary opened his eyes. "He didn't mean to do it. I was trying to stop him." His voice was quiet and breathless.

"Stop him from doing what?"

"Going after Martha."

"Martha? Why Martha?" I asked, looking up at James, who was listening, wide-eyed.

"I told him there couldn't be any more."

"Did David kill Reuben?"

"Reuben accused me of stealing some money."

"And the others? Did David kill the others?"

"I tried to stop him. He kept telling me that each one was the last and I believed him every time."

"Why did he kill all those poor people? And Jack? Jack was just a boy!" I felt an intense anger rising within me. You knew and you didn't tell anyone?"

"Penny," whispered James, reaching out a hand to try and calm me. "Don't be angry with him. Now is not the time."

I looked back at Hugo. His eyes were half-closed, but they were still fixed on mine.

"Don't harm him," he whispered. "He didn't mean it. God will forgive us both."

His eyes moved from mine and stared straight ahead. His breathing slowed and his lips moved no more.

CHAPTER 47

J ames and I left the chapel as soon as the doctor arrived.

"We have to protect Martha!" I said. "We have to get to her before he does. How could Hugo and David have called themselves missionaries? David killed all these people and Hugo kept silent about it! How can they be men of God?"

"I share your anger, Penny," said James, "but we need to save it for later. David Meares cannot be allowed to get to Martha. We need to have every officer in London searching this area now! Do you have any idea where he might hide? Quick, there's someone up there!"

We ran a short distance up the road to find two constables calling at doors. James told them to alert Chief Inspector Cullen in Lumber Court and then arrange for a telegram to be sent from Bow Street station instructing all police stations and divisions to search for David Meares. The constables ran off to summon help.

I was hit by a sudden realisation. "I suppose we should have known who the murderer was long ago."

"How?"

"Adam de Vries. It's an anagram. We should have realised it. Adam de Vries is an anagram of David Meares."

"Of course." James sighed. "David Meares. A quiet, hard-working missionary whom I never suspected. He's been taunting the police and even leaving us clues, and still I didn't suspect him!"

"He can't have got far."

"Indeed, but he will be helped greatly by this thick fog."

We moved as quickly as we could in the direction of Martha's home off Queen Street, checking each doorway and courtyard as we went. We asked everyone we came across if they had seen David Meares. A few people thought they had seen a man in dark clothing, but no one could be certain that it was him.

Narrow streets led into a maze of alleyways and court-yards. The fog was close and thick, and I felt alarmed by how little we could see around us. The air felt like a damp, cold blanket on my face. Each time a figure came out of the fog I jumped. James held his revolver firmly in his right hand.

"It's safer to stay inside," he told the people we encoun-tered on the street. "There's a fugitive about, and we've almost got him."

"We'll 'elp find 'im, mister," said a group of boys who looked like they might have been part of Ed Keller's gang.

"If you see him, holler loudly and we'll find you," said James. "But be careful!"

Now and again, we encountered a constable who was also searching for the killer.

"Keep it up," James said to him encouragingly. "He won't escape us."

He lit his bullseye lantern, but its beam was quickly absorbed by the dense fog. The walls dripped with damp and the ground was wet and slippery under our feet. The thought that we could encounter David Meares with a knife at any moment was terrifying.

"Are we nearly at Queen Street?" asked James.

"I hope so. I'm finding this fog disorientating."

The murmur of a child's voice startled me. I looked around, thinking I had imagined the noise before noticing two small, huddled forms at the base of a wall. I walked over to them and bent down. Two dirty, round faces stared back at me from beneath matted hair. It was a girl of about six and a boy who was just two or three years old. They looked familiar.

"You shouldn't be out here," I said as soothingly as I could. "It's dangerous. Where are your parents?"

The girl shrugged. "Dunno."

"Where do you live?"

"'Ere." The girl looked at me, wide-eyed and wary and I recognised her as Hettie, the girl I'd seen in Nottingham Court. The little boy was Will who'd been pushed over by his brother in the argument about marbles.

"It's not safe here," I said. "You must find somewhere inside."

"Why's it not safe?"

I looked up at James, who sadly shook his head.

"We can't leave them here," I said. "They live in Nottingham Court. We need to take them home."

"Ma don't want us at 'ome," said the girl. "We ain't goin' back there."

She stood up and held out her hand to the little boy.

"C'mon, Will, let's go."

He got up and took the girl's hand.

"Where will you go?" I asked.

She shrugged and began to walk away.

"Don't go!" I called out.

The children stopped and stared at me, solemn-faced.

"Stay with us for now. You'll be safer that way."

"Penny," warned James. "We can't—"

"I'm not leaving them," I snapped as I got to my feet. "I want to keep them safe. They can't just be wandering around St Giles with this man about. If they stay with us then we know they'll be all right."

"I understand," he said resignedly. "Perhaps you can take them into the next pub we come to and wait there with them until this is over."

"You need me to help find Martha," I replied. "And I know David better than you. I might be able to talk him out of doing anything foolish."

"The man is deranged."

"I want to help you, James. I don't want to leave you facing him on your own."

James sighed. "Instead you're bringing the children along to face him too?"

"He won't hurt the children."

"How can you be sure of that?" He scowled.

"James, we don't have time to argue. Let's continue searching. I'm sure the children will behave themselves. Come on, Hettie and Will. Come with us and do what I tell you. You must do what I say. You'll do that, won't you? We'll keep you safe."

We continued on our way with the children following closely behind. Having promised to protect them, I felt even more nervous that we would encounter David. I prayed that some of the other police officers would find him before we did.

We turned a corner and heard voices, then out of the gloom came Fenton and Pilkington.

"I've never seen fog like it," said Fenton. "Blakely, what's happening? Some constable found us and said the killer's roaming around here. *Children?*"

He glared down at Hettie and Will, who shrank back from him.

"I'm looking after them," I replied. "It's not safe for them to be alone."

"It's certainly not!" said Fenton.

"We need to protect Martha Nicholls," said James. "David Meares is after her."

"David who?"

"One of the missionaries, I'll explain when we have time. Martha lives in one of the courtyards off Queen Street. You can get there faster than us as we have these children in tow."

"So I see," said Fenton.

"You two head back the way you've come. Queen Street leads off Seven Dials."

"I'm aware of that, but I'm not even sure where Seven Dials is in this fog," said Fenton. "I thought I knew this place, but it's a labyrinth."

"Ask people for directions, but be quick!"

Fenton's eyes narrowed, as if he didn't want to take orders from James.

"What are you waiting for, Fenton? We don't want another murder on our hands!"

"Very well."

"Good luck," said James.

My feet were damp and cold.

"Do you think someone could be sheltering him?" I asked.

"You think he has an accomplice?"

"I don't know. Someone could have let him into their home without realising what he has done. He's known as a missionary around here, and anyone who has recently encountered him won't yet know about his crimes."

"It's possible, isn't it?" said James.

We paused in a narrow alleyway and heard the noise from a nearby gin shop drifting up the street.

"We should ask in each pub in case anyone has seen him," I said.

"I agree. We must try everything we can think of."

"And if someone's sheltering him, he could be anywhere in this place."

I looked up at the walls around us, where a few lights could be seen flickering dimly in the windows. We asked in the gin shop whether anyone had seen David Meares. Some people didn't know who he was, while others gave conflicting reports of sightings. When James told them why we were looking for him, a mixture of panic and excitement passed through the crowd.

"I'm goin' 'ome and lockin' meself up till yer've got 'im!" said a woman with only a few teeth.

"I think you'll be safer staying here for the time being," said James. "Wait until we have him in our custody before you leave."

We stepped out of the gin shop and back into the street. Everything was still and silent outside, with many of the drinkers heeding James' warning to stay where they were. The children stayed quiet and obedient, and Will sucked his thumb.

"It won't be long now," I said to them, but I felt guilty about reassuring them when I had no idea what was to happen next.

I detected movement in the fog ahead of us and waited for the figure to emerge, assuming it was one of the constables, but no one materialised.

James put his hand on my arm and brought me to a stop. "I think I saw someone walk into that doorway," he whispered.

"I'm sure I saw someone too. Do you think he's hiding

from us?" I kept my voice as low as possible and held my breath as we slowly approached the doorway.

Was David Meares hiding just inside it?

As we drew nearer, I saw that it wasn't a doorway at all, but the entrance to a dark passageway.

"Do you know where it leads?" whispered James.

"No idea."

We peered into the passageway, but it was too dark and foggy to see much.

"Hello?" called James.

There was no reply, but we heard footsteps running away from us.

James quickly lit his lantern.

"Let's go!" he said.

We stumbled into the darkness, following the beam of the lantern. I took hold of Hettie and Will's hands, and all we could see ahead of us was a swirl of mist and fog. We heard only the echo of our own footsteps.

The passageway came to an end and opened out into a courtyard. I could just about see the high walls around us. To my right was a pair of large wooden doors, which looked like they belonged to a warehouse. There were no lights in any of the windows.

"I heard something come from this way," said James, moving off to the left.

But just at that moment, I heard footsteps from the right side of the courtyard.

"No, definitely this way," I said, moving towards the sound so that I didn't lose it.

"David?" James called out. "Is it you?"

James and I drifted apart, but I made sure that I could still see the faint beam of his lantern. Keeping Hettie and Will close to me, I made my way around the edge of the courtyard, passing the warehouse with its broken windows and a rickety staircase, which led down to a basement room.

"David?" I heard James call again. His voice was further away, but so long as I could still hear him and see his lantern I felt sure that I would be safe. If I caught sight of David I knew that James was close enough to be swiftly by my side with his gun.

The children and I reached the corner of the courtyard and then continued along the next side. I could see boards nailed over windows and a narrow gap between two buildings, which was wide enough for a man to hide in.

"David?" I said.

I heard only silence.

I turned around to see where James' light was, but it was no longer there.

"James!" I called out. "Hettie, Will, tell me if you see his light."

I looked around frantically and then I heard a clatter as if something had fallen to the ground.

"James?" I ran carefully with the children to where I thought the sound had come from, soon reaching the other side of the courtyard.

He wasn't there.

"James!" I cried out, hoping that someone would hear me.

I hadn't wanted to alarm the children but I knew they were frightened now because they were clinging to my skirts.

"There you are," I said with relief as he emerged from the fog on my right. "You had me worried for a moment!"

But when I saw the figure more clearly, I realised that it wasn't James at all but a taller man, dressed in a long dark coat and wearing a Pulcinella mask, which covered his eyes and nose.

CHAPTER 48

A cold fear gripped my stomach and the children hid behind me. The man's dimpled chin and straw-coloured moustache were familiar to me.

"David?" I asked cautiously.

I could see the gleam in his eyes through the dark holes of the mask. He was staring at me, and in his right, gloved hand was a knife.

"Have you done something to Martha? Where is she?"

David said nothing, and with a chill I realised that the vision of the man who stood in front of me would have been the last thing many of his victims had seen. I fought the urge to run and kept my feet rooted to the ground. I knew that if I ran away we might lose him again in the fog. I had to stay and hope that James would swiftly find us.

"Give me the knife, David." I slowly held out my hand in vain hope.

"No." He lifted his hand and brandished the weapon wildly.

"Run to that wall over there!" I instructed the children. Hettie and Will did as they were told and huddled together. I decided to keep David talking in the hope that it would distract him from harming anyone.

"Why are you doing this, David?" I asked. "Why are you after Martha?"

"She upset Hugo. They all did."

"You know that Hugo is dead?"

"Is he?" His voice had a slight quaver to it. "It was an accident. I became angry with him."

"I don't understand."

"He wanted me to stop, but I couldn't sleep for thinking about what they had done to him. He didn't need to tell me how much their words hurt; I could see it in his face. I saw how the rejection affected him. For every person who accepted his help, there were half a dozen who ignored or insulted him. Have you ever felt such deep hatred for someone, Miss Green, that you wished they were dead? That's how I felt about them. He told me God would forgive them, but I could see that his heart was wounded."

"But you killed him. I still don't understand."

"I didn't mean to, I was seized with rage. He forgives me, I know he does."

His mouth widened into a macabre grin, which made me shiver.

"It's been amusing, hasn't it? All this has caused quite a stir and I didn't even have to hide! I could watch the police searching for me, even at the funerals." He cackled.

"You called yourself a missionary!" I retorted. "You pretended to be helping people and they trusted you. They believed what you told them. How can you pretend to serve God and commit such evil acts?"

"The people I killed rejected Hugo. And by doing so, they rejected God."

"So killing them was a noble act, was it?"

"I believed it to be. Not one of them was worthy."

"But why Martha?"

"Hugo was a friend to her. He made sure she could attend Mrs Baxter's funeral. And Mr Turner's funeral, too. You saw how much he helped her, didn't you? But she refused to pray with Hugo. She took his help when she wanted it, but refused the most important help of all. I can't tell you how much that upset him."

"Where is she?"

He shrugged in reply and I shuddered, terrified that he might already have tracked her down. I glanced quickly around me, desperately hoping that James would emerge from the fog. The only sight which reassured me was that of Hettie and Will remaining crouched by the wall. I prayed that Fenton and Pilkington had found Martha safe and well.

"I saw what you did to Jack. It was a brutal act. Why did you do it? Jack was only a boy!"

"And a thief since he'd been old enough to walk. He stole from you, remember?"

"And I forgave him! As men of God, you and Hugo should have done the same."

David laughed and I hoped I could keep him talking.

"Why did you write the letters?" I asked.

"You're a writer, aren't you, Miss Green? You understand the power of words. Haven't you ever wished that your words could create such panic? Nothing you write will ever have the same effect as my letters. The police didn't take me seriously at first, but they soon learnt, didn't they? They had only a matter of hours to locate every possible Mr Turner in London!" he laughed. "When I killed, people had to listen to me. The power was intoxicating."

"And the reason you scattered those cards about with the name Adam de Vries on, that was about power?"

"Of course. It's all part of the same game. I heard about you and the inspector making the journey to Leinster

Gardens. Oh dear, I am sorry." He laughed again. "I thought you knew that the address wasn't real. It was supposed to be a joke!"

"A joke which only you would find funny?"

"I've always had a queer sense of humour. Do you know what I enjoyed most about the panic the murders caused? The numbers in our congregation increased threefold! I'd never seen Hugo so happy. He finally had a decent flock. That was all he had ever wanted."

"And he was complicit in what you were doing."

"I'd be lying if I said he was proud of me. He didn't like what I did, but he couldn't bear to give me up. He would never have told the police; he loved me too much. He didn't want to lose me, and he thought he could make me stop. He tried hard to make me stop and told me that each one must be my last. I couldn't stop, though. I realised that in the end. I will never be able to."

"Was Hugo afraid of you?"

"I suppose he was. Everyone is after me now, aren't they? They're going to hang me."

He lifted the knife and held it up to his throat. He grimaced and began to push the sharp edge of the knife against his neck.

I winced and turned away. "David, stop! Put the knife down! Throw it away!"

I looked back and his eyes were still glittering out at me through the mask. His mouth was fixed in a strange grin and he bared his teeth. A trickle of blood ran down his throat.

I didn't want the children to see what he was doing to himself.

"Stop!"

I took a step towards him and swung my bag at his arm. It knocked his elbow and dislodged the knife from his neck, but

I shivered when I saw the blood oozing from the gash that had opened up there.

"Drop the knife!" I shouted.

His mouth twisted into a snarl and he lunged at me with the blood-stained blade.

Two gunshots rang out and I ducked and covered my head. Then a figure came hurtling out of the fog and knocked David to the ground. The knife fell from his hand and spun across the cobbles.

I crawled forward, grabbed the handle of the knife and rolled away from David. I looked up to see James kneeling on David's chest, pinning his arms to the ground.

"James!" I cried out. "Is he dead?"

"No. I don't think any of my shots reached him, although he's losing a lot of blood from this cut on his throat."

I got to my feet and dashed over to the children, who looked up at me with large, frightened eyes.

"It's all right," I said. "You're safe now."

Finally, I could reassure them with real certainty.

The gunshots had alerted the attention of a number of people. Within moments, a small crowd had gathered around us, including many police officers. I handed the knife to one of them.

Then my legs were unable to support my weight any longer and gave way beneath me. I sat down by Hettie and Will and tried to suppress a wave of nausea.

CHAPTER 49

"The preparation for this trial will be quite straightforward," said James. "I don't think I've ever encountered a suspect before who has spoken about his crimes with such enthusiasm."

"It begs the question whether there is any need for a trial!" said Mr Sherman. "Just hang the fellow and then London can get back to business."

"At least we stopped him from getting to Martha Nicholls," I said. "I wouldn't have been able to live with myself if he'd harmed her."

"And he had a fairly nebulous reason for doing so," said James. "I think the man became so fond of bloodshed that it seemed that any reason at all would do."

"Adam de Vries," said Edgar. "Why didn't I solve that anagram?"

"What was the missionary's justification for killing the boy?" asked Frederick.

"He was never a missionary," I said. "Not in the proper sense of the word."

"David Meares' explanation for each murder was that he was exacting revenge on Hugo's enemies," said James. "Over a period of many years, he had developed an all-consuming loyalty to the man who had rescued him from a pickpocketing gang in Salford's slums. Anyone who exchanged a cross word with Hugo Hawkins incurred the wrath of his protégé.

"Apparently, Jack Burton reminded Hugo of David as a boy. Hugo had almost succeeded in saving Jack Burton. The boy regularly attended chapel for some time, but then he stopped coming and no longer wanted to have any contact with the missionaries. This rejection deeply upset Hugo, and this made David angry. Perhaps David also harboured some jealousy towards the boy. Perhaps he worried that Jack would eventually become his replacement. He followed him for a number of evenings and eventually found his opportunity to cut the boy's throat when he was trying to escape having snatched Miss Green's bag."

"He did it extremely quickly," I said. "And to think that he stood in that courtyard a short while later as if he'd had nothing to do with it!"

"It's the best cover," said James. "Running away rouses suspicion."

"You'd have thought he'd have been blood-stained," said Mr Sherman.

"His clothes were dark and it was night-time," I replied.

"And Hugo didn't notice?" said Edgar.

"I'm sure he knew what David had done that evening, but he couldn't bring himself to betray his fosterling," said James. "The swift murder of Jack Burton was in stark contrast to the murder of Ernest Larcombe, the pawnbroker. David lay in wait for him in his shop, prepared with the knife and a bottle of chloroform. Ernest Larcombe didn't like the missionaries. He accused them of interfering in people's lives and believed most people in St Giles were far too sinful to ever be granted redemption. I've heard accounts of the many drunken arguments Larcombe had, and it seems that a number of them were with Hawkins."

"And Larcombe's sister, Mrs Baxter? Was she involved in any of these arguments?" asked Edgar.

"She may have been. However, there was a separate conflict with Mrs Baxter. Sometime earlier, Hugo had requested that her tours of St Giles should call in at the missionaries' chapel. Apparently, he wanted the wealthy visitors to hear about the work he and David were doing, and I suspect that he would also have welcomed some donations from them."

"That must have been the true reason," said Edgar. "Money."

"Mrs Baxter stood her ground and refused to include the missionaries in her tours. Clearly, the stand-off between the two escalated until David put a brutal end to it."

"And Mr Turner, the philanthropist?" asked Frederick. "Was he actually a philanthropist, or did his interest in fallen women extend beyond charity?"

"Sadly, the latter," said James. "E Division spoke to quite a number of these women, who explained exactly what Turner's relationship with them had entailed. They were desperate for money, of course, and he had plenty of it."

"And a wife and children at home in Chelsea," I added.

"Indeed. And perhaps we can find some worthiness in Hugo's character in that he was concerned about Turner's motives. He confronted Turner and, as you can imagine, the antagonism would have increased from that moment onwards. Turner was murdered in his own home, and he probably allowed David in because he must have recognised him from St Giles. He would have been interested to find out why the missionary should be calling himself Adam de Vries."

"And David didn't give him any time to find out, did he?" said Edgar.

"Murdering Reuben was senseless," I said.

"All of the murders were senseless," said Edgar.

"Reuben O'Donoghue had been supportive of the missionaries to begin with," said James. "Despite a propensity for fighting, he donated money to the mission in the belief that he was helping the poverty-stricken. He was far from wealthy, but he had some modest income from his rag shop."

"And he wanted to know what Hugo was doing with the money," added Edgar.

"They served up soup on cold days," I said, "but perhaps Reuben thought they could have done more with the donations they received."

"Reuben thought that Hugo was keeping some of it back for himself," said James. "I asked my colleagues in Manchester to make some enquiries at the mission Hawkins worked in while he was in Salford, and there was an accusation that some of the donations there were finding their way into his pocket."

"So that's why Hawkins and Meares came to London," said Edgar.

"Probably. But two people had also had their throats cut in Salford, in the vicinity of the mission where Hawkins and Meares worked."

Edgar's mouth fell open. "You think Meares murdered those people too?"

"It's possible, and I'm sure he'll confess to the murders if he was responsible for them. The man seems strangely proud of his crimes."

"And the first couple of victims, Mrs O'Brien and Mr Yeomans?" asked Mr Sherman.

"I'm told that Mrs O'Brien was always first in line for soup, but never joined the missionaries for prayers. Hugo tried to help her after her husband abandoned her, but she never appeared grateful for his work. Like Larcombe, Mr Yeomans considered the missionaries an imposition. Apparently, he once told Hawkins that if there really was a God then he wouldn't allow anyone to live in such poverty as there is in St Giles."

"An extreme view," said Mr Sherman.

"Extreme enough to cost Mr Yeomans his life."

"For a while, life was going well for Hawkins, wasn't it?" said Edgar. "Whenever someone antagonised him, his friend silenced them. I wonder who would have been next?"

"Surely he and Ed Keller must have fallen out?" I said.

"You'd be surprised, Penny. I spoke to Ed Keller after we arrested Meares and, apparently, he had a good relationship with the missionaries. There was an agreement that the Seven Dials Gang looked after the chapel in return for a weekly payment."

"With Hawkins falling out with so many people, it was probably a necessity that his chapel was guarded," said Mr Sherman.

I kept quiet, but I realised that Keller's friendly relationship with Hawkins helped to explain why he had stopped attacking me the moment Hugo Hawkins had ordered him to let me go.

"Thankfully, E Division have managed to arrest Ed Keller for selling stolen property, and I'm hoping he'll be spending some time in Newgate," said James, catching my eye and giving me a subtle smile.

Mr Sherman lit his pipe. "Well, there won't be much space in tomorrow's edition for any news other than this. Who would have thought that two missionaries could have caused such a terrible fear to sweep through London for as long as seven weeks? Mr Fish and Miss Green, you'd better get your stories written up in time for deadline. We need to trounce *The Gazette*'s sales tomorrow."

"That shouldn't be too difficult," laughed Edgar. "Clifford's only just been released from his police cell. He's got rather a lot to catch up on!"

CHAPTER 50

Dear Ms Green,

Legend says that the falls of Tequendama were created by Bochica, who struck the rocks with his golden staff to drain the Bogota savannah after it was flooded by the angry god Chibchachum. I read this in An Historical, Geographical and Topographical Description of the United States of Colombia. *I wonder if your father was aware of this legend when he visited the mighty falls? It will be interesting to find out whether he alludes to it in his diaries or letters.*

I also wondered if you would like to accompany me for a walk in Hyde Park on a Saturday afternoon when the weather allows? You would be most welcome to bring a chaperone, of course.

Perhaps you can reply to me at your earliest convenience.

I remain

Your most truly

Mr Francis Edwards

I felt my face flush hot. I hadn't noticed the small piece of paper this message was written on among the other papers

Mr Edwards had given me. I had no idea how I would respond to him. I folded his note and placed it in my biscuit tin while I gave it some thought.

◊✤◊

"What an ingenious idea!" said Eliza. "Onions growing in old packing cases!"

"Sixpence for 'alf a dozen," croaked a reptilian-looking woman wearing four or five tattered shawls.

"Of course." Eliza gave her some coins and came away with six onions wrapped in newspaper. "So this is the notorious Seven Dials?" She looked around her. "It doesn't seem so bad, although the pubs appear rather busy for this time in the morning."

"They're always busy," I replied.

"Which way is the chapel?"

"It's on Neal Street, just up this way."

"I think it's extremely sensible that they're pulling the houses down around here. Some of these buildings are extremely old and people need new, sanitary dwellings."

"They do, although I'm not sure that the current residents will be permitted to live in the new ones."

"What will happen to them?"

"I don't know. Perhaps they'll be moved on to another rookery somewhere. Perhaps out in the East End. It looks as though Hettie and Will will be accommodated in one of Dr Barnardo's homes there, their mother is unable to care for them any longer. I'm planning to visit them soon."

"Poor children, they deserve a proper home don't they?"

"They do."

"You haven't told me how you're progressing with Father's book. Has your work on it completely stalled?"

"No, I've just begun work on it again."

"It's the massacre, isn't it? It put you off the idea."

"I won't mention it in the book."

"Of course not. But the knowledge that he did it has dampened your enthusiasm for the book, hasn't it?"

"I'm still enthusiastic, Ellie, I—" I faltered, unsure what to say.

"It has changed your opinion of him."

"Does Mother know?"

Eliza shook her head. "I don't think so. She could never bring herself to read his diaries in detail. If she did know, perhaps she would cope with the news better than you and I. The older generation seem to have more tolerance of barbaric acts than we might."

"Is that what you think it is? Barbaric?"

"Perhaps that is too strong a word. I think that it's difficult for the two of us to pass judgement when we have never travelled in those parts of the world. Father was a brave man and I think we should feel proud of him. It's important to continue with the book so that we can acknowledge the good work he did."

"I'll get back to it when I feel ready."

We turned into Neal Street.

"There's still quite a crowd gathered here," I said.

We walked up to join them.

"That's an unpleasant smell, isn't it?" said my sister, wrinkling her nose. "Burnt timber."

Even after the night's rainfall, wisps of smoke continued to rise from the ashes of The Mission of Faith, Hope and Charity. A group of people stood staring at the spot where the chapel had once been. A few picked their way through the embers, hoping to find something they could salvage.

"The buildings either side of it have gone too," I said. "It's fortunate that no one was injured. I know I shouldn't say this, but I'm pleased that someone burnt it down. It was never a proper chapel. They weren't proper missionaries. It makes me angry that people like them use the cloak of religion to hide their wickedness."

"Does anyone know who started the fire?" asked Eliza.

"A few do, but they ain't sayin'," said a stocky woman in front of us, wearing a headscarf. She turned around and gave us a smile.

"Martha!" I cried out. "How are you?"

"I'm a'right. 'Appy they got 'im at last. David Meares? I never would of thought it, but 'e were a quiet one now I comes to think of it. Kept 'imself to 'imself, didn't he? Now we knows why!"

Thankfully, no one had explained to Martha Nicholls that she had been David's next intended victim.

"I'm so sorry about what happened with Winston."

Her smile faded slightly. "Yeah, well, the police didn't know what they was doin' 'alf they time, did they? Seems hev'ryone was a suspect at one time or another. I'm just 'appy Winston ain't been out murderin' no one."

"As am I. This is my sister, Eliza. She wanted to see the remains of the chapel."

"Nice to meet yer. Where d'yer live then? Not round 'ere, I can tell!"

"Bayswater," Eliza replied. "How long have you lived in St Giles?"

As my sister and Martha talked, I noticed two men standing apart from the crowd, pointing at the smoking ruins. It was Inspector Fenton and James. I walked up to them.

"Good morning, Miss Green," said Fenton. "I don't suppose you've heard who carried out this act of pyromania? We're on the hunt for the persons responsible."

"Do you need to find them?" I asked. "I don't think the false missionaries need their makeshift chapel any longer."

"Someone has carried out an act of arson, Miss Green!" He scowled at me. "Perhaps someone in this crowd has heard something."

He strode off to speak to the group of onlookers, his boots echoing noisily against the cobbles. James and I were left alone.

His tie was black, but his face looked brighter than it had been for a long time.

"Are you ready for David Meares' trial?" I asked.

"I think so. Hopefully it will be nothing more than an uncomplicated formality. The man is freely admitting his guilt. Will you be writing about the case?"

"Yes, so I'm sure I shall see you at the court from time to time."

"Yes, you will." He smiled. "I haven't yet thanked you for your help with this case, Penny."

"I'm not sure I did much. There were many people working on it."

"You stopped David Meares from cutting his own throat. If he'd been successful, the victims wouldn't have received the justice they're due."

"I hit him with my bag! It wasn't what I'd describe as an heroic act."

"It was brave, Penny."

"Anyone would have done the same if they'd had a large carpet bag with them."

I glanced around the street, wanting to say words which I knew were inappropriate. Instead, I settled on something mundane. "I suppose life will return to normal now and we shall see less of each other now that the case is over."

"I suppose so."

I wondered if he felt as saddened by this as I did. I watched him take his pipe out of his pocket.

"Has the future Mrs Blakely not discovered your little habit yet?"

"Not yet." He gave me a clandestine wink.

"I won't tell her," I said with a smile.

James laughed. "You've never met her!"

"No, I haven't, and I don't suppose I'm likely to either. Perhaps I will someday, who knows?" My words stalled as I toyed with the idea that I might be invited to the wedding.

I was trying to say goodbye to him, and yet I couldn't bring myself to do it.

"I should say good luck with the wedding preparations," I continued, "and I hope that your special day goes well." I felt a lump rise into my throat.

"The wedding's not until September, Penny!" James grinned and rested his hand on my arm. "I sincerely hope that we will work together again before then."

We held each other's gaze until we heard the footsteps of Inspector Fenton approaching.

"I hope so too, James."

THE END

THANK YOU

Thank you for reading *The Rookery*, I really hope you enjoyed it!

Would you like to know when I release new books? Here are some ways to stay updated:

- Join my mailing list and receive a free short mystery: *Westminster Bridge* emilyorgan.co.uk/short-mystery
- Like my Facebook page: facebook.com/emilyorganwriter
- View my other books here: emilyorgan.co.uk/books

And if you have a moment, I would be very grateful if you would leave a quick review of *The Rookery* online. Honest reviews of my books help other readers discover them too!

HISTORICAL NOTE

St Giles Rookery occupied an area of London which is now part of modern day Holborn, Covent Garden and the theatre district in London's West End. It was already becoming an overcrowded poverty stricken area in the seventeenth century and by the first half of the nineteenth century it was one of the worst slums in Britain. William Hogarth immortalised the area's lawlessness and depravity in a series of etchings, one of the best known being *Gin Lane*.

By the late nineteenth century Victorian social reform and philanthropy had gained strong momentum and attempts were made to clear and rebuild London's slums. Areas such as St Giles attracted many from the middle-classes who either wished to help the inhabitants or tour the poverty stricken streets out of curiosity. Evangelical missionaries began establishing themselves in slum districts from the 1830s onwards and by the end of the nineteenth century there were hundreds of missionaries helping slum dwellers with practical needs as well as spiritual.

The church of St Giles-in-the-Fields was rebuilt in the eighteenth century and still stands today. Seven Dials has retained its layout and character despite some redevelopment, and Neal Street is a popular shopping street in the Covent Garden area. Neal's Yard, famous for the organic beauty company which uses its name, provides a good idea of how the narrow crooked streets would have once looked. Although these days the buildings are brightly coloured and house trendy eateries and boutiques.

I've read some interesting contemporary accounts of London's slums. *The Bitter Cry of Outcast London* is a harrowing read written by a clergyman, Andrew Mearns, in 1883. It created a sensation at the time and helped pave the way towards housing legislation. *Dottings of a Dosser* documents the depressing adventures of a nineteen year old journalist, Howard Goldsmid, who went undercover and stayed in the very worst of London's lodging houses in 1886. Lodging houses – or 'dosshouses' – provided shelter for homeless people who were able to find a few pence to stay the night. Many dosshouses were overcrowded, unsanitary and run by unscrupulous landlords.

The houses at 23 and 24 Leinster Gardens had to be demolished in the 1860s to make way for a train tunnel connecting Paddington and Bayswater. The facades of the two houses were reconstructed and behind them is a section of railway line which was left open to allow the steam engines to vent off. The facades are extremely convincing and have featured in a number of hoaxes over the years as well as being a filming location.

Ye Olde Cheshire Cheese pub was a favourite with Fleet Street journalists for many years. The newspapers and journalists have since moved out of the area but the pub is still popular and retains its seventeenth century charm and cellars which date from the thirteenth century. The gloomy, warren-like pub has counted literary figures such as Dickens, Conan Doyle and Tennyson among its regulars.

Brookwood Cemetery in Surrey was built by the London Necropolis Company in the 1850s when the capital was running out of space to bury its dead. At the time of its opening, the cemetery was the largest in the world. The London Necropolis Railway ran funeral trains from Cemetery Station, just behind Waterloo Station, down to Brookwood – a journey of about thirty miles. The mourners travelled in the passenger carriages and the coffins were carried in a separate windowless carriage. The train stopped at two halts in the cemetery: the North station for non-conformist burials and the South station for Anglican burials. The railway ceased operation after its London station was bombed in WWII, a commemorative piece of railway track remains at Brookwood Cemetery.

The iconic circular Reading Room at the British Museum was in use from 1857 until 1997. During that time it was also used as a filming location and has been referenced in many works of fiction. The Reading Room has been closed since 2014 but as I write this (in summer 2017), it's just been happily announced that it will reopen and display some of the museum's permanent collections. It could be a while yet until we're able to step inside it but I'm looking forward to it!

Plant hunting became an increasingly commercial enterprise as the nineteenth century progressed. Victorians were fascinated by exotic plants and, if they were wealthy enough, they had their own glasshouses built to show them off. Plant hunters were employed by Kew Gardens, companies such as Veitch Nurseries or wealthy individuals to seek out exotic specimens in places such as South America and the Himalayas. These plant hunters took great personal risks to collect their plants and some perished on their travels. The *Travels and Adventures of an Orchid Hunter* by Albert Millican is worth a read. Written in 1891 it documents his journeys in Colombia and demonstrates how plant hunting became little short of pillaging. Some areas he travelled to had already lost their orchids to plant hunters and Millican himself spent several months felling 4,000 trees to collect 10,000 plants. Even after all this plundering many of the orchids didn't survive the trip across the Atlantic to Britain. Plant hunters were not always welcome: Millican had arrows fired at him as he navigated rivers, had his camp attacked one night and was eventually killed during a fight in a Colombian tavern.

If you've read the historical note in *Limelight* then you'll know that women journalists in the nineteenth century were not as scarce as you may think. Eliza Linton became the first salaried female journalist in Britain when she began writing for *the Morning Chronicle* in 1851. She was a prolific writer and contributor to periodicals for many years including Charles Dickens' magazine *Household Words*. George Eliot – her actual name was Mary Anne Evans - is most famous for novels such as *Middlemarch*, however she also became assistant editor of *The Westminster Review* in 1852.

In the United States Margaret Fuller became the *New York Tribune*'s first female editor in 1846. Intrepid journalist Nellie Bly worked in Mexico as a foreign correspondent for the *Pittsburgh Despatch* in the 1880s before writing for *New York World* and feigning insanity to go undercover and investigate reports of brutality at a New York asylum. Later, in 1889-90, she became a household name by setting a world record for travelling around the globe in seventy two days.

My research for *The Rookery* has come from sources too numerous to list in detail, but the following books have been very useful: *A Brief History of Life in Victorian Britain* by Michael Patterson, *London in the Nineteenth Century* by Jerry White, *London in 1880* by Herbert Fry, *London a Travel Guide through Time* by Dr Matthew Green, *Women of the Press in Nine-*

teenth-Century Britain by Barbara Onslow, *A Very British Murder* by Lucy Worsley, *The Suspicions of Mr Whicher* by Kate Summerscale and *Journalism for Women: A Practical Guide* by Arnold Bennett, *Dottings of a Dosser* by Howard Goldsmid, *Travels and Adventures of an Orchid Hunter* by Albert Millican, *The Bitter Cry of Outcast London* by Andrew Mearns, *The Complete History of Jack the Ripper* by Philip Sugden and *The Necropolis Railway* by Andrew Martin.

THE MAID'S SECRET

A Penny Green Mystery Book 3

The truth is rarely simple.

Victorian industrialist Alexander Glenville is a man with many secrets. Fleet Street reporter Penny Green is tasked with working undercover as a maid in his home, but tragedy strikes when Glenville's daughter is poisoned.

Penny's insider knowledge is crucial for Scotland Yard's murder investigation, but someone in the Glenville household already suspects that she's more than just a servant. Can Penny and Inspector James Blakely solve the mystery before Penny's cover is blown?

Find out more at: emilyorgan.co.uk/maids-secret

GET A FREE SHORT MYSTERY

Want more of Penny Green? Sign up to my mailing list and I'll send you my short mystery *Westminster Bridge* - a free thirty minute read!

News reporter Penny Green is committed to her job. But should she impose on a grieving widow?

The brutal murder of a doctor has shocked 1880s London and Fleet Street is clamouring for news. Penny has orders from her editor to get the story all the papers want.

She must decide what comes first. Compassion or duty?

The murder case is not as simple as it seems. And whichever decision Penny makes, it's unlikely to be the right one.

Visit my website for more details:

emilyorgan.co.uk/short-mystery

THE RUNAWAY GIRL SERIES

✶

Also by Emily Organ. A series of three thrillers set in Medieval London.

Book 1: Runaway Girl

A missing girl. The treacherous streets of Medieval London. Only one woman is brave enough to try and bring her home.

Book 2: Forgotten Child

Her husband took a fatal secret to the grave. Two friends are murdered. She has only one chance to stop the killing.

Book 3: Sins of the Father

An enemy returns. And this time he has her fooled. If he gets his own way then a little girl will never be seen again.

Available as separate books or a three book box set. Find out more at emilyorgan.co.uk/books